PRAISE FOR
THE BRASS BED

"More fun than pillow fighting naked!"
—VICKI LEWIS THOMPSON,
author of *Talk Nerdy to Me*

"Hip, hot, and highly imaginative. I want the
sequel. (And I want the bed.)"
—HARLEY JANE KOZAK,
author of *Dating Dead Men*

"Funny, frisky, and far-out! Jennifer Stevenson's
writing is naughty and irresistible."
—JULIE KISTLER, author of *Scandal*

"A perfect meld of humor, fantasy, and sex. Jewel
Heiss is the sassy heroine I want to grow up to be!"
—CECILIA TAN,
editor of *The Best Fantastic Erotica*

"Hot sex and hysterical humor. It doesn't get any
better than this."
—KATE DOUGLAS, author of the Wolf Tales series

"An out-and-out winner—fun characters, rollick-
ing story, and fantastic sex!"
—MINDY KLASKY,
author of *The Glasswright's Apprentice*

"Once you get into *The Brass Bed*, you won't ever
want to get out."
—PHIL AND KAJA FOGLIO, Studio Foglio

By Jennifer Stevenson

THE BRASS BED
THE VELVET CHAIR
THE BEARSKIN RUG*

TRASH SEX MAGIC

*Coming July 2008 from Ballantine Books

The Velvet Chair

Jennifer Stevenson

BALLANTINE BOOKS • NEW YORK

The Velvet Chair is a work of fiction. Names, characters, places, and incidents are the products of the author's imagination or are used fictitiously. Any resemblance to actual events, locales, or persons, living or dead, is entirely coincidental.

A Ballantine Books Mass Market Original

Copyright © 2008 by Jennifer Stevenson

Smoking Pigeon copyright © 2008 by Julie Griffin

Published in the United States by Ballantine Books, an imprint of The Random House Publishing Group, a division of Random House, Inc., New York.

BALLANTINE and colophon are registered trademarks of Random House, Inc.

ISBN 978-0-345-48669-1

Cover design and illustration: Tamaye Perry

Printed in the United States of America

www.ballantinebooks.com

OPM 9 8 7 6 5 4 3 2 1

For Rich, my sweet love

CHAPTER 1

Jewel Heiss squinched her eyes shut. She was so tired that her hair hurt. Her clothes stank of gasoline. She and her partner Clay Dawes had spent a satisfying day measuring gas, writing tickets to stations whose pumps filled shy, and sitting in traffic. Only one part of her body was in a good mood, and she was even tired of that.

"I'm gonna become a nun," she muttered.

Late Monday afternoon, the staff room at the Chicago Department of Consumer Services was empty. They were the first team back in the office.

"That would be a waste." Clay put whitener in her mug and black coffee in his. "Take tomorrow off. Get some sleep."

She sighed. Sleep sounded so good. "I can't."

"Why not? I'll babysit Randy. We can do gas stations."

Randy was her sex demon. Her source of fantasies-come-true. Some nights, it was so good she wanted to die in his arms. Some days, she never wanted to set eyes on him again. Once an English earl, Randy had possessed a brass bed for two centuries, after his mistress complained that he was a lousy lover and put a curse on him: *Satisfy one hundred women.*

The curse was only kind-of broken.

He sure knew his way around a bed, though.

"You need an eight-hour break from each other," Clay suggested.

"There's a catch, right?"

"Well, we might go shopping."

"You don't shop. You shoplift." Clay was a mostly reformed con artist. "But it's a lovely idea all the same." Clay had been using the possessed brass bed to sell fake sex therapy when Jewel met him. He wouldn't be reformed now if she hadn't ruined his scam by scoring Randy's hundredth notch in the bedpost.

Now Randy was celebrating his freedom in her apartment, in her bed, with Jewel. Over and over and over.

The boss, Ed Neccio, waddled into the staff room, his hands full of files. "You two get in here." He went into his office and drew the blinds shut. "I've got an important case for you. Siddown. Heiss, you look whipped. Don't your partner let you sleep?" He leered perfunctorily and passed across a thick file. "This is totally stop secret hush hush on the QT confidential, like nobody ever knows nothin' about it, okay?"

Clay mouthed, *Stop secret*? at Jewel.

"That means no blabbing to my wife, Heiss," the boss said. "You two are chummy, but I'm telling you this is classifired. You talk in class, you get fired. *Capisce*?"

She muttered, "Yeah, yeah."

Ed aimed his bushy eyebrows at her. "The Fifth Floor's got an interest in this one."

Jewel groaned. She lifted the cover of the file with a fingernail. "Looks like this one's stale." She recognized signatures from three different divisions of the department. "Gee, I get to bat cleanup for Digby and Britney?"

"To hell with them," Ed said, slapping the file shut. "This is the important stuff. Number one, it's fraud. I dunno how or where. That's your job to find out. Guy runs a psychic spa thingy, you get fortune-telling with your facial and shit. Got a million ways to service customers, each one shadier than the other. Every team we send in there, he *gets* to them somehow."

"You try Building Codes and Safety?"

"They went in first. Clean as a Pekingese's asshole. His permits are in order," Ed admitted. "But the guy's a crackpot. Calls himself a magician. Thinks the city handles the hinky shit all wrong. Wants to start a new era of peace an' magic an' age of aquariumoon is in the seventh house and Jupiter lyin' with Mars. He's running for mayor." Ed returned to coherence.

"Oh," Jewel said. "Has it hit the press yet?"

"No. That's why this is a rush job."

"Shit," she echoed. "I get it."

"Fabulous," Clay said. "What do you get?"

Ed waved a dismissive hand. "Explain it where I don't hafta listen. Couple more things." He tossed down another file. "Consumer complaint. Woman claims her brother is getting rushed by a gold digger trying to sell him a magical machine."

"Should be open-and-shut," Jewel said. "Find out what her claims are, make a ruling."

"He's a millionaire. You gotta at least pretend to use kid gloves."

"No problem," Clay murmured, leaning over her shoulder.

Jewel thought, *Clay and a millionaire. Scary combination.*

"No problem," Ed muttered, as if thinking the same thing.

Clay peered closer at the file and stiffened.

Then Ed took her breath away. "So, listen, you two. On both these cases . . ." He hesitated. "I guess I gotta authorize you going in undercover."

Jewel choked on a gasp of ecstasy. She sat up.

"Don't get excited. You're still no *Alias* bitch. Uh, woman. Person." Ed appealed to Clay. "Keep her outta trouble? Fill in the gaps in her expertise." He rose. "Now, scram."

They stood.

"One more thing. Know that punk kid you're always protecting? He's selling something again, some kinda consumable. If you give a shit, take it away from him before the Department of Health busts him for not having a pushcart license."

"Sure, okay, fine," she muttered. Inside she was wooting. *Undercover!* Jewel was sick of inspecting gas stations.

In the empty staff room, Clay flicked the top folder away from her. "Okay, let's split these up. You take the political case and I'll deal with this little gold digger thing."

"Forget it." She pulled a chair close to him. "Listen. While nobody's in here but us."

He sat. "The Fifth Floor?"

She nodded. "The thing is, it doesn't matter who runs against da mayor, we know he'll win. But it's the campaign fuss. The media circus." She lowered her voice. "This guy's platform is totally against Policy."

They exchanged glances. The Fifth Floor had a lot of policies, but only one with a capital Pol. The Hinky Policy, the reason for their tiny division's existence.

"Yeah, yeah, we don't see magic, we pretend it's normal, and we cope," Clay said.

Jewel winced. If she had to define hinky, she wouldn't use the word magic. That was kind of the whole point of the Policy and the Division. You just knew hinky when you saw it.

"Don't say that word."

"So?" Clay opened the skinny file. "Why's he dangerous?"

"So he can screw up the city. Suppose the nut goes on TV with something hinky? What if he starts giving the public *advice* about how to deal with the hinky stuff? Other cities are getting sick, but Chicago is da city dat woiks. We work hard at that."

"Other cities." Clay looked up from the file he was reading. "Brussels."

"Brussels is actually doing okay," she said. "But—"

She met Clay's eyes.

They both said, "Pittsburgh."

"First thing is to figure out why these other teams flopped. Oh, hi, Britney," she said in a louder voice as her friend came into the staff room and slumped into a chair. "Run some background on the parties concerned, if you're so excited about the gold digger case. I'll talk to Britney about this spa."

Clay took the file to a workstation. His heart was racing. He hid behind his computer screen, opened the file, and glared at the names burning on the single page inside.

A Ms. Ernestine Griffin (44) had phoned in a complaint against one Sovay Sacheverell (30?), whom she accused of trying to sell a magical antique to Ms. Griffin's brother—*her brother?*—one Virgil Thompson (70). *Blah, blah, blah, she told me all this on the phone.*

Between every word, a dozen had been written and scratched out. That was Griffy. Never could tell a story in a straight line. Clay leaned his head on the screen and breathed softly. *This is what I get for refusing to help her. I can't believe she called this in over my head.*

He glanced at Jewel. She was deep in a girl-type pow-wow with Britney, the Blonde to End All Blondes.

He turned back to the file and the computer.

A quick background check on Griffy, as he'd expected, yielded a pinup poster for her first and only Atlantic City revue. It was probably on the Web because of the famous movie star standing next to her in the chorus line. A bimbo of Griffy's vintage didn't leave a big paper trail, not when she'd scored so young.

The Sacheverell woman next. Vassar degree but no social mentions. Hm. He tried the last name, then the first. A Sovay Claire once played on a high school soccer team in south Florida. He traced Sovay Claire for a while and found a head shot at a Vegas talent agency. Zowie. Major brunette. He printed it off. If she wasn't the right Sovay, she'd draw Jewel off the scent.

But there wasn't much else.

Fishy, that Vassar thing. Long way from south Florida to Vassar. He tried a few different spellings of Sovay, and hit the jackpot with Sauvée. Society wedding, the major brunette in white next to a millionaire. Society wedding, the brunette again, with a different millionaire. Clay got a bad feeling. He narrowed his search to the five spellings of Sovay and the word "wedding."

Five different mentions.

He googled the bridegrooms and, on a hunch, asked for "obituary."

Dead. Every one.

Oh, Virgil.

Okay then.

Drawing a deep breath, he googled Virgil Thompson.

Here we go. Author of essays on fake Shrouds of Turin. The articles went back twenty years, which startled Clay.

Member of the Amateur Mechanical Engineers Society of Great Britain. Lots of old-timey engravings of whiskered guys showing off Rube-Goldberg-like apparati. With every picture he found the note, "From the collection of Virgil Thompson."

Breathing deep again, Clay opened AFIS, the fingerprint tracking system.

Nothing.

Clay searched under AKA Virgil Athabascan, Virgil

Marconi, Virgil Dante, Dante Virgil, Inaeas O. Virgilius. He scratched his head and came up with nine more aliases.

Nothing.

Well, he hadn't expected to find anything. His old man was good.

With care, he wiped the record of his search off the system.

Good grief. How was he going to finesse this one?

CHAPTER 2

Britney put her head close to Jewel's. "Tell me about your new partner." They both glanced at Clay, who seemed to be deep into his computer.

"He's weird," Jewel whispered. "You know every guy I work with hits on me."

Britney grunted. "I can't believe that one isn't after poontang. Those eyes. You look so pooped, I figured you two—"

"It's not that. I think he wants to know me better."

Britney gasped. "You mean he doesn't want sex?"

"He probably would if I said yes. But I think he wants to get under my skin."

"Don't they all. Honestly!" Britney sounded exasperated. "Where have all the brainless horndogs gone? Now Digby wants to get all, like, serious. After three weeks! 'What makes you tick, Britney?' Like I want to bare my soul 'cause we've done it. What if I just want to get laid?"

"Exactly!" Thank God for Britney, who made sense.

At this point Randy himself sauntered into the staff room with a garment bag over his muscular shoulder. Tall and dark, with hot black eyes that could see through women, he really didn't need to be magical, too.

Before she could chew him out, Clay beckoned him over. The staff room was filling up with investigators dumping their day's paperwork. She took the thick psychic-spa file to the copy room.

When she got back to the staff room, Clay had moved to the conference table. He had playing cards in his hands and he was surrounded by investigators. He seemed to be teaching a class.

"So now Randy signals to me what he's holding. Don't look at me, Randy, look at somebody else. Good. So you've got two aces and a king?"

"Queen," Lolly said, looking at Randy's cards over his shoulder.

"That's the other eyebrow. Okay, good. Wait two beats, *then* look at me." Clay turned his head. "Now I'm looking away so I can signal my hand. What have I got? Not you, Randy. Someone else tell me."

"Uh, three hearts?" Sayers blurted.

"Very good, Sayers. But what's wrong with that interpretation? Three hearts is a bridge term. What card is high? I'll give the signal one more time," Clay said.

"Lemme try," said Finbow the Monosyllabic.

It was miraculous. A dozen contentious, competitive, bad-mannered investigators reduced to a schoolroom.

"No cards in the staff room!" Ed bellowed from his office door, and everybody got up fast.

"You were supposed to stay with the car," Jewel told Randy.

"I grew bored with the automobile." Randy sat in Jewel's chair, looking smug. "Did we earn anything?" he said to Clay. Clay slapped some money in front of him and he pounced on it.

"Would you mind not corrupting this man?" she said.

Clay was looking in his wallet. "Honey, you have no idea how corrupt this guy is. He must have been born with a deck in his hand."

"Very nearly," Randy said, stuffing money into his pocket.

"If you've been teaching him—"

Clay's voice dropped. "Okay, here's how I think we should handle this. You chase after the street vendor."

"Now, wait a minute—"

"Then you two check out the spa while I go to Thompson's and wriggle into the woodwork. You and Randy show up after I'm in."

"Randy is not on this team," she stated. Randy looked up with a wary expression. "How about the background check?" Her tired heart was dancing. *Undercover!*

Clay tossed some printouts on the desk. "Complainant is a former Jersey showgirl. Her brother, the millionaire, collects antiques, crackpot stuff. Newage." He pronounced the word to rhyme with sewage.

She smiled. "Real, or fake?"

"The machines are fakes. The gold digger looks like the real thing," Clay said. He tapped a picture. "And she's got the right bait for her mark. This here is a well-known piece, been in several private collections over the last century. Keeps disappearing."

Jewel took the picture. "What is it?" She turned it upside down. "Is this a chair in the middle?"

"The chair is Hepplewhite. Valuable antique itself. This unit here—" he pointed to a chunky box covered with dials and Frankenstein switches "—is the CPU, if you will. The tubes and wires probably do something like convey mystic vibrations to the subject. The straps, I'm guessing, keep him from flying out of there like a scalded cat when the current comes up his rear end."

Yowch. "Did they even have electricity back then?"

"Sure. Remember my brass bed? The one you wrecked for me? Many devices of that vintage favored the juice."

Randy took the picture from Jewel. "Hamilton's Celestial Bed was electrical. Built in 1795 to treat impotence in men."

"So this guy collects swindling machines? Kinky."

Clay shrugged. "This is the Katterfelto Miracle Venereal Attraction Accelerator Apparatus, otherwise known as the Venus Machine. It makes you irresistible to the opposite sex."

"What's it worth?" she said, studying the picture.

"Maybe half a million dollars. If it's stolen, we can bust this gold digger tomorrow. Won't even have to infiltrate."

"Not so fast," she said. "Check the stolen property angle, Mr. Underworld Connections. If this is the real thing, then who owned it before her and did they part with it voluntarily? If not, she's holding stolen goods. If it's still in somebody else's possession, we've got her on counterfeiting antiques."

Randy pricked up his ears. "We are investigating a lady?"

"That's no lady," Clay said, tossing Randy another picture.

"*You* are not investigating anyone," Jewel told Randy. "You're my driver."

"But you don't let me drive." Randy took the picture.

"Hey, he could sleep with her, read her mind, and tell us all her secrets," Clay suggested. "Save time. That the new suit?" he said, indicating the garment bag Randy had draped over Jewel's chair. "How's it look?"

"I made them replace the buttons," Randy said.

Distracted, Jewel squinted. "How did you pay for it? Oh, no. You didn't use my credit card again, did you?"

"I have my own credit card now. The shop offered me one."

Uh-oh. "What did you use for a job reference?"

He drew himself up to his full height. "They didn't ask."

She slapped her head with one hand.

"And a social security number?" Clay said, sounding amused.

Randy waved that away. "I made one up. Why? Is it important?"

Jewel slapped her head with both hands. "Argh!"

"Is this the suspect?" He picked up the Sovay picture.

"Don't change the subject," Jewel said. "You do not 'make up' a social—"

Randy ignored this. "What is your parlance? She appears to be 'hot.'"

Jewel rolled her eyes. "You are such a horndog!"

"No, seriously. He can, like, read women's minds in bed, yuh?" Clay looked innocent. "Our secret weapon."

"I should like to be a secret weapon," Randy said.

"By boning suspects? I don't think so. We need a new angle on this spa," she said.

"You puzzle on that," Clay said. "Let me take the point on the machine. I'll go in undercover. Then you come in after me."

"We'll meet in the morning and talk it over then."

Clay cupped a hand at his ear. "Sorry, I didn't catch that." He pooched out his kissy-face lips at her and his blue eyes crinkled.

"*Nyet, nein, non,*" she said. "You don't go in alone."

He cocked his shaggy blond head. "You're just saying that."

"I am your senior partner and I say we go in together." She felt her blood pressure rising to almost normal levels. God, what she wouldn't give for a full night's rest.

Clay said, "You know, if you got some sleep, your judgment wouldn't be impaired. I know Randy didn't do anything but nooky for two hundred years, but can't he spare you shut-eye time?"

"I am present," Randy said stiffly.

"Dude, you're *omni*present," Clay said, squaring off with her glowering incubus. "Look at this woman. Dark circles under her eyes. Her hands shake. Her hair's a mess."

"Hey!" Jewel said. "I am present."

Clay shook his finger at Randy. "You may not remember what being human is like, but a person who misses sleep loses judgment, endurance, mental acuity—" Jewel swiped at him and he ducked "—and her reflexes go. This isn't about finding the hundredth woman to make you human, is it?" he sneered. "It's your ego."

"Sh!" Jewel flapped her hands. "Don't talk about it here!"

Randy inflated his chest, his long black hair bristling. They were the same height, but Clay was actor-slim. Randy looked like he bench-pressed taxis.

She began, "Can you two please—"

Randy said with sinister softness, "Jewel is your senior partner. She chooses her own bedmates."

"So you'll leave her alone tonight?" Clay said offensively.

They were nose to nose.

Randy looked like thunder. "She did not choose you."

Jewel picked up the files and headed for the car. They would knock it off when they saw their audience was gone.

Probably.

CHAPTER 3

In the middle of the night, dead exhausted and fuzzy in the head, Jewel rolled over in bed and realized something was different. Blindly she reached out. Her palm touched warm skin.

Then she remembered.

This wasn't different. It was the same, the new same. Different from how things used to be, back when she had privacy and loneliness and perpetual body-hunger.

Her sex demon was in bed with her.

She groaned.

Awake again? she heard him say inside her head.

"Why do you ask if you already know?" she said aloud.

He rolled to face her. His hand slid up her leg, around her bottom, up her back. He pressed gently, so that her back arched and a lot of muscles stretched.

Give him this: The first week, she used to wake up sore. Now her body was getting used to him, though her brain was still in first gear. She arched more and her belly touched his marvelous schlong.

"You want me to ask," he said aloud, his voice husky.

Tired, tired, she was so tired. Her eyes were gluey with unfinished sleep.

He traced a circle on the small of her back. Two square inches of skin woke up. She squeezed her eyes shut. "No, no."

He moved in again, nuzzling her throat with dream-soft lips.

Her eyes closed. "Can't it wait? Please . . . uh . . . mm." Friday, two hours of sleep. Saturday, three hours, but then he did that thing with the swings and the vat of chocolate pudding. Sunday he had magicked himself into a football offensive line, and she'd slept ninety minutes. She was losing short-term memory. Her eyeballs were dry. She couldn't think.

The thing was, he did it for her. He always did it for her.

He bit down, his teeth sharp against the curve of her neck. Every muscle in her back zinged down to her tingle-tangle, and she arched up tight against him.

Then he was spinning her back toward sleep, into demonspace, where he could be anything and do anything and she loved it.

He floated in grayness.

Where are we?

As always, he replied, *Somewhere between your desires and mine.* He reached for her.

She flinched and floated out of his reach. *If you would please listen to me!*

In her head, in demonspace, his voice gonged, *I listen to you every moment. I can count your breaths. I know when you want me, before you know.*

But why does it have to be all night, every single night? Her throat tightened. Everything was such a contest with him.

You are my equal here, he said, answering the thought. She had no mental privacy, here in his world.

I'm trying to tell you, not tonight. Don't you ever rest?

When I know you are satisfied.

She rolled her eyes. *I am satisfied every single night!* she yelled into the faceless clouds. *And don't tell me*

*how many breaths I took since the last time we did it,
because it's pissing me off!* Suddenly she was back in her
bedroom, her eyes full of exhausted tears. "You *don't* always know what I want, and I never asked for this
mess!"

That wasn't fair. He hadn't asked for it either.

"Don't you ever settle for a quickie?"

He said, sounding shocked, "I have learned to make it
last."

God yes. He'd learned it well. "Okay, maybe less
magic sometimes?"

"But you love the magic!"

This was true. "But I shouldn't." She felt guilty. She
looked away from his nine-inch temptation and tried to
assemble a reasonable argument. "My job is to mini-
mize magic's impact on the city. I'm not paid to play sex
games with it. Bad things happen to cities that don't
fight magic. Pittsburgh is total chaos." That made sense.
She must be waking up. "New Orleans is above water finally, but half of it is blue zones, and tourists are disappearing. Most of 'em are crackpots, all voodoo-happy,
like a bunch of doped-up runaway teenagers, letting
their hair grow in the Haight in the Summer of Love."

He blinked.

She stretched out a hand. "Don't you get it? We can't
let magic take over our lives!" Actually, she loved how
magic was taking over her sex life. She just wished her
sex life didn't interfere with her sleep.

He said, "How does their hair grow in hate? Or love?"

Beating against his colossal ignorance made her
tireder.

"Look, I'm going to sleep now. I can't catch you up on
last century's cultural revolution."

He reached for her hand. "After we—"

She slid off the bed. "Oh, no. No, not 'after we.' 'We'

every night. And in the daytime on weekends. And whenever you—" *Whenever you disappear on me.* But she was too whipped to go there. "Just—just no." Her treacherous bimbolimbo twanged, but she walked away. "I'm sleeping on the couch. Alone."

"Wait! Jewel!" Real panic was in his voice.

She turned at the door. "No."

"No!" he yelled like an echo, his hands reaching for her.

While she watched, he vanished.

"Well, that takes care of that." She felt defeated, which was totally unfair.

She could get all the sleep she wanted now. As long as she didn't go back to bed.

She staggered out to the living room couch, crawled under her ugly yellow hand-crocheted afghan, and fell asleep before her head hit the cushion.

Twelve fabulous, dreamless hours later, her cellphone rang.

"It's me," Clay said, insufferably cheery. "I'm on my way to the Thompson place."

She sat up. "What? No! You can't go in alone!"

"I thought you were going to the spa with Randy."

"*You* wanted me to go to the spa. What you're going to do is wait for me, and we'll do this together." She rubbed her head. She felt great. She should sleep on the couch more often. "What time is it?" Her phone said 10:30. "Dear God, did I sleep."

"You needed it. So I've thought up the coolest cover story. Two layers. You'll love it."

"You can't just move into a millionaire's house."

"Bet?"

"No bet. Meet me at Wolfy Shekel's in an hour and a half. We'll have breakfast and discuss our approach."

Jewel hung up, stretched until every vertebra popped,

and put on her swimsuit and shorts, detouring past the bed.

Five minutes later, Clay was face-to-face with his father for the second time in a month. Almost a record.

"It's an honor to have you under my roof," Virgil said at his most urbane. "But why?"

Clay ground his teeth. This was even harder than he'd expected it to be. "Maybe I'm here to see Griffy."

Virgil raised his eyebrows. "She's at home, I believe."

The service elevator opened and a burly bald guy in a black suit pushed a room-service cart into the collection room.

"What's with the help?" Clay said, mystified.

His father shushed him. "Thank you, Mellish, we'll manage. Ms. Griffin will come upstairs to pour."

Clay waited until the elevator closed behind Mellish. "But you hate servants." He realized that Virgil must be involved in another scam. He wouldn't lay on hot and cold running help if he only wanted to replace Griffy. Sovay might be just a mark.

At this moment Griffy peeked around the door. She squealed, "Clay, honey! You came after all!"

Clay gathered her up for a big hug. "Mm-mm! You sexy thing!" When his lips were near her ear he whispered, "What are you up to?"

Griffy squeezed him back. She pushed him away to give him a smile. She was thinner than he remembered, in full showgirl war paint, and her blond hair was cut in a new bob, but she had dark circles under her eyes. "You'll stay until the birthday party?"

"There is no birthday party," Virgil stated.

"I'm sorry, honey," she said in an odd tone. "The block party. I just can't help thinking of it as your birthday party."

That was weird. Virgil had just laid down the law

and Griffy sort of skated over it, instead of knuckling under.

"I have a houseguest," Virgil said. *That would be the gold digger*. "If you stay, I'll need you to take another name."

Clay let go of Griffy. "She knows my name?" What was Virgil up to? And, darnit, he had just revealed that he already knew the houseguest was a she. How did Virgil do this to him?

"No, no. Dawes will do," Virgil amended. "But you're not my son. You don't know me, you don't know Griffy."

To Clay's amazement, Griffy made a protest in her throat. Virgil rounded on her with a *What?* look in his eye. Griffy said nothing. Clay got goose bumps.

Virgil said, "You can stay Clay Dawes, but you're not my son, you're, hm, a shill, a fool, a bumbling worshipper of new age theories, a woo-woo wonder, a clown." Clay felt every word like a punch in the gut. "I happen to have a use for someone like that right now."

"I want him here for the birthday party," Griffy said.

Virgil inclined his head. "You can stay five days. I'll be through with you by then." It wasn't clear from his gesture or his glance whether he was talking to Clay or Griffy.

Griffy stumbled out, looking pale.

When she had gone, Clay blurted, "Why are you torturing her? That woman has put up with you for eighteen years! You don't have to marry her or anything but, if you plan to dump her, wouldn't it be decent to pay her off and pack her off?"

Virgil started fiddling at his workbench. "Got a job going. Oh, and for the next five days, she's my sister."

"*What?!*" Clay already knew this, and it infuriated him.

"You can remind her. I have to keep correcting her tells. She's like a sheet of glass."

Clay exploded. "I can't believe you're running a con in your own house!"

"Job came to me," Virgil said, peering through a loupe.

"She deserves better than this!"

"She gets what she's earned."

"If this is just a job, you owe her an explanation!" *I've got to stop shouting.* How did Virgil do this to him? Anytime he wanted, *bam!,* he could destroy Clay's hard-won Buddha calm.

Virgil aimed the loupe at him. "The last time you got foolish over her, you stomped out of my house and didn't come back for three years."

His chest got tight. "You asked me to come back."

Virgil held still. "All right, I asked you to come back." He took the loupe out of his eye. "So is this another fit of gallantry?"

"I won't abandon Griffy, and neither should you." Why couldn't he tell the old man off?

Because last time he went off on Virgil, he'd had to leave the house at age seventeen and support himself through college. Virgil had canceled his credit cards, appropriated his bank accounts, and sent a repossessor after his car. Clay considered he'd got off lucky.

"So you've come to keep the old man honest?" Virgil showed his teeth. "Then I guess you had better stay, if you want to protect her interests." He stuck the loupe in his eye and turned back to his tinkering. "You've gone sentimental, boy."

He glowered at his father's back. Without thinking it through, he lashed out. "I'm here on business."

"Good. Maybe you'll finally make some money."

"It's not a con. I'm done with that. I told you a week ago, I'm an investigator with the Department of Consumer Services."

"Yeah, yeah."

Clay hardened his voice. "The department received a complaint against a Sovay Sacheverell. My partners will be showing up today. I expect you to cooperate." Wow, he sounded like Jewel, facing down a crook and laying down the law.

Virgil turned toward him with amusement and disbelief in his face. "Why should I bother helping you?"

"Because your new girlfriend is a black widow?"

"Blah. You can't even make an arrest. You're here because Griffy boo-hooed on your shoulder and 'you want to see justice done,'" Virgil said meanly. "Like last time, when you thundered at me to 'do the right thing.' That was about Griffy, too."

"If you think you can con a murderer, you're playing with fire. Worse, you're playing with Griffy's life. What if she decides to get rid of Griffy first, to clear her path to you?"

"Murderers make excellent marks. They don't dare scream when you take 'em," Virgil said.

Clay noted that he hadn't responded to that last question. Griffy still meant something to the old man. But what? "You have to cooperate with our investigation."

"Who complained?"

Clay stood tongue-tied, caught off guard again.

Virgil waved a hand. "I don't need you and your flat-footed friends clumping around in a delicate job."

He's not willing to talk about Griffy. In a sick way, that was a sign of hope.

Virgil changed the subject. "Speaking of explanations owed, that explanation you gave me for losing my brass bed sucked sour owl stool. What really happened? I suppose you fell for some girl and gave her all the money."

"I still have my money. You got yours."

"I don't have my bed," Virgil said. He looked up again and Clay felt paralyzed, facing those snaky eyes.

"The bed got crushed. It was, uh, special."

"What was so special about it?"

And Clay told him. He hadn't intended to. The words just fluttered out of him on their own. "—Because his mistress turned him into an incubus, and he spent two hundred years giving orgasms to women." A sinking feeling gripped Clay. Virgil could get him to betray himself or anyone else. "The bed got crushed. The guy's magical. He gets stuck in beds and my partner, uh, gets him out." It sounded so dumb when he said it out loud.

His father snorted. "And you believe this fairy story."

"It's true."

"You take the cake. There's a master con man in this story somewhere, but I'm not looking at him." Virgil turned away as if the sight of Clay made him sick. "Get out of here. I'm sure Griffy will be glad to talk to you."

Sweating, Clay got out.

Now to get Jewel organized.

He found a corner on the back stairs and phoned her. "Did you order breakfast?"

"I'm at the beach."

"Whoa, what happened to the case?"

"I'll be in Wolfy Shekel's in half an hour. Where are you?"

"So you'll bring Randy?"

"No, I will not bring Randy." She sounded guarded.

"Why isn't Randy coming?"

"We had a fight. As a matter of fact, he's stuck in my bed back at my apartment."

"In your bed? Like when he was stuck in that brass bed for two hundred years? And you left him there? That wasn't nice."

She went off like a bomb. "Darnit, I needed the sleep! You said so yourself!"

"I didn't say you should trap him. I can't believe you did that. He must be freaking out, the poor schmuck."

"Since when do you care if I'm nice to Randy?"

"I don't. But we're gonna need him."

"Randy is not a city employee."

"Three cases at once? This will be tough. He might be the cover you need. He seems to know more about the Venus Machine than you do. Plus the mind-reading-while-boning-the-suspect thing. He's a person, Jewel. Treat him like one."

In a small voice she said, "He might not be stuck. He's done this before, disappeared on me and then turned up running around loose in my apartment. Buying stuff on my Amazon account." Now she sounded worried.

Clay tsked. "You can't ignore his humanity—"

"I guess you're right. I'll call you when I'm done."

CHAPTER 4

Jewel had been ready to head home when Clay called, but, at the thought of excavating Randy from bed, she took her shorts off again and plunged into the lake for another ten minutes.

Her shoulder cut through the waves against the slap and heave of the surf. Around her, gulls bobbed, tossed and struggling with motion, but she slid like a sea lion, moving with the water, never against it, thrilled by the incalculable power of the lake and yet comfortable in its arms.

Then she turned onto her back, resting. The water was bracing-cold, the sky pale blue. Far overhead, a white egret oared its way slowly along the lakefront on a five-foot wingspan. What was that like? To fly fearlessly?

She tried to imagine it. Suppose the water was air. Pretend the waves were wind.

She filled her lungs and dove.

No, this was nothing like flying. The waves churned sand off the bottom and scoured her skin. Floating water weed hung down, wobbling with the surf, defying gravity. A pair of pinky-orange gull feet scrabbled below the surface overhead, and she eeled forward and popped up beside the bird. It made a guttural noise of surprise and burst into flight. Jewel laughed.

At length her hands and feet went numb. She gave up and let the water push her ashore.

On the bike ride home, she remembered Clay chiding her. *That wasn't nice.* Why did he care? Trying not to feel guilty, she bumped the bike up the steps of the Corncob Building.

She was fed up with having a sex demon for a roommate.

"You try having headbanging sex for three weeks straight with no sleep."

Said out loud, it sounded ungrateful, as well as mean.

She sighed. In defiance of the Hinky Policy, she picked up her phone and hit speed dial.

"*Ask Your Shrink, you're on the air, caller.*"

"Yeah, hi, this is, um, Coral."

"*What's on your mind, Coral?*"

"It's my boyfriend. He won't let me sleep. I mean, totally won't let me sleep. He can do it all night, and I'm starting to see pink elephants, know what I'm saying? I'm afraid I'll get in an accident." In the elevator, she punched twenty-three.

"*Slip him a sleeping pill,*" Ask Your Shrink suggested, and Jewel blinked in shock. "*Perhaps he has a sleep disorder.*"

"The thing is, I've kind of locked him in my apartment. Bedroom. Because then I get to sleep on the couch."

"*Is your boyfriend underage? Debilitated in any way?*"

"Heck, no." He was over two hundred years old and he was friggin' magical. "He could get out if he wanted," she lied. Now she felt terrible. Clay was right. She was a jerk.

"*When you say he's locked in your bedroom, Coral, do you mean for the night?*"

"Um, no, he's pretty much locked in. I think." That

sounded worse. She burst out, "I can't get anybody to see how hard it is." The more she said, the rottener she felt. Ask Your Shrink probably pictured her chaining this guy down and bringing him bread and water only if he, like, performed. "Oh, never mind." She hung up and stuffed the phone back into her pocket.

Imagining Randy stuck in bed, all verklempt, worried she'd ever come back for him, she raced her bike to her front door.

Maybe he was in her bathrobe, using her credit card online.

She burst into her apartment and stood in the hall.

No sound.

No Randy in the living room at the computer or the TV. No Randy in the kitchen. No Randy in the bedroom.

She stripped and flopped on the bed. "Randy?"

No tingle. No cuddly come-fuck-me vibe. *Sulking.*

Staring at the ceiling, she wondered if the woman who had cursed him for being bad in bed all those years ago had known what she would be doing to the lucky girl who won the Randy Raffle. Probably not. When you had magical revenge available, you were probably trigger-happy.

"Randy?" She reached out into the darkness in her mind.

Sweet heat exploded in her chest. Her eyes drifted shut with pleasure, and she heard him say in her head, *You came back!*

"I always come back." Her body, freshened by a good night's sleep, yelled a big yahoo.

And fell backward, cartwheeling into that cloudy night sky in demonspace.

Not like swimming at all.

She screamed.

He caught her from behind as they flew, or fell. The clouds rushed up to meet her face. *You want it.*

Yes, I want sex! But I don't want— She turned in his arms, struggling with his strength. And because she was in demonspace with him, she could be as strong as he. *I thought you could count my breaths!*

So I can.

She felt them lift up into the air, *always in the air, he knows how scared I am of heights.*

They grappled body to body.

They were so high there was nothing to see, above or below, but the turbulent curling bellies of thunderclouds, purple, blue, black, and every shade of gray. There was no ground in sight at all. Fear clutched her chest.

In the peculiar half-light of demonspace, his eyes burned down on hers, big and black, so intense that she froze, helpless.

Fear and exhaustion met the core of her strength.

This time she wouldn't cave. She refused to swoon and let him scare her into holding still while he did his magic deed.

With that thought, she felt her shoulders bunch up. Extra muscles sprouted to pull her a few inches out of his grasp. Without surprise she realized she had grown a pair of big leathery snow-white batwings.

She pulled her knees up to her chest, set her feet against his belly, and kicked.

He spun away, falling. In seconds, he was a speck, far below.

Randy! she screamed. She squinted down through the clouds.

He fell and fell and fell.

She beat the air with her wings, making great flaps of wind, drawing a bead on his shrinking body. Then she aimed her head down, put her arms at her sides, folded her wings until they touched her ankles, and plummeted after him.

Randy!

He didn't seem to get any closer. Frantic, she opened her wings and beat down hard, accelerating her plunge. Now he was a starfish spinning below her, now child-sized, now a naked man falling slack with his eyes closed. She shot past him and tumbled over herself on air as hard as asphalt, trying to brake and keep him in view past her own ankles.

In another moment she was pacing him. She seized him in her arms and, with one powerful wingstroke, carried him up through the clouds, cradling him. He was dead weight in her arms.

Randy?

He opened his eyes.

You saved me.

A little sneaky something in his tone, in the lines around his eyes, made her pause in midair.

She gasped. *You—you big faker!*

She opened her arms and let him fall.

He slid down her body, clutched her ankle, and stopped with a yank that set her rolling again.

Let go of me!

Very well, since you will have it so.

In another instant he had his own pair of batwings, oxblood red, making a mighty wind as he hovered before her. Even his flesh reddened. Every muscle on his big naked body swelled. Including the sonic red boinkwurst at his groin.

She backpedaled in the air. *Wait. I want to negotiate a—*

He bounded into the sky over her and spread his dark red wings, his face dark with lust and testosterone-flavored greed. For once he looked demonic in a not-good way.

Jewel had had enough.

She was *not* going to be intimidated anymore.

She too leaped up, letting her wings out with a *flump* like a parachute opening. His equal, was she? Thinking of comic books, she flexed and stirred her fists at him, bulking her muscles up until she had big bulgy thews.

Come and get it, fool, she said, beckoning him with a hamlike hand. Ew, the hands seemed a little too hulky. She smoothed them out and added long white fingernails.

He looked startled. *I don't want to fight with you.*

Shoulda thought of that when you were scaring the shit out of me in the air! Come on, demon. Put 'em up.

Her demon reared back on his wings.

Sissy! she yelled. *Sunday driver! Big fat lord on the outside, melted marshmallow on the inside!*

His face darkened. *You take advantage of my need.*

You take advantage of me every single night! she screamed, and a jet of flame shot out of her mouth with the words.

Whoa. She shut up, startled.

You want it! You want me! he screamed back. Fire billowed out of him and played over her bare skin, leaving sootmarks and a sizzling thrill wherever it touched her.

Just like a man. Throw dirt on her and then blame her. She flung out her wings, letting them expand even bigger, letting them glitter like huge white diamonds, burning away the soot, sending blazing white light into his angry eyes.

You make me what I am, he grated. *I offer you nothing you have not imagined or wanted deep in your heart.*

She'd never bought that and she never would. *Quit trying to scare me!*

He recoiled from her and his face and body swelled inhumanly. His wings caught fire. His legs joined into a block-long oxblood-red tail that whipped out behind him with a crack like thunder. He pulled his neck back like a fighting cock about to strike. His neck elongated.

He opened a mouth full of foot-long fangs, flared the crimson ruff around his neck to its fullest, and screamed a long, angry blast of fire at her.

But Jewel reacted as if he were a dark red mirror. Her own ruff flared, white as mink, sparkling as the sun on water. Her own long sinewy body uncoiled.

His flame licked her like jalapeño bath oil.

Oh, lord. That felt *good*.

Against her will she felt that old heat, that zing, that shimmy-shimmy-coco-pop undercarriage goodness.

He'd done it to her again.

As he sent another gout of flame at her, she darted straight through it and bodyslammed him, wrapping him with her tail boa-constrictor style. He wrapped her in turn, sending pulses of raw desire through her straining muscles.

I know what I want, she panted. God, this was exciting. Like riding a green horse. Like mountain-biking down a switchback. Like wrestling, for the feel of body on body.

Their tails tangled, knotted, tightened on each other, and their scaled bodies lengthened, twisting this way and that, striking sparks as they slid against each other.

She wanted him so much she was dizzy with it.

Furious with lust, she opened her jaws as far as they could go, then farther, calling up the fire in her belly. His throat came in view. With a roar of white-hot flame she chomped down, shutting her eyes and pulling him to her with her claws, grappling with his thrashing, glowing body, tasting him, feeling his muscles move in her jaws.

When she opened her eyes she saw the impossible.

He clung to her face-to-face, his dragon's eyes dark as old lava.

He opened his mouth wide. Wider. His fangs were the height of tall buildings. Wider still.

The impossible happened every night, in demonspace.

His dragon-dick found her opening and slid home, and she squeezed around him like she would never let go. *I love this.*

Down inside his throat, she saw the heart of his volcano.

All right. Let's do it, she thought, and she dove into the fire. Her wings expanded. Her tail thrashed, knocking against his gullet. He swallowed her down, down into the spiralling sparks, even as she swallowed him into her burning center.

They reached the magma core at the same moment.

The fireball blew them into a million tiny pieces.

Jewel found herself lying in bed, tangled with two hundred pounds of sex demon. Her body sang like a comet tail, all sparks inside, sooty, sweaty, stinky, satisfied. Randy's naked body was curled around hers. She sighed.

With one hand she ruffled his hair. "You're a pain in the ass, but you are *so* good at that."

"I know," he said, his breath cool on her shoulder. "And yet it angers you. I don't, er, 'get it.'"

"I know, buddy, I know."

Now she saw soot on the ceiling, walls, closet door, venetian blinds, rug. "Time to get up. Gotta go to work."

Randy looked at the soot all over the room. "My powers increase while I am with you."

"Yeah. My cleaning bill increases. Unless you care to spend the day washing and repainting this place. You understand what I was saying in there—out there— wherever we were? I don't want you scaring me for the hell of it. It's rude."

He smiled, sooty and naked, looking unfairly adorable. "Sex is rude."

"It can be. But can we please try something else?"

He blinked. "Very well. But I don't see—"

In the living room, her cellphone rang. She crawled out of bed and went to answer it. "Heiss."

"I'm in," Clay's voice said. "Be here this afternoon sometime. I'm a well-known criminal, insinuating my-self into an innocent antiques collector's home so I can burgle the joint or something. Think you can remember that?"

"What do you mean, you're in?" This was what came of Ed hiring an ex con artist for her partner. "I told you to wait!"

"Too late. My cover is set up now. You and Randy don't have to pretend to be anybody. You're you, a six-foot DCS fraud cop with razor blue eyes, and Randy's your partner. I don't know you guys are coming."

"Randy is not coming!"

"We need Randy."

This was the man who swore up and down, three weeks ago when she busted him for selling fake sex ther-apy, that he never used an accomplice. "What do we need him for?"

"Lots of things. He knows about magic. He has pres-ence. He'll impress the marks."

"He'll screw up and do something suspicious."

"Thus drawing attention away from you. He's foreign. That'll get him slack, and at the same time distract peo-ple from any little undercover slips you might make," Clay said, putting his finger on Jewel's insecurity. "We're still training you there. Randy's a pretty good liar. You suck, girlfriend."

"Thanks," she said. He had a point.

"Plus he's a hunk and we may need one," Clay said with unprecedented modesty.

"Jewel?" The hunk came out of the bedroom. "Do you want to shower first?"

Jewel put the phone on her knee, swearing hard but silently. She looked at Randy. He might clean up okay.

She bit her lip. "Go shower and put on some nice clothes. No tee shirts or jeans."

Randy disappeared into the bathroom.

She said to the phone, "I'm going to have to kill you."

"That's part of your cover."

"I'll enjoy it." She spread the yellow afghan over the couch and put her sooty behind on it. "Don't hang up yet! Brief me. Who's in the house besides you?"

"Besides the old guy, there's his sister and the gold digger, plus a bunch of servants, butler, cook, maid, chauffeur. You can ID them when you get here. I'm kind of hampered."

"You? Mr. Omniscient? I'll write that in my diary. Did you bring those background files with you?"

"Uh-oh, someone's coming. Gotta go." He hung up.

Jewel counted to twenty. Then she showered and picked out some navy polyester.

Clay was insubordinate and sneaky, but they'd worked well together at the gas stations. He might be trainable. The big question was, what could she do with Randy? Randy was in her head, in her every-other-personal-thing. He was a miracle in bed, but out of it he was impossible. She couldn't stand having him around.

Yet she couldn't dump him. The terms of his curse were explicit. The hundredth woman he satisfied was the only one who could rescue him. He'd been out of bed for weeks now, yet things like today kept happening. Apparently, he still needed Jewel.

The curse, recorded on parchment by his pissed-off mistress two centuries ago, also specified that, to be free, he had to "love" his rescuer, whatever that meant.

No way did Jewel want to go *there*. Randy seemed equally reluctant to discuss it. The "relationship conversation." God, she hated that.

"Did you make coffee?" Randy said, reappearing, rubbing his head with a towel.

She sent him a look.

He said hastily, "Very well, I shall make it."

She headed for the shower. His coffee sucked, but at least he had volunteered. For the next twenty minutes she was allowed to hope they might be getting somewhere.

Their shoes left soot-prints from their front door to the elevator.

Then that cute stockbroker from down the hall stepped into the elevator with them and Jewel smiled at him and Randy stiffened like a pillar of ice until the poor guy went to stand in the extreme far corner of the elevator.

Another reason to establish cooperation.

"Guys are gonna smile at me," she told her possessive sex demon when they were on the parking ramp. "Get used to it."

"They mean you harm."

She rolled her eyes. "This is not 1811, dude. I am not 'ruined' just because I've slept with a guy—"

"Or several hundred 'guys.' "

She couldn't stick her tongue out at him and drive down the spiraling exit of the parking ramp at the same time. "So how many women have you had? Not counting your other ninety-nine satisfied customers."

He sniffed. "It is said, *Vulpus est index anima*. Yet men's souls do not always reveal their minds in their faces."

"I thought you flunked out of lord school." She pulled out of the Corncob Building onto Dearborn and aimed the Tercel north.

He was silent until they got to a stoplight. Then he put his hand over hers on the gearshift. "Jewel."

"What?"

He said nothing, and she looked into his eyes, big and black and full of soul. He said gently, "I wish you could know what is in their minds when they look at you. If you could know what they want from you before you open your thighs to them."

His sincerity punched her over the heart. She swallowed. "Must you be so coarse?"

"Their thoughts are not so well-looking as their faces."

She said, "You've been in all the dirty little corners of my mind. I'm in no position to criticize."

Horns honked behind them. He removed his hand and faced forward. "Ah. Well. I'm different."

"That you are."

CHAPTER 5

Pink smog blanketed the air over Lake Shore Drive again, so Jewel detoured past the John Hancock Tower. Regs forbade her to make contact with a suspect without her partner's knowledge, but she consoled her Wisconsin dairy-farmer's conscience with the thought that she was only looking.

Besides, she wasn't alone. She had Randy with her.

Scoping him from the corner of her eye, she admitted he looked hot. And rich. Too rich for a city employee, really. How did he *do* that? Two weeks ago he'd owned two tee shirts and a pair of jeans, which he had to keep washing because she absolutely refused to wait on him. In honor of this case, he wore the dark Blass suit he'd charged using a fake social security number, and the collarless black silk shirt Clay stole from Field's for him the night they sneaked in and she had to have sex with Randy in the home furnishings department.

She felt like a frump in navy polyester. There was no help for that, either.

A lighted cigarette fell out of the sky onto her windshield. Moodily, she flicked on her wipers. Even the pigeons thought her car looked like an ashtray.

"What are we looking for?"

"Buzz. Remember him? He sold you a genie in a bottle."

"The djinn merchant, yes. A boy with spots."

"Yup. Only he's selling potions now. Ed gave me a chance to shut him down before he throws the case over to the cops. Keep an eye peeled. Goddam potions," she muttered.

"Do not profane. It puts off the marks."

"You know, don't you, that card sharping is not a job skill." Her hair was blowing around, already half out of its ponytail and sticking to her forehead. Randy's hair was black as a crow's wing and kind of shaggy. In that suit and collarless shirt, he looked like a hot Euro-bum. "You need a haircut."

"I had thought of letting it grow. I saw a musician on television whose queue I admired."

"His what?"

"Tied back," he said, trying to hold his hair in a pony-tail. "Still too short," he grumbled.

"It's a mess."

"I was unaware that my personal appearance is subject to your whim."

She played her trump card. "If you're working with me, you need to look more like an investigator."

He turned toward her, his eyes glowing, and she almost rear-ended a bus. "I shall be an investigator?"

"You'll be my assistant." Chee, give him a finger and he took an arm. "C'mon. We'll hit the Salon on the Mile."

Randy cried, "There! I see him!" and pointed.

"Who?"

"Your potion merchant!"

"Buzz? Where?" She was spang in the middle of the intersection of Ohio Street and Michigan Avenue. Gunning the Tercel, she peeled past fifty-seven honking cars trying to sneak left turns through the red light.

Buzz straddled his bike on the sidewalk, his back-pack over his shoulder. The kid was so scrawny. He was selling something to a tourist. Didn't he eat? Her heart pinched.

She squealed to the curb at a hydrant and threw the flashers on. "Wait here."

She let Buzz finish his deal with the tourist before coming up and laying a hand on his handlebar. "Dude, long time no see."

Buzz's richly pimpled face broke into a smile. "Hey, Officer Jewel." He threw his leg over the seat and she ducked to keep from getting brained by his size-twelve sneaker.

"What's in the backpack today?"

Buzz's smile weakened. "Would you believe lunch?"

"Nope."

"It's my homework?"

"I would think I'd died and gone to heaven if you were in school right now. Somehow I doubt it."

He shrugged. "No harm a guy trying, right?" He pushed at the bike. He was like Clay's good twin. The broke, hungry, needy, teenage runaway version.

She gripped the handlebar. "What's in the backpack?"

With a sigh, he showed her a little bottle the size of a Tabasco bottle, with a fancy-schmantzy label.

She grabbed it. " 'Imparts radiance to the aura and enhances the powers of the second chakra.' What the f-fruit."

"You should try it. My customers love it."

"Famous last words." Hell, Ed was right. This could get him in real trouble. "Where'd you get this and what's in it?"

He said, "It makes people feel good about themselves."

"So it's a drug."

"It's a potion," he corrected. "It's, like, in beta testing. Before we put it on the market big time."

Jewel groaned. "That does it." She snatched for the backpack strap, but he was too quick for her. Off he zinged, pedaling fast.

She sighed, put the potion in her purse, and got into the car.

"Why trouble yourself with him?" Randy said. "Ed can turn the matter over to the authorities."

"I *am* the authorities. Sometimes you can be such a lord." Jewel paused the Tercel beside a handful of tourists taking pictures of one another lighting cigarettes and holding them up for pigeons to grab. She leaned out the car window. "That's against the law!"

One kid wearing a baseball cap backwards looked at her with his mouth agape. "Why?"

"It's a fire hazard," she said with a straight face, and drove on.

"He's only a street urchin," Randy said. "You lie—you claim that vermin do not smoke—but you allow Buzz to run tame, though your employer commands otherwise."

"They're not smoking. They use the tobacco for nesting material. The cops would put Buzz in jail, which would make a real criminal out of him."

"I repeat, why do you care?"

She sagged against the seat. "Why do I wear myself out, rescuing you from the consequences of your lordly temper?"

"Ah. So Buzz is one of your strays."

"Look, he's only like sixteen. He ran away from something bad. He's clean . . . ish. He's making zero dollars, and he's so skinny it hurts to look at him. But he's working. He's not taking drugs or dealing drugs. Conventional ones anyway. In fact, he's a good example of what you could be, if you didn't have me, but you did have a work ethic and street smarts."

"I am aware how obliged I am to your generosity."

Now she'd done it. Insulted his lordship's ego. "Let's get your hair cut."

Clay found Griffy in the kitchen, "helping" the cook.

"Miss Griffin, I can take care of this," the cook said.

"Oh," Griffy said, looking flustered. "Let me—those pans go in the top—all right, I'll—"

Clay disentangled her and led her out to the front hall. "You shouldn't help the staff."

Griffy collapsed onto a settee. "They live here now! They've been here two days, ever since Virgil brought that woman home. I think he hired them to spy on me. That butler, Mellish, he watches me. I'm a nervous wreck!" A tear leaked out the corner of her eye. "Virgil's put me in a separate bedroom. He's getting rid of me. But first he's going to torment me until I lose my mind. I should have gone to college. I'm too old to strip," she mourned.

"Naw. He's salting the mine—uh, dressing the place up so the gold digger will think he's worth seducing. It's a scam, I'm positive." Clay sat beside her and held her hands. "Listen, I wasn't going to tell you this."

"Because I can't keep a secret," she said with resentment.

"Because you have enough to worry about," he said, though she was right. How did Virgil expect Griffy, of all people, to cope with the web of lies he wove around a con? "The thing is, I need you to do something for me. You were right, he's out of control, and I'm sorry I didn't listen to you before, and I *really* wish you hadn't complained to the department," he said, his soothing tone slipping.

"But Clay, you wouldn't believe me."

"I guess this will teach me, huh?" He won a smile from her, and moved on to his forlorn hope. "So I've got two people from my division coming in to help out. Can

you do me a huge favor? Don't talk to them about me?"
He kept his face pleasant, but inside he was squinching
his eyes shut and crossing his fingers.

"Oh, no." She shook her finger at him. "Not you, too!
What is it with you and your father? Secrets, secrets!
You know I'm no good at remembering what's a secret
and what isn't."

"Well, it was pretty clever of you to use the Consumer
Services hot line to get me here."

She dimpled. "But that's your job, isn't it? Stopping
con artists from stealing from people?"

"We don't chase off gold diggers."

"But that's stealing, too!"

Clay gave up.

Lunch with the gold digger was a revelation. Sovay
Sacheverell was one of those women who flaunted. Sovay
She was gorgeous and classy and hard as nails, down to
the English accent. Jewelry, skin, youth, class, clothes—
she flaunted them. And she never stopped talking.

"Griffy, this mousse is marvelous, your cook must
give me the receipt." Yes, she said "receipt." "As I was
saying, the Venus Machine disappeared in the eighteen-
fifties during a house party of the Company of the
Apostles—I don't know if you know of their secret
society?—At the home of Viscount Urgyff, who was a
cousin of the head of the Anglican Church. It turned up
thirty years later in Prague." Sovay laughed a rippling
silvery laugh. "Collectors can be such fiends, don't you
agree, Virgil?"

Clay's ears hurt. He simpered at Sovay, which she
seemed to take as her due, but her real audience was Virgil.

Virgil ate it up. In a sickeningly phony, feeble-old-man
voice he said, "That's quite a story, quite a story. I remember hearing old Simonson, or was it that Pharsee
collector, what was his name, ben Haroun? al Harim?

I'm sure it was one of those, yes, he talked about a similar thing happening in 1948, or maybe it was 1947, hm. Hm. I'd have to look it up. Anyway it was most amusing and instructive, what he had to say about the behavior of collectors, indeed it was. Coffee," he said to the butler. The butler poured coffee. Virgil sipped. "Mmm. Tigers! That's what he collected. Knew I'd remember it."

Rigorous training provided by the doddering fool across the table kept Clay from rolling his eyes.

Sovay leaned toward Clay and put her elbows on the tablecloth. "And your area of expertise is so fascinating, Mr. Dawes. I had no idea there was a branch of psychical research called *sexualis imaginarium*."

The look Clay shot his parent would have killed if he'd had the safety off. "Not many people do." He lowered his voice. "Everyone talks about sex, but when it comes to the nitty gritty of psychic phenomena in the bedroom, they're afraid to explore."

Sovay leaned forward even farther. Her breasts made Griffy's look like prunes. *Yes, I see them, they're spectacular.*

"But how many of us experience such a thing?" She touched her chest, as if nobody had noticed it.

"Everyone," Clay stated. "Every single one of us goes through extradimensional space during the sex act."

Sovay sucked in a deep breath. "That sounds dangerous!"

"It is. That's why so many people prefer mystery novels," he said, looking deep into her eyes. "Or playing cards."

Virgil clapped his hands. "Cards! I want poker!" he cried as if he, too, preferred cards to sex in extradimensional space. "Griffy, get the table ready."

"I—I need to go to the kitchen," Griffy said, and Clay saw that her feelings were hurt.

"We can play three-handed," Clay suggested.

Virgil doddered. "Of course! Do you know milking-stool poker? Three handed. Sudden death. Good way to lose a lot of money," he said with a senile chortle. He patted Sovay on the hand. "You can trim the pants off me, young lady."

Sovay laughed. "I can try!"

Griffy blundered away from the table.

Clay was heartened to find that Virgil didn't object to skinning his gold digger at milking-stool poker. He followed Virgil's signals. Between them they took six hundred dollars off the lovely Sovay.

She only laughed and paid up on the spot.

Cash, he noted. *Hm. Wonder which room she's in.*

CHAPTER 6

To Jewel's relief, Randy submitted beautifully to the haircut. He didn't even make remarks about the sexual orientation of the hairdresser. Jewel sat for a trim.

"Pretty quiet in here, Leo," she said. For a Michigan Avenue salon, it had a lot of empty chairs.

"Business sucks," Leo said, concentrating on Randy's head. "Ever since Bruce let that kid in here, we're in the toilet."

Jewel got goose bumps. "Bad stylist?"

"Bad peddler. Came by a month ago selling love potions," Leo said, giving her a heart attack, "and since then we see fewer regulars every week. Bruce claims there's no connection."

Bruce, snipping away at Jewel's hair, murmured, "I don't see the connection."

But Jewel saw. Buzz was at it again.

Leo said, "I ran into one of my regulars at the chocolate counter at Neiman's yesterday, she's missed three appointments, her hair and nails were a *mess*. Know what she told me? 'I like myself the way I am.' Did you ever? I said, 'Darling, it's not about who you are, it's about what you look like to other people,' and do you know what she said? 'If I love me, they'll love me.' " He shook his head. "This was a nice haircut once," he said to Randy. "I've never seen a cut like this."

Bruce glanced over at Randy. "Where did you have it done?"

"London," Randy said, watching the scissors flash in the mirror.

"Figures," Leo said.

Jewel wondered how Buzz could be singlehandedly undermining the beauty industry in the most expensive neighborhood in Chicago. When she caught up with him again, she'd ask him.

An hour later she pulled the Tercel up to a meter a block from the Thompson residence on Marine Drive, which acted as a frontage road for Lake Shore Drive. "You don't say anything, you don't talk about the department, you stay out of my way."

Randy nodded. Too excited to argue, she guessed. *Poor guy. I guess I haven't been respecting his personhood.* He looked seriously hot in that Blass suit. It was way too nice a suit for a city worker. Alas, he didn't own anything else appropriate, so they were stuck with it.

She felt seriously hot, too, but that was because her pantsuit was plastic.

Holy crap, the Thompson place was one of those limestone landmark mansions with a lake view. Marble front steps. Woof.

She led Randy up the steps. He knocked.

An actual butler answered the door. Jewel blinked. Randy cleared his throat, and she sent him a *shut up* look.

"I'm Senior Investigator Jewel Heiss with the Chicago Department of Consumer Services. I want to see Mr. Virgil Thompson. In private. Official business."

The butler shut the door in their faces.

"You should have permitted me," Randy said. He knocked again, pushing Jewel to one side.

The butler opened the door.

Randy said in his most languid tone, "Lord Pontarsais

to see Mr. Thompson." He flicked his fingers and a card appeared.

Jewel stared. *When did he get a visiting card?*

The butler examined the card, bowed again, and stepped back. "If you would step this way, milord." He parked them in a front room full of dead animal heads and disappeared.

"You have any more of those cards?"

Randy handed her one. *Randolph Llew Carstairs Athelbury Darner, third Earl Pontarsais*, it read in tight, loopy script. Clay must have bought him the cards.

"You realize there may be an Earl Pontarsais alive right this minute."

Randy favored her with a look of pitying hauteur. "I'll fight him for it."

"I don't think," she whispered, "they still do trial by combat in Wales."

The door opened. "In here? Thank you, Mellish. Ah, hello, good afternoon, I'm Virgil Thompson." Thompson was an old guy with a bald head like a turtle's, about three inches shorter than Jewel. "Lord Pontarsais." Thompson shook hands with Randy. "Marvelous. And your lovely, lovely lady friend?" He took her hand and gazed up at her as if she were Mount Rushmore.

She gave Thompson a businesslike smile and repeated her credentials. "We're sorry to disturb your privacy, sir."

"Not at all, not at all." Thompson appealed to her in a fossilized way. There was a gleam in his turtle eye, as if he might at any moment say *Yowza* or *Hotcha, cutiepie*. "And how may I serve the lovely hand of the law?"

"Sir, I'm sorry to inform you that a known criminal was observed entering your home yesterday."

"You terrify me," Thompson said, looking unterrified. "Is this man a burglar?"

"No, sir, he's a con man. He calls himself Clay Dawes.

Perhaps he insinuated himself into your house as a guest. He's a very smooth talker. We've had him under observation for weeks. When we realized he was in your home, we felt it was time to reveal our presence. In confidence, sir, if you feel you can keep the secret."

Turtlehead Thompson blinked at her. "Oh, I can keep a secret. With confidence. Yes, he came by yesterday posing as an aficionado of old machines. I have a remarkable collection, you know. It happens that a friend has brought me a valuable antique for repair and appraisal. Of course he's after that."

"Perhaps. It wouldn't do for us to make assumptions about his motives yet." Now to see if she could talk her way into the house. Jewel shot Randy a warning look.

"Ye-e-es, I quite see." Thompson's pale blue eyes got bright. "My goodness, how exciting! I feel as if I were in a film about master thieves." He turned a mischievous smile on Jewel. "So you must become my guests, too." He tapped his lips with a skeletal finger. "But not as fraud investigators."

This was almost too easy. "Uh, of course not."

"No, no. You must fit into the decor. Hm." The turtle head turned from Jewel to Randy and back. "I have it. You shall be psychical investigators. I am considered something of an expert in the history of such matters, so no one will feel any surprise at your visit. Lord Pontarsais can remain himself, but perhaps we should disguise his name a little? Lord, hm." Thompson looked at Randy's visiting card.

Randy's eyes sparkled. "You might style me Lord Darner. I have a personal interest in supernatural phenomena."

Virgil Thompson bowed. "Very neat. And you, my dear? Perhaps you are his hired expert."

Jewel set her foot on Randy's toe and leaned forward. "I'd rather be his hired debunker. Trailing him around the country, keeping him from spending money on fakes and bull—and nonsense." She smiled another warning at Randy.

"What fun! A believer and a skeptic. We shall call you, mm, Julia Hess. That way if Lord, er, Darner happens to forget and calls you by your real name, it won't be noticed." Thompson rubbed his hands together, looking tickled to death to be in a complicated intrigue. "You should send for some other clothes, however, my dear," he said, eyeing her polyester. "You look so *federal*." Well, that was a new way to describe her wardrobe. He clapped his hands. "How thrilling! You must stay as long as you like. Corner this criminal. He won't suspect a thing."

"Mr. Thompson, you're being very cooperative." Jewel shook his hand again.

"Oh, call me Virgil. Everyone does. And now you must meet my sister Griffy, who keeps house for me." For a hundred-year-old fossil, Virgil had the sexiest twinkle in his eye.

Jewel twinkled back at him. She felt like hunting Clay up and singing Nyah-nyah at him. *I'm undercover! Woohoo!*

Griffy was charmed with the new guests. She guessed right away that they must be Clay's partners. The man was handsome in a very stiff, English way, and Jewel was tall and righteous-looking, with an FBI chin, exactly the sort of person you could trust to chase away scheming floozies who tried to ruin a good woman's relationship.

"Griffy, this is Lord Darner, the prominent British supernaturalist, and his assistant, Julia Hess."

"Call me J-Julia," Clay's partner stammered.

Oh, good grief. More secrets. Well, she just wouldn't worry about it. Who cared what their real names were? "I'll show you to your rooms."

"Room," Lord Darner said. "One room will suffice."

Julia looked grumpy. Griffy wondered if they were getting along. *He thinks they're together and she doesn't.*

"Our bags will be coming later," Julia said, showing her teeth at Lord Darner.

Yup. Trouble. Maybe it was only a tiff.

"Come with me, Lord Darner," Virgil said. "The women can put their heads together while you and I have brandy and a cigar in my collection room. I can't wait to show you my latest toy."

"This would be the, er, antique machine?" Lord Darner said.

Julia looked nervous. "You're not going to b-buy it, are you, Lord Darner?" she said. She seemed to have a stammer.

"Not a chance!" Virgil cackled. "*I'm* going to buy it. Since I'm appraising it, I'll offer the owner double what it's worth. Can't let it out of the house, now that I've seen it!" He towed Lord Darner away.

Julia sighed. "I hope he doesn't do something stupid."

"Men!" Griffy said. "If you saw all the junk he's got up there. I'll show you around. You must be good with people."

"Well, I like to see justice done."

Griffy's eyes widened. "That sounds so strict!"

"I like to think of myself as cruel but fair." Julia was looking at the grand staircase in the foyer. "Wow, some house."

"The marble kills your knees going up and down-stairs. And it's awful to clean. Oops, I wasn't supposed to say that. We have all these people from Household Temps now. I can't keep track of the stuff I can say and can't say," she complained. "At least you know I'm not Virgil's sister. Well, how could I be? He's twenty-five years older than me!"

"Mmm," Julia said.

"Wait 'til you see this woman," Griffy said darkly, thinking of that female fiend, Sovay Sacheverell. "She looks like his granddaughter. But I'll say no more, it isn't nice, and you'll make your own professional decisions. It won't be easy. Virgil is *determined*." She caught herself on a gasp and covered her mouth. "In eighteen years, I've never seen him like this."

Julia came to the top of the stairs and looked down at Griffy with kind eyes. "You love him."

Griffy sniffled and wiped the tears away from her mascara with one finger. "The old buzzard," she gulped.

"I was thinking turtle," Julia said.

Griffy felt a warm place in her heart. "I won't worry anymore. I know we're in good hands."

She tried to smile, and Julia smiled back.

Hm, Jewel thought. It almost sounded as if Griffy knew she was a cop. But how could Virgil have told her the truth already?

While Griffy went off to get their room ready, Jewel went into the ladies' cloakroom in the foyer and called Nina. The cloakroom was as elegant as a ladies' room at the opera house, with a pink silk sitting room and a lavatory beyond.

"Where have you been?" Nina wailed. "I need girl talk!"

"Me, too." Jewel lowered her voice. "I'm undercover. I need a favor."

"And I need a big old drink with salt around the rim."

"Please, I'm serious. I need you to go to my condo and pick out some clothes for me and bring them to me."

"Don't tell me you're sleeping around on Randy already!" Unfortunately, Nina knew all about Randy.

"I'm *undercover*," Jewel hissed. "I'm on a case."

"So Randy's all alone in your apartment?" Nina had

been one of Clay's best customers, back when he was selling bogus sex therapy on Randy's brass bed.

"Back off. He's on the case with me."

Nina laughed. "Just testing. So I get to dress you up?"

"Raid my closet." Jewel thought of her closet and groaned. She had two kinds of clothes: the polyester body-bags she wore to work, and weekend slutwear, which was no longer appropriate. The slutwear would have to do. She gave Virgil's address. "About a week's worth. Tell the butler they're for *Julia Hess.*"

"Wow, an alias *and* a butler! Evening dresses? Jewelry?"

"Who do you think I am, Paris Hilton?"

"Relax, I've been wanting to buy you clothes for years."

"Nina—" No point asking Nina not to go off the deep end. Nina lived on the high-dive board.

Her friend gave an evil laugh and hung up.

Jewel came out of the cloakroom, hoping to find Clay, but Griffy pounced on her for more girl talk.

Randy didn't turn up until suppertime. The butler made a noise in the front hall like Ringo Starr beating gently on the biggest garbage can lid in the world, and here came Randy, sauntering downstairs with Virgil and Clay.

With them slithered a woman who made Jewel feel fat, homely, ill-groomed, badly dressed, badly made-up, poor, and short.

Short, if you please. Jewel was six feet tall.

Up close, she realized Sovay Sacheverell was five-ten, tops. Must be the tight gold dress that made her look taller. She had snake hips, fabulous legs, and shoes to kill for: black, shiny, pointy, and strappy, with little bows in the back. Jewel tried not to look at her face. Too depressing.

Also the English accent.

"Julia, delightful to meet you, I've spent the most marvelous hour with your *too* exciting Lord Darner. Isn't he rugged?" Sovay sat beside Virgil and fluttered beringed fingers. "He says he measures psychical vibrations in antique furniture." She eyed Randy across the wineglasses and gold plates.

Sovay's scarlet mouth curved, and her eyes were a glorious hazel, and her hair was black and thick, and her throat was a miracle of smooth whiteness, and Jewel hated her with every drop of her blood.

Jewel felt it was too bad that she couldn't cite Sovay Sacheverell for homewrecking. Griffy was in pain, and charming, dithery old Virgil wasn't paying attention.

Maybe she would end up busting Sovay for something else.

Randy drank Virgil's wine with a look of deep satisfaction on his too-exciting, rugged, fascinating face. "A nice young claret," he said, pursing his lips.

"A connoisseur." Virgil toasted him. "Drinkable, I think."

Randy sniffed the glass. "Oh, very." He was in his element, surrounded by beautiful women and expensive food. Now Jewel realized she was a poor hostess as well. The most she'd ever given him was a thorough grounding in take-out Thai.

"And your expertise is?" Sovay said to Jewel.

"Debunking phonies," Jewel said, sucking down claret.

"A skeptic! How challenging!" Sovay smiled, and Jewel knew the challenge would be between them. This bitch would get Randy in bed for practice. Because her focus was obviously on Virgil. "Virgil-darling, she would be perfect for our experiment."

"What experiment?" Clay said. He was wearing what Jewel thought of as yacht-club casual: boring hundred-dollar khakis and a silky polo.

Jewel's brain caught up with her ears. "What experiment?"

Virgil clapped his hands. "The Katterfelto Venus Machine. It hasn't been used in more than two hundred years. It's way out of adjustment, but we'll tinker. We may get a buzz off it."

Jewel knew the whites of her eyes were showing. "Randy?" Call her superstitious, but the mention of two hundred years reminded her of the brass bed. She'd had as much fun as she could stand with that.

Randy ate a green bean. "Katterfelto boasted that he had enhanced the charms of beauties who later made advantageous marriages. He wouldn't name them, but everyone knows he meant the Gunning sisters. One of them married two dukes."

"Two dukes!" Sovay said, showing him her cleavage.

Randy's eyes gleamed. Jewel could have sworn the bitch's hand was on his thigh under the table.

"Surely that's not possible!" Sovay looked as if she would have tried it, if she had known bigamy was legal with dukes.

"Miss Gunning married her dukes random-tandem, not as a team," Randy murmured, dangling his wineglass in his fingers and looking at Sovay under drooping eyelids.

Jewel felt her hackles go up. The butler came by with the claret again and she drained her glass so he could refill it.

Virgil patted her hand. "Now, don't spoil our fun." He reminded her of the family lawyer back in Homonowoc, Wisconsin. Dusty and old-fashioned on the outside and funny and sexy underneath. "I rely on your good sense to offset the placebo effect. We'll play a few hands of poker and then see how this thing works. Bordeaux?" Before she could answer, Virgil pointed to one of the forest of crystal wineglasses in front of her and asked

Randy, "You're familiar with Hamilton's work with electricity?"

"The Celestial Bed man," Sovay said, erupting into a fountain of flimflam about the effect of electricity on latent auras and psychic contagion of charismatic individuals on personal property. Virgil, Randy, and Sovay put their heads together and talked newage with great energy.

Jewel's eyes glazed over. She tasted the Bordeaux. She tasted more claret. In desperation, she turned to Clay, whom, she remembered now, she was supposed to be investigating. "And what do you do, Mr. Dawes?"

Clay smiled his crinkly-eyed smile. "I've always wanted to explore my theories of sexualis imaginarium with a skeptic. Do you ever dream about sex?"

He was just like them. She felt tongue-tied.

"My experiments," he said with a straight face, "show that partial submersion in REM sleep, or a hypnogogic state mimicking REM sleep, is ideal for those moments of transcendent, extradimensional eroticism that—"

She felt herself going down for the third time.

After dinner they all moved into another room and the men, plus of course Sovay, sat down to their poker game with a bottle of old Scotch. Jewel hid out in a corner with Griffy, who hadn't said a word throughout the meal.

Griffy looked depressed.

"Cheer up," Jewel said. "It can't last."

"I'd like to kill her."

Looking at Virgil's turtle head and his slow fumbling with the cards, Jewel was surprised Griffy wanted to hold on to him. Maybe she didn't have any palimony paper.

Griffy watched Sovay. "She doesn't even like him." She turned to Jewel. "*You're* doing okay. What's Lord Darner like?"

"Moody." The butler brought a tray and glasses to

them and, against her better judgment, Jewel accepted champagne.

Griffy frowned. "But Lord Darner cares about you."

"How can you tell?" Jewel put her chin on her hand. Randy was laughing at Sovay. She'd never seen him look so relaxed. Something twinged inside her chest.

Just then, Randy looked at her. She flushed, as if he'd caught her feeling something about him. He spoke to Virgil.

Virgil put his cards down. "Julia! Can you play poker?"

"I suck at cards," she called back. But Virgil sent Clay over to get her.

Griffy said, "I'll order drinks for upstairs."

Clay put his hand on Jewel's elbow and watched Griffy go with a grim expression on his face.

"Do I have to do this?" Jewel complained.

"Yes." Clay didn't look happy. But by the time they were seated at the poker table he was the life and soul of the party.

Jewel expected to hate poker, but a funny thing happened. She started winning.

"Julia, you brute, you can't raise again!" Sovay cried. "How long have you been a blonde?" she added, *sotto voce.*

"All my life," Jewel said. Bottle-brave, she said, "Five or fold."

"So difficult when the color begins to fade. The choices that beset one," Sovay said, tossing five dollars into the pot.

"See you and raise you," Clay said.

"I'm in," Virgil said, and Randy echoed him.

And where was Randy getting the money to play cash poker?

Duh. Clay must be leading her sex demon into temptation.

Virgil poured her a long Scotch. Clay and Randy fawned on Sovay, but Virgil flirted with Jewel. And for the first time in her life, tiddly with three kinds of wine and Scotch and victory, she won.

Then Virgil proposed they all go take a look at the Katterflibbertygibbet Machine upstairs. "Maybe our hardened skeptic will prove it's a fraud. Ante up, my dear," he said, twinkling like her Homonowoc lawyer. Jewel felt at home. "You're on a winning streak."

"Yes, a skeptic is irresistible to a certain type of man," Sovay said through her teeth.

"Do you type men, as a rule?" Randy asked Sovay languidly.

"Oo, what type am I?" Clay asked Sovay, frisking like a damned puppy.

CHAPTER 7

Which was how Jewel found herself sitting on an elegant green-velvet-padded chair with a curvy gold frame, surrounded by a Rube Goldberg machine made of mahogany and teakwood, copper-inlaid dials, brass switches, and mother-of-pearl buttons in gleaming, important-looking rows. It had more class than her car. She felt underdressed again.

"What does this thing do?" Her voice sounded far away.

"In theory, it'll make you irresistible to men," Clay said, examining the machine. "It's in nice condition."

"I've cleaned it," Virgil said. He leaped around the machine like an aged spider monkey, twiddling this, unscrewing that, adjusting and clanking and throwing levers. Clay and Randy hemmed and hawed and talked newage. Randy sounded well-informed on supernatural phenomena, as well he should. Griffy came in, trailed by the butler and a drinks cart.

Sovay accepted a martini from Griffy with a "Thank you" that blended condescension toward a social inferior with a case of sulks, and would have made Jewel want to stab her to the heart with a swizzle stick.

Jewel lounged on the green-velvet-padded chair, feeling not quite ready to pounce on evildoing.

"Ready!" Virgil threw the switch.

She didn't feel a thing.

True, getting out of the velvet chair she tripped over a silver-inlaid rosewood potentiometer and fell on her ass, but that was the Scotch.

"You've been had," she announced to Sovay from the floor.

"Jew—Julia!" Clay cried. "Are you all right?"

Randy leaped forward to help her to her feet. It comforted her to see concern on his face. "You've suffered no hurt?"

"Only my pride." She dusted off her fanny. All three men and the butler goggled at her. "No worse than falling off a donkey." They stared. "Well?"

Clay swallowed. "I think this case has sprung a leak."

She glared at him. "And I'm looking right at it." *This is the last time I take you undercover anywhere.* Had she said that out loud? She'd had too many Scotches. "Can I go to bed now?"

"I'll help," Randy and Clay said.

But Virgil was at her side before the words were out of their mouths. "My dear, thank you for your cooperation. Perhaps it is time to say good night."

"You think I'm drunk," she blurted. "Well, I'm not so drunk I can't tell this thing is a big old drunk of junk. Very impressive, but a junk of hunk," she enunciated.

"Coffee, Griffy?" Virgil said, putting his arm around Jewel.

Griffy sent Jewel a wounded look and poured a cup.

"How do you feel?" Clay said.

"You're a phony, too!" Jewel accused, then put her hand over her mouth. *Would Julia Hess say that to the person Clay was pretending to be?*

"Any ill effects?" Virgil ushered her to a lab stool by his workbench.

Her ears buzzed. "I'm telling you, that thing's a fake."

"Check the settings," Clay said, and Virgil went to

fiddle with the Venus machine. Randy leaned on the bench beside her, sleek and dangerous, like a Doberman pinscher guarding a baby carriage. Virgil called out numbers and Clay wrote them down.

Sovay didn't say a word. She stared at Jewel with loathing.

Jewel ignored her. She could have told her the men were hoping she would fall on her ass again.

She felt itchy. One of those low, slow, tingly itches.

Everybody drank coffee while Clay and Virgil conferred.

"—Calibrated too high, or else we're seeing a placebo effect of extreme magnitude," Clay said.

"Shouldn't think so," Virgil said. "Still, I'd like to measure the green tones in her aura. I have a Kirlian camera here somewhere." He blinked around the collection room.

Clay said, "In fact, you and I and Lord Darner could spend the morning recalibrating. If we can get rid of the women for a few hours," he added in bald English. Jewel's jaw dropped in amazement. "Why don't you ladies hit a spa tomorrow? When you get back, we'll be ready to take a Kirlian shot of Julia's aura."

"I have an account at Giorgio lo Gigolo," Griffy said.

"There's that new place up in the Hancock Tower," Clay said even more brazenly. "I hear they do colorimetry. Newfangled aura reading," he explained to Jewel. "Get a second opinion."

Somebody had better explain to this dope how to conduct a fraud investigation before he dug a hole they couldn't climb out of. "You," she said, "are babbling."

Griffy said, "No, I've heard of them. They tell fortunes. And you get a massage!" She turned to Jewel. "We'll all go. My treat." After a pause she said to Sovay, "You'll come, won't you?" with what Jewel considered heroic niceness.

"Of course." Sovay inclined her head as if she were doing Griffy a favor.

Griffy looked more cheerful.

The pressure of all the suspicious looks flying between Virgil, Clay, and Sovay was giving Jewel a headache. "I'm going to bed," she announced.

"I'll take her downstairs," Clay said.

Randy glared. "There is no need for you to trouble."

"Clay will take me downstairs," Jewel told Randy. "Go flooze with your English flirty." Besides, she needed a chance to remind Clay exactly who was senior partner on this gig.

Randy turned his shoulder and offered Sovay coffee-sugar.

"Hunk of drunk," Jewel muttered as Clay held the collection room door for her. "Bunco hunk of attitude."

"That coffee was awful weak, wasn't it?" Clay said, supporting her down the marble staircase to the second floor.

"I'm not a cripple," she grumbled. They were out of earshot now. "Listen, buster. You do not, *not*—" she drew breath "—commingle cases!"

"You're tiddly, officer." As he opened a bedroom door, he twinkled at her, and she felt an urge.

"What I mean is, we're working on two cases but we mustn't mix them together." She flumped down on the bed.

"More efficient, I would think." He helped her off with her shoes. Then he squeezed her right foot in both hands.

"Oh my God." She groaned. "What were you thinking, initiating contact with Thompson? You could get us into deep shit here!"

He twisted gently, sending good feelings all up her leg and into her hoopla. "Better?" he said.

"Don't stop that. I'm serious." It was hard to act serious

when she was so, so loaded, and his touch was so good. "You could screw this case royally. If we do get evidence, it might be ruled in—mmMMoh—inadmissible because you tangled the cases."

"It's only a spa day with the girls. I thought you would like a chance to scope the joint."

"Well, stop thinking. Oh, and another thing." She had to pause because he'd switched feet and was now working his thumbs into the arch of her left foot, bringing muted ecstasy. "What the hell and a half have you been telling Griffy about me? I admit she could get secrets out of a stone with that face, but I would think *you* could keep a secret." *I must be sobering up. I couldn't have said that ten minutes ago.*

"She is innocent," Clay said with a solemn face. "You believe that, don't you?"

"Yes." Somehow Jewel was on her back on the bed. She felt grand.

"Good." He pulled off her polyester pants. "Tell Griffy to buy you some clothes while you're on the Magnificent Mile."

"Nina will bring over some of my weekend clothes." *Something to make Randy look at me, not at Sovay.*

"Good, because these things are dreadful."

She got up on her elbows and found him kneeling between her thighs. "Hey."

He kissed her and pushed. She fell on her back. "Hey yourself." He tossed her pants away. "I propose a detente. You're right, we're outclassed here. We need to pull together."

The ceiling swam over her. He continued working the polyester off her unresisting body. She had that old familiar feeling, the feeling that she was making a colossal fool of herself and would regret it in something like twelve hours.

Although not right now.

This isn't so bad, she thought, repeating a mantra from sluttier days. *I like him.* Which was true. Working with Clay for two weeks hadn't inspired her with confidence in his honesty or his urge to follow orders, but she liked other things about him. He was kind, patient, and more polite than her average fellow investigator, though that might be because she'd dated and dumped most of them. But she had to keep her mouth shut around him. Clay couldn't be trusted with secrets.

"Why is it," she said aloud, "that a confidence man betrays your confidence?"

"How much did you drink?" he said to her left ear as he groped behind her back. He grunted. "Lift up, I can't get this bra undone."

She giggled. Randy never had trouble getting her naked.

"I remember doing you," she accused. "You're normal."

Clay licked the hollow of her throat. A frisson shot down her side into her buttock. She yelped.

"That's good, is it?" he panted. "Ah."

The bra strap snapped open and her breasts, always uncomfortable in traction, eased apart against his naked chest. When did his chest get naked?

He threw the bra over his shoulder. "I hate these things."

She said, "I do, too, but they keep me out of trouble."

He lifted himself in a push-up over her. The heat of his body between her thighs was distracting. "Trouble? You? Hard to believe, Officer Teflon."

"True. There's a reason I dress like this. It keeps my coworkers happy."

He squinted at her breasts. "Naw."

"Okay, it keeps the men from thinking lustful thoughts about me. Look like that if you want, but I couldn't keep a partner. I mean, I tried. Ed set me up with every guy in the department." The more she talked, the more everything sounded like sex. "I mean, Ed made me their partner." In a small voice she confessed, "I did them all. It didn't help."

"This partner thing is important to you."

"I need a partner. I can't do any important work without one. This is my first big case in forever."

Clay seemed thoughtful. She lay on her back, watching his face change, relaxing into the idea of normal sex with a normal guy, feeling unbelievably grateful to him. "Thanks for picking me and not that Sovay bitch."

He glanced down at her body, lifting himself higher into a one-handed push-up as he looked. Her skin heated as if he were licking her.

She smiled.

He sighed. "Officer, this is killing me, but I think we stop now." And he rolled off her.

"What?"

He flipped the coverlet over her bare body.

"Hey!" she said. She sat up. "That's not funny!"

He knelt on the bed, pushed her back down, and slowly, slowly snuggled against her, keeping the coverlet between them.

"You're right, it's not funny." His face was so close, she could smell both wine and whiskey on his breath. His eyes glazed over. His hand pressed down on the coverlet over her breast, making her roll hungrily toward him.

Then his face changed. "Oh, brother."

He slid away again. She smiled while he took off his pants and shoes.

Then he put on a pair of pajamas.

Her smile faded.

He lifted the sheets and got into bed. Now there were lots of layers between them. From arm's length away he reached over and brushed a lock of her hair off her forehead.

Jewel watched with speechless resentment.

"The thing is, officer, I like working with you. I don't want that to blow up in our faces because I took advantage of you when you were drunk."

"I've screwed men on dumber excuses," she blurted.

"And lost your partner every time. Ain't gonna happen. Not tonight." He looked at her so tenderly that lust climbed into her chest and twisted into something else.

To her horror, she felt her eyes prickle. "Do you want a punch in the nose?" Unwelcome feeling was rising in her throat.

"Might take my mind off my johnson." She laughed, and he said, "If it's any comfort to you, you are hotter tonight than I have ever seen you."

Her breath caught. Her throat went hard. "Con man."

Eye to eye with her, he said, "Jump me tomorrow and find out if I'm lying."

He put his hand out and closed her eyes, and she turned over so he wouldn't see her face crumple.

Clay got up and turned the light out, then lay back down under the covers beside her. *Close one.* His fingertips were wet where he'd touched her eyelids. He wondered until daylight what he wanted.

CHAPTER 8

Jewel's head hurt. She skulked in the alley behind Virgil's house, leaning her burning face against the cold brick garden wall, until Nina drove up in the Beamer with a suitcase. Nina tried to give her a hard time about the soot all over her bedroom, but Jewel stonewalled her, promising girl talk later.

Then she snuck back up to Clay's room.

Twenty minutes later she came downstairs, showered, dressed, still hung over. Griffy sat at one end of the big table. All the men were waiting on Sovay at the other end.

When Jewel came in, all the men turned toward her.

"Julia! Would you care for coffee?" Virgil said.

"Can I get you some ham?" Clay said.

"Orange juice or cranberry, Miss?" Mellish said, holding her chair for her and leaning very close.

"Where were you last night?" Randy demanded.

Sovay scowled. She was lovely, even while scowling.

"Coffee," Jewel grunted, avoiding Randy's sizzling-hot eye.

The butler poured coffee into her cup.

Griffy said, "How are you feeling this morning, Julia?"

Jewel cut her eyes to Clay. "Uh." He looked smug. She remembered scolding him for unprofessional behavior.

That would have been while he was trying to unhook her bra. She swallowed coffee around a lump.

"Yes," Virgil said, "how are you feeling this morning?" He smiled at her with understanding. "Any ill effects?"

Besides the damage to my work relationship? "I think it was the Scotch," she said huskily. Her skull was splitting straight down the center of her forehead.

"Now might be a good time to take those Kirlian photographs of your aura," Virgil said.

"I'd like an aspirin," she confessed.

"A spa day will make you feel wonderful," Griffy said. She looked at Jewel with a mixture of sadness and envy. "We have a nine-thirty sauna, then a treatment, lunch, and another treatment. You have time for those photographs if you hurry."

Jewel's eyes felt like coarsely-sanded golf balls. "Let's hurry," she croaked.

An hour later she felt great. Not just less painful but wonderful. In fact she felt fabulous.

Virgil had taken her back upstairs to what she couldn't help thinking of as his laboratory, where he took her picture with a device that made her teeth buzz. Much newage was spoken, especially about her green tones, whatever the fuck those were.

Randy was in a huff, which she could understand but was in no mood to encourage. After all, she had no proof he hadn't spent the night elsewhere, too. She refused to meet his eye.

With all the men frisking around Jewel, Sovay was huffy, too.

So far, her day was a net win.

She swaggered into the John Hancock Tower. Every man in the lobby turned to look at her. The snake Sovay trailed behind her, shoved in front of her, or strode beside her, expensive heels clicking, but nobody cared. It was Jewel they saw.

She should work undercover more often.

Now that she was masquerading as Lord Darner's hired debunker, Jewel had on some of her pre-Randy, pre-Clay, pre-six-months-of-celibacy slutwear, such as today's tight little red top with the bunch in front that made her tits look bigger than God, and a pair of jeans that mostly fit.

None of the guys in the lobby seemed to have any complaints.

And she loved it.

"The elevator to ninety is up the escalator," Griffy said, consulting a building map.

Jewel didn't want to hide in an elevator yet. "Let's get coffee." She sashayed to the lobby Starbucks, reveling in the feeling that she could have any man she saw.

She hadn't felt like this since college. In the order line, three guys in window-washer coveralls turned around and stared at her, their jaws dropping. A paunchy tourist festooned with cameras gawked in her direction. His wife hustled their children away, looking miffed. The shoeshine guy whistled at her.

"Boy, that Venus Machine sure works," Griffy said.

"It must," Jewel said. "Yesterday I felt frumpy. Today—!"

"Today you're only half frumpy," Sovay said. She bent and rubbed a speck off the toe of her shoe, and her breasts almost fell out of her dress.

Jewel noticed that nobody else was looking, and smiled to herself.

"But how can it work?" Griffy said. "I don't under-stand!"

"It must have been intimidating to grow up with an intelligent brother," Sovay said. "For a slow child."

Jewel stepped between them. "It's just the power of

suggestion," she said to Griffy, wondering if that was true.

Through Starbucks's window she caught the eye of two men in suits, smoking outside the building. They were looking in at her. They sucked on identical huge phallic cigars and their palms were flat against the window and maybe she only imagined she saw a string of drool hanging off the side of one guy's jaw.

The lime-green-haired boy with big round spectacles taking coffee orders began to ask her, "How can I help—" and the words died in his throat.

"Double shot grande latte no foam cream to go," she said with a smile that made the barista reel.

I could get used to this.

CHAPTER
9

At the spa, Alex, their Beauty Guide, a youth of ethe-real good looks and iffy sexual orientation, spoke of Ayurvedic practices, turbinado sugar scrubs, and hydrat-ing shirodhara massage techniques. They could be rubbed, scrubbed, or packed with alarming products such as Amazon Basin bat oil, Potowatomi mineral baths, and soothing fluid marine flora reductions.

Griffy and Sovay took it all in solemnly.

Jewel thought Alex looked familiar. Had she ever dated him? Since she hadn't made a practice of chasing gay guys, maybe not.

She also found a stack of pamphlets entitled *Magic Is Afoot!* by Dr. G. K. Kauz, illustrated with a cartoon of a wizard waving a wand. *Holy crap.* She pocketed one, her blood running cold.

"I thought this was a psychic spa," she said. "Don't you have anything for my soul?"

Alex spread his arms angelically. "*Mademoiselle*, of course we won't neglect your soul. We have many meth-ods for spiritual cleansing and development, via active or passive energy flow."

She decided to push. "I need my aura tones checked. I've been told they're too green."

Alex looked at her with new interest. "Some practi-tioners rely on the naked eye, which is biased. Using our director's patented psychespectrometer, our colorimetricians measure every shade in your aura up to five hundred twelve precise tones, each with unique significance and treatment indications."

Patented. Jewel made a mental note. *That's a provable claim of material fact.* She said, "Can you treat my aura, too?"

"But of course."

"If it's broken or stained or something?"

He raised his chin with such saintliness that his perfect skin glowed. "Stains and breaks are mended every day," he uttered. "We make the process as pleasant as possible."

And that was almost a claim to practice medicine.

Sovay said, "I'll have the Hot Stone Relaxing Regimen and, to follow, the Lymph Drainage Facilitating Bastinado with Spring Salix Matsudana Twigs."

Jewel shot her a curious look. She'd once dated a guy who was into whippings.

"I need to relax," Griffy said, stating the obvious.

"Then may I suggest to *Madame* our Ultimate Triumph of Soul Mare Tranquilium, a two-hundred-minute experience with facial, mineral bath, massage, and seven-layer sea vegetable wrap. *Madame* did say she would be using Diner's Club?"

"My treat," Griffy said, waving at the other two, and glowed under Alex's look of startled respect.

"Perhaps you wish to make your nutrition selections now, rather than waiting for the midday sustaining ritual? The spa tends to fill up with office workers at lunch," he translated.

Jewel decided on a Rhodochrosite Crystal Chakra Cleanse with a massage and a marine flora reduction wrap, and after lunch an aura reading on the Institute's *patented* psychespectrometer. This would leave her, she calculated, forty minutes for loose snooping, while Griffy finished her Ultimate Triumph.

They were led to a locker room, lovingly undressed by small elderly women wearing kimonos, and laid out in a sauna. This was depressing. Sovay looked even better naked than clothed.

"In fact," Jewel remarked later to Griffy as they took their massages, "if you play the who's-what-bitch game, I look like an overweight golden lab and she looks like an afghan hound."

Griffy moaned under her masseuse's hands. "Who's what bitch?"

"Everyone's a bitch. Except you. The question is, what kind." Jewel felt her back start to loosen up.

"Oh, you are not overweight."

"See? You're not a bitch."

"Well, I think you look majestic. You're so tall and strong-looking. And your hair is beautiful. It just falls like a blond river. And you have nicer eyes than she has. I think brown eyes are kind of sneaky. Blue eyes are honest," Griffy said, in the teeth of the evidence under her own roof.

"Maybe you're an Irish setter, but blond," Jewel said.

The door opened, and Jewel's masseuse gasped. "Excuse me, this room is private!"

At the door, the baristo from Starbucks peeked in. His lime green hair seemed to stick straight up when he saw Jewel. "I brought you another latte."

Jewel stammered, "Uh—thuh—thanks."

He set the latte cup on the massage table by her nose. "You need anything, call downstairs." He smiled a trembly smile.

Griffy's masseuse flapped her hands at him. "Go, go!"

"Uh, here's a discount card!" He shoved it through the crack as the door shut on him.

Jewel looked at the latte cup. It had hearts drawn all around the top in green magic marker. She laughed.

"What the heck was *that*?"

"It's the Venus machine," Griffy said. "Venus was the goddess of love, wasn't she? She probably blessed the machine, and the machine blessed you."

"I don't think it's love on his mind," Jewel said. She felt pretty good. It didn't suck being a love goddess. "Just the power of suggestion."

The door opened. Her masseuse made a noise like an offended chicken. Jewel recognized the man peeping in as Griffy's chauffeur. "I'm Mike," he said, taking off his cap and looking at her as if she had just invented ice cream.

Jewel waited, but he didn't say anything else. "And? Nice to see you, Mike, but we're busy in here."

"Um, did you leave a scarf in the car?" He held up a tan plaid wool muffler.

Wool? In July? Jewel kept a straight face. "No, Mike, I didn't, but thank you for asking. Griffy, is that your scarf?"

He did a double take at the next table and looked embarrassed. "Oops." He backed up.

"Mike!" Griffy said in a scandalized voice.

"Sorry!" He left. The masseuse banged the door shut. Griffy said, "Well!"

Jewel laughed again, her belly shaking her whole body. "Don't even start with me. Did I leave a scarf in the car. What next!" The masseuse squished her shoulders. She relaxed. "Still, I don't see how the power of suggestion made those guys follow me ninety floors upstairs."

"You don't think it's kind of wonderful?" Griffy said. "Virgil said that Venus is related to the navel chakra. Maybe the Venus Machine did something to your navel. Does your navel feel funny?"

"No, but my head feels like it's gonna come off at the roots," Jewel said, grunting under the masseuse's powerful hands.

Her masseuse now began slapping her thighs.

"*Ow!* Hey! Knock it off!" Jewel twisted her neck to send a frown behind her. "If I want a spanking I'll go to a club."

The masseuse bowed. Then she laid something piping hot on the base of Jewel's spine.

Jewel jerked upright. The hot thing rolled onto the floor.

"I think I'm full up on new things. No. Please, no."

The masseuse protested in Ubangi or Ukrainian or something.

Jewel was firm. "I'm done. I want a shower. Shower? Water?" She mimed a showerhead. "Shh-shhhh-flflflfl-shhh?"

The masseuse yanked a hose down off a ceiling-bungee.

Jewel tried to take it from her. "I'll do it myself."

Griffy said, "You have to go back to the locker room for a shower. Haven't you ever been to a spa?"

Clambering off the table, Jewel wrapped her terry-cloth robe around her. "I think this one time will do me."

Jewel sneaked back to the locker room, showered off the oil, and donned a fresh puffy white terry robe. High time she started acting like an investigator. Her phone had eight messages, all from Ed. She went out into the elevator lobby to call him back.

" 'S'amatter with you," he groused, "I been calling all day."

"I'm undercover, boss, remember?" The lobby floor was cold under her bare feet. She huddled into a corner and turned her terry-robed back to avoid the eyes of elevator passengers.

"You done anything about that nutcase in the psychic salon?"

"I'm there now."

"Hurry up. They're holding election press conferences any day. Get something on him, fraud, code violation, somethin' looneytunes. Feelin' up the customers, I don't give a damn."

"Fifth Floor leaning on you?" Jewel said sympathetically.

"Commissioner. Seems to think his job's on the line."

"So I guess if I screw up we get a new boss."

"You wish. I'm Shakman exempt, they can't fire me for political reasons. But the whole friggin' city could go to hell in a hanky. You gotta think big picture."

Someone male came out of the spa behind her. "Hi, Jewel!"

She stiffened. *Who knows me here?*

"Ed," she said, hunching lower over the phone. "Check out a patent for me. For a 'psychespectrometer,' whatever that is, and I have no clue how you spell it."

Ed grunted. "And you think I do?"

"The patent's in the name of the spa guy."

"Gustavus Ka-flim-flam-a-ram-a Kauz?"

"That's him," she said.

"Oh, you're on the phone," said the voice behind her. *Oh God, what if it's someone I dated?*

Ed said, "The Fifth Floor has a file on Kauz. You want it?"

"Dear God, yes." She stuck her finger in her free ear. "Talk to you tonight or tomorrow."

"Speed it up," Ed said, and rang off.

She stood holding the dead phone to her ear. "Uh-huh," she said to the dead phone. "Okay. Uh-huh."

The guy behind her said, "Some other time, I guess."

In that moment she recognized the voice as Buzz's and turned to see him disappear behind closing elevator doors. She noticed two more things: His backpack was bulging, and he looked furtive, as if he too had decided not to be recognized.

It's a potion. I'm, like, beta testing it.

Beta testing for a spa, maybe?

Hot dog, she thought, tapping her phone in her palm. *I've been undercover one day and I've already detected something.*

Two suited guys also holding huge, phallic cigars came out of the second elevator and spotted her. "It's her!"

"There she is! Hey, foxy lady!"

They stuck their cigars in their faces and reached for her with both hands.

In the nick of time, someone opened the spa door.

Jewel swept past them into the spa, barefoot, with her nose in the air.

The guy holding the spa door for her was Griffy's chauffeur.

In the waiting room, latte-boy looked up and smiled.

Feeling hunted, Jewel pretended she didn't see them. *Jeez. Now I'm starting to worry about my green tones.*

"There you are!" Alex fluted. "Are we ready for our chakra cleanse? By the way . . ." He leaned closer to her. "My partner still talks about you. You look better than ever!"

"Thanks," Jewel said pallidly. Not for the first time, she wished she'd kept a little black book during her slut years. It could have helped her place these guys. "Uh, tell him hi."

Her chakra cleanse began alongside Griffy's treatment. They were bathed on adjoining massage tables with the bungee-showerheads, which Jewel instantly coveted. Then they were laid on their backs, schmeared in fragrant green muck, and wrapped like mummies in what seemed to be huge sheets of sushi-wrap.

"Seaweed?"

"Dehydrated marine flora," Jewel's attendant corrected. "Let that soak in." She turned the lights down and dialed up the Muzak. "I'll leave the door ajar in case you need something." She left.

"How about a quart margarita and a straw?" Jewel muttered.

Griffy giggled. "I can't move my lips."

"I can't move anything. What's this you're having again?"

"Some kind of ultimate soul tranquilizer."

"Man, I should have asked for that. My nose itches."

They lay there companionably, listening to dronymoany music with tinkles. Jewel could see out the sliver of open door, across the hall, into the waiting room. A familiar-looking, dark-clad shoulder was visible. The chauffeur maybe? His back was to the doorway.

"You do this kind of thing often?" she said.

"Mm-hm," Griffy said. "Usually I go to Giorgio lo Gigolo."

"It would drive me scatty. I guess I bore easily."

"Oh, but you have such interesting work!"

What was her cover? Randy's flimflam debunker. "Lord Darner's not up on American culture. Not that he'll admit it."

"Men are so fragile. Inside, I mean," Griffy said. This didn't sound much like Virgil, but Jewel didn't say so. "They're easily fooled by appearances."

"Huh," Jewel said, thinking of Sovay.

"And yet here we are, improving our appearance for them! That Venus Machine really works. Maybe I should try it."

"I didn't need it. A switch to turn guys off, maybe, yeah."

Griffy gave a sad laugh. "Well, I'd like to try it."

Jewel said, "Girlfriend, have you ever thought that

you are a fabulous woman, and Virgil is lucky to have someone like you to love him? You don't need to change. He does."

"Maybe," Griffy said forlornly. "But men don't change. Do you like Clay? I think he likes you. Of course, he won't change, either."

Great, everybody knew Jewel had slept with Clay last night.

"He's nice enough after the weirdos I've dated. Like the guy who ties you up, and the guy who wants to play pretend-stalker, and—" *Whoa, dial back the girl talk.* "I had way too much fun in college," she finished.

"College!" Griffy sighed. "Clay must be a breath of fresh air."

"So far, yes," Jewel admitted. "He's been attentive and generous and patient and nonjudgmental."

There was a smile in Griffy's voice. "Love is wonderful."

Jewel bridled. "Has Clay told you he's in love with me?"

"Clay doesn't tell anyone anything. He talks a lot and he seems to be telling you stuff, but when you think about it later, you didn't learn anything. Have you noticed that?"

"Hell, yes." Something was odd about this conversation. Griffy seemed to assume that Jewel and Clay knew each other well. She'd sounded like that yesterday, too. As if Clay had blabbed to her. But why would he do that?

"He's like his father that way. I gave up trying to figure Virgil out years ago."

"His *father*?" Jewel put the clues together. "Clay is—he isn't *Virgil's* son?" That would make Griffy— "Holy crap!" she blurted. "That sneaky, lying weasel—"

"Oops," Griffy said in a small voice.

Jewel lied, "I guessed anyway." But her head was exploding. No wonder Clay wanted to handle this case on his own!

Never in a million years would she have guessed. She would kill Clay. So this was how Griffy knew all about Clay's job, and Jewel being his partner. She felt like a fool.

If Virgil was his father, then Clay had known it when they took the case. And since he went to Virgil's house before Jewel and Randy got there, he must have lied to Virgil about them somehow. But how? What lies did he tell? And why?

On the other hand, if Virgil knew who Clay was, what the heck was he up to, pretending they were investigating Clay?

Complex, too complex!

"So you complained to the city?"

"Clay was annoyed with me about that. He said the city can't stop Sovay from taking Virgil from me."

"He's right." *Although we may bust her for the Venus Machine scam, if we can figure out the scam part.* "I can't believe Clay didn't tell me that he told you about us. Doesn't that bother you? To be lied to and shut out?"

"I don't know. Should it? Maybe I'm not that interested in something a person doesn't want me to know. I pretty much take people as they come. It's not very complicated, but then I'm not very smart," Griffy said humbly.

"You're plenty smart, Griffy. At least you're not screwing two men at once," Jewel blurted.

"Two? Oh, of course. You're with Lord Darner."

Jewel groaned. *The girl-talking mouth got away that time.* "Now I'm wondering if I should tell you."

"No teasing! Lord Darner is your other partner?"

"Clay told you way too much."

"Oh, no, I figured out who you were right away. So you—you work with both of them?"

"Randy is my siamese twin. My bodyguard. He's glued to me for life."

Griffy gasped. "You're *married*?"

"No, that's what's so unfair about it." *Relationships, ugh.*

"Uh, Jewel, I don't think Clay is the marrying kind."

"I don't want to marry Clay!" she burst out. "I don't want to marry Randy either. What would be the point? He already haunts my pussy!"

Griffy snorted. "For real?"

Jewel yearned to pour it all into a female ear. "I spoke figuratively."

"How does that work, then?"

"You want the long version or the short version?"

"I want to hear the part you want to tell me," Griffy said, which brought Jewel up with a start. *I so suck at undercover.*

She frowned. The mummy-wrap around her forehead crinkled.

"He lives with me. He sleeps with me. Whenever he's in a bed with me, he, like, disappears into my—I don't even know if this is true—but it feels like he's inside my mind and my body at the same time. It weirds me out. What's sick is, I love that. But the weirdest thing is I'm getting used to it. It's like, you reach out in the night, and you feel that warm lump under the covers, and you think, 'He's still here!' And it feels good, it feels safe, because he hasn't left you."

Griffy said softly, "Sometimes I wonder if Virgil is going to leave me."

Jewel pulled herself together. "Virgil? He's a hundred and one!"

"I wonder. He's had a lot of girlfriends, you know. He won't marry. He was married a long time ago to Clay's mother and it was awful. She took him for everything, I'm guessing."

"Well, he's not gonna leave you. He wouldn't dare."

"Why wouldn't he dare leave me?" Griffy sounded vulnerable.

Jewel felt guilty for trying to comfort her. What if she was wrong? "Because he'll never get a deal this good. You're gorgeous, you're the kindest thing in nature, and you love him. You love his kid. Why on earth would he leave that?"

"I guess I know all that. But I feel dumb around him."

"I bet he loves that, too."

"Gosh. I bet you're right! Tell me about Randy."

All Jewel's grievances came up in her throat. "Have you ever had a boyfriend who had to get laid, *all* night, *every single night*? Whether you were drunk or asleep, or had the flu, or you're just mad at him? No matter how you feel when you go to bed, there he is with his permanent erection."

"Been there," Griffy said, yawning. "That was Virgil, once." She gave a sleepy sigh.

"And this is the part that sucks. *He can always make me come*. Every single time. It's like an obsession with him."

Griffy laughed. "Oh, now I'm playing my violin for you."

"I knew you wouldn't understand."

"Try me."

"Well, think about it. If I'm drunk, if I pass out, if I'm just asleep? He can—" *Keep Randy's secret, Jewel.* "I don't even know what he does to me when I'm asleep. It's like he gets inside my dreams. I have horny dreams until I'm creaming. And then, *wham*!"

"He must love sex."

"I wonder. Sometimes I don't know if he's loving it or

not. At first I thought so. But we've been inseparable, twenty-four-seven, for weeks. I know him better now. I think he's afraid to miss a chance." *Because of the curse.* The sting in the curse's tail came back to her at that. *You must love her, Randall*, his magician-mistress had written.

He never missed a chance to make her come. But did he love her?

Hell, did she *want* him to love her?

See, this is why I don't do relationships. "All I know is, it's driving me out of my mind."

"I've known guys like that," Griffy said wistfully. "Only they weren't desperate to make me enjoy it."

"He may be holding on to the kennel door," Jewel mused.

"What kennel door?"

"My grandparents hated dogs, which was odd, since we had a farm. They made my dogs stay in a kennel at night. Not one of those dogs liked going in the kennel at bedtime. And yet, if a dog got in trouble, he'd run for his kennel and curl up inside."

Griffy sounded fuddled. "So Randy—"

"Sees my pussy as his kennel." Over Griffy's laughter, she said, "He could be sick of sex by now—you would think so—I bet I would be, in his shoes. But if we ever have a fight he, like, uh, runs away, and then I don't see him again until I go to bed. And there he is, like a bad, horny penny."

"That's normal," Griffy said. "Some men want a relationship, and they think they know about sex, and they think that should be enough for us. Really they're desperate, 'cause they don't have us figured out, and they don't understand themselves, and sex is easier than love. They're praying that sex is enough. And it never is."

And you just described how screwed up I am, Jewel

thought. For a dumb blonde, Griffy had a grip on important things.

Griffy's mummy-wrapping rustled. "The whole secret is—"

The masseuse came in. "Ready for our exfoliation?" She wheeled Griffy out, leaving Jewel in the dark about the whole secret.

Jewel drowsed, wondering how come people who seemed dumber than she was always had longer-lasting relationships.

There was a muffled shriek. The door opened again.

"—Put them in lost and found," said a woman at the door.

"But his wallet and everything," someone said in the hall.

"Trust me, he'll notice if his wallet is missing. And his shoes. Hello," the woman said, closing the door and advancing on Jewel, carrying a lighted candle and a wicker basket. "Have you ever had your chakras cleansed before?"

"Uh, no. Don't I get out of this stuff first?" Jewel said. The seaweed mummy-wrap was making her sweat.

"Your chakras lie parallel to your endocrine glands." The woman lightly touched Jewel's wrappings in a line from her pubic bone up to the crown of her head, dip-dip-dip, little touches that felt odd. "This is energy work."

Jewel felt like she was about to have a mammogram. Her nipples tightened.

"Should I be memorizing any of this?"

"No need." The chakra cleanser lit more candles around the massage table. "Relax and allow it to happen."

Jewel lay still. She felt antsy. She thought about wriggling. She wanted to rip off the mummy-wrap. The green gunk they'd schmeared her with made her skin tingle. The candlelight dazzled her eyes. She thought about shifting her hand under the wrappings into her crotch and jerking off, which shocked her.

I wish she hadn't said "energy." Now I have some.

"Om mane padme hummmm," said her chakra cleanser.

Jewel realized she was horny. Good thing she was a girl. If she was a guy she'd have a hellacious boner.

"Ommmmm. Ommmmm."

"So what is my chakra?" Jewel said. Her chin itched.

"You have seven chakras." The attendant did that tapping thing again and Jewel spasmed like a hooked fish. "Relax. Close your eyes and go into the music."

There was music, Jewel realized, a mealy-mouthed tinkly sound. It made her think of ice in a glass of Long Island iced tea. She closed her eyes. Maybe a mint julep. She pictured making a julep, picking the mint, grinding it in a pestle with a swivel-hipped motion, her nostrils filling with peppermint scent. Now the woman was touching her brow with minty stuff. *Nice.*

Jewel's julep-making fantasy popped away. "The thing is, I'm not very relaxed," she blurted, squirming.

"Listen to the music. Wait for the low tones."

And then do what? I can't move a freakin' muscle. Just breathing, she could feel the seaweed wrap chafe her nipples.

Jewel closed her eyes again. She thought of walking ankle-deep in the creek on a hot summer day, and the smell of mint plants in the marsh out behind the back forty. The music hit some deeper tones. *Huh.* She thought about lying on her back in the sun, crushing peppermint plants under her. Bobby Wiflheimer was with her, and he slid a finger into her panties.

Her eyes popped open. Her breathing was shallow and fiery. "How long does this take?"

She thought about an alien bursting out of her chest— no, not an alien, more of a big old donkey schlong— tearing out of this goddam mummy-wrap and—

She must have drifted off. Her eyes opened again. "How long?"

"Shhh, you're doing beautifully. Now we'll open your second chakra." The attendant held something over Jewel's tummy, not touching her. The restless feeling in her ying-yang jumped into high. "Do you hear the low tones?"

A deep-voiced flute began playing. "Yeah." Jewel's eyes closed. She lay under the stars by the creek, alone, thank goodness. Her nerves sang with damped-down lust, lust that slept because she lay still. Nothing moved. The gleaming creek didn't make a sound.

And yet, now she felt she was not alone.

Finally, she thought. *I can't seem to do this on my own.*

Do what? she wondered, and then she felt a sly presence like an invisible smile. It seemed far away, and yet also touching her, putting its finger on a nerve running up the middle of her body, a nerve that zinged and jumped.

She felt two powerful impulses. She wanted to jump up, run around, scream, find the intruder and beat the smile off his facelessness with her fists. She also wanted to lie still and let the intruder make her desire swell like an ocean wave.

Far away, the attendant Ommed again. Her fingertips touched the mummy-wrap here and there.

Jewel didn't feel a thing. Her whole mind focused on locating that invisible smirk, that mischievous poking, teasing presence. Just when she thought she'd found it under her tailbone, it melted away, then returned, tracing a circle around her nipples, counting hairs on the inside of her thigh, tickling the roof of her mouth until her eyes rolled up in her head. The longer she lay still, the less she felt she could move. And yet she felt an urge to thrash and squirm.

Slowly, so as not to attract the notice of the chakra cleanser, she tightened every muscle in her buns, and felt a momentary rush. *Oh, yeah.*

Then someone began to moan. *Is that me?* No, it was the new-age Muzak. It moaned the way she wanted to moan. Only she mustn't. She mustn't move or speak. That woman would know.

With that thought, Jewel felt a great stillness fall on her, like a heavy hand clamping the back of her neck, like a heavy blanket of winter coats piled on the bed, like an ocean wave rolling over her so heavily, no grain of sand shifted under her.

And the invisible smiler swooped in, shadowing her thoughts, filling her lower body with bliss.

The invisible finger touched a nerve in the hollow of her right buttock, sending a shiver up to her right ear. She could hear the nerve twang like an electric guitar note fuzzing out, a sound so alive that it bashed around inside her belly, trying to get out. The guitar-note got louder. It crawled sizzling up her side, up her shoulder, to the base of her throat.

If I don't come soon, she thought, *I'll scream.*

She drew in a long breath.

The invisible smiler put a firm thumb on the trigger between her legs.

Jewel arched her back and screamed. Sexual release flew out of her in all directions. At last she could move. She thrashed back and forth and half-rolled off the massage table, her flying legs knocking over candles and chakra-cleansing equipment, until strong arms grabbed her around the waist from behind and she lay still again, quivering like a scared horse, her eyes rolling.

The overhead light flashed on.

The attendant stood by the door, gasping, her hand splayed on her heaving chest.

On the ceiling, bits of seaweed wrap stuck to ceiling tiles and light fixtures. The walls were spattered with the green gunk they'd schmeared on her.

And, of course, underneath her, a very familiar woody prodded her in the back.

"Don't move," Randy said in her ear, "or you will roll off."

Well, it was a huge scene. You'd have thought this was some low-class joint where nobody ever did anybody on a massage table before. Masseuses and manicurists came to the door to peek. Hairdressers and holistic healers gabbled in the hallway. The chakra cleanser had hysterics. Jewel lay still while bits of her mummy-wrap dripped off the ceiling onto her, and Randy clung tight to keep her from falling off the table, and voices in the open doorway said words like, "fat, exhibitionist, deviant, sexual perverts."

Then her two stogie-smoking fans shoved to the door.

"It's her! Wow!" said stogie fan number one.

"Move, I want to see!" said stogie fan number two.

"That lady is a lady, you jerks!" said the green-haired kid from the latte shop.

"Miss Hess, are you all right?" said Griffy's chauffeur. *Thanks for telling them my name. At least it's not my real name.*

"If you get a picture, I want one." That was the shoeshine boy from the main lobby.

A flash went off, and Jewel recognized the paunchy tourist from downstairs, grinning at her behind a formidable camera.

At that she struggled out of Randy's grasp and rolled gracelessly off the table, away from view.

Now the gawkers were saying, "Hunk."

"I most humbly beg your pardon," her naked sex demon said at his lordliest to her chakra cleanser. "It was unforgivable of me to distress you, madam." His highbred voice seemed to calm her.

"Oh, well—it's not—you—I—"

Jewel stuck her head up in time to see Randy bow and kiss the chakra cleanser's hand. "So sorry to have troubled you."

Her whimpers turned to simpers. "Oh, sir."

The camera flash went off. Jewel ducked behind the table again.

"Hey!" cried the chivalrous barista. "You can't take her picture without her consent!"

Scuffling broke out in the hall. Something crunched. The tourist yelled. When the fighting seemed about to become general, Randy shouted, "Silence!"

And lo, they all shut up. Under the massage table she saw Randy's bare feet and ankles move into the hall.

Jewel crouched behind the table, silently swearing.

Eventually her worshippers were shooed out of the hallway and, she hoped, out of the spa. Then Randy said at the doorway: "Perhaps one of you might bring her a hot cup of tea? Too good of you. And if someone could find my clothes?"

The sound of the chakra cleanser's hiccups receded.

Jewel heard the door shut. She stood up. "Well!"

Randy was looking at the walls and ceiling. "Interesting. I suppose you couldn't tear it away in time." A flap of seaweed fell on his upturned face and he picked it off, studying it. "The pressures involved must be sufficient to—"

She socked him on the arm. "You followed me!" she hissed.

"You are not safe here. With tones so green, you need protection from lewd men," he said with a straight face.

"I was doing fine until you showed up!" she lied.

He took her robe off its hook on the wall and hung it around her shoulders as someone opened the door.

"Excuse me please? Hello?"

Jewel yanked on her robe, hiding behind Randy's altogetherness and blushing.

A tubby little guy wearing rimless spectacles and a white lab coat over a gray suit and tie appeared at the door. "I am the Institute's director, Dr. Kauz." He handed some folded clothes and a pair of shoes to Randy "Yours, I believe?"

So that was Randy in the waiting room! Jewel put it all together at last. *Uh-oh. He was listening to me dish on him to Griffy. That's why he zapped into the massage table.*

Jewel yanked her fluffy belt tight and stepped out from behind her sex demon. "I'm sorry. He follows me everywhere. Get—" she hissed to Randy "—dressed."

Dr. Kauz was looking at the walls and ceiling, his little mouth hanging open.

"You should not be alone with him," Randy murmured.

She pointed at the door. "Wait for me in the waiting room."

Randy shrugged into his trousers and shirt, then turned smoldering black eyes on her. "I shall be near, if you need me."

"Or even if I don't. Now scram."

With a dark look at Dr. Kauz, Randy scrammed.

"Most remarkable," Dr. Kauz said to Randy's back. Then his watery blue eyes bugged out at Jewel. "*Himmel!* You must be the lady with the too-green aura!"

She looked at her green-schmeared arms. "There was a lot of seaweed," she began. Then she remembered Virgil tut-tutting over her Kirlian photographs, a hundred years ago this morning. "Uh, that's what they say."

He looked her up and down with awe. "You wish to shower. Then if you would step into the next room, my psychespectrometer will pinpoint the trouble."

"Can't be too soon for me," she muttered.

CHAPTER 11

Jewel congratulated herself on getting the spa director's attention. After her shower, Kauz led her in triumph through the spa, his spectacles flashing, his round face flushed.

As they passed through the dining area, she saw Randy drinking coffee with Sovay, Griffy eating salad alone, and three window cleaners in coveralls plastered to the outside windows, their hands cupped against the glass, looking in. She avoided meeting their eyes. Everyone was staring at her.

"Julia, are you okay?" Griffy said.

"I'm fine, I'm fine," she kept saying.

Randy, Sovay, and Griffy got up and followed her.

In the psychespectrometer room, Dr. Kauz explained the principles of colorimetry. It had something to do with refracting and sublimating implied light given off by the human body, in effect, the aura, blah, blah, blah. The machine itself looked like a big-ass, white-panel-faced fluorescent light fixture, hanging perpendicular to the floor, with wires connecting it to several monitors and a printer. Behind the panel was a chunk of humming hardware that Dr. Kauz called "the transformer."

He made her stand in front of the psychespectrometer while he fiddled with the controls.

Griffy said, "This is Julia Hess. She's suffering from—"

"*Stumm!*" Kauz touched his lips. "I see very well how she is suffering." He picked up Jewel's hand very gently. The round spectacles flashed. "*Fräulein*, kindly stand there." He switched on the spectrometer and squinted into an eyepiece. "*Mein Gott*," he blurted. "Look at this." He switched on an overhead monitor, and Jewel craned her neck to look. She caught her breath.

The monitor showed a moving form in blazing acid green.

"Yow." Griffy stared. "What is it, Doctor?"

Jewel scratched her cheek, and the image on the monitor scratched with her.

Kauz seemed transfixed. "Vot happened to her?"

"Is she supposed to be that color?" Griffy said.

"She is not!"

Sovay slumped against the door. Randy loomed beside her, eyeing the equipment with suspicion.

Jewel stared at her green self. She swallowed.

"How should she look?" Griffy said.

"I demonstrate. If you would exchange places?" Kauz waved to Griffy and she sat. Her rainbow-colored image appeared. Kauz tapped the screen. "Miss Julia's chromatic distribution should be more diverse, *so wie*. Exchange again, please?"

Jewel returned to the psychespectrometer. Again the scintillating acid green image filled the monitor.

Kauz seemed fascinated. *Maybe I can lure him over to Virgil's house.* She felt very Clay-like, very undercover.

"How does such a woman survive in this world?" Kauz mused.

"That Venus Machine did it!" Griffy said. "They put her in it last night and she's been different ever since."

"Machine?" he said, peering into the eyepiece again and twiddling a knob. "Charged. Like cloudful of lightning." He shook his head. "Incredible."

"My—my brother is appraising a machine for this

lady," Griffy said, nodding toward Sovay. "It's a Catty-wompusomething."

"Kat-ter-fel-to," Sovay pronounced with scorn.

Kauz jerked his head up. "Katterfelto?" The round spectacles filled up with his boogling blue eyes. "Can it be—is it possible that you mean Katterfelto's Miracle Venereal Attraction Accelerator Apparatus?" He spread his hand over his chest. "Has it reappeared?"

"I guess it works," Griffy said. "Ms. Sacheverell owns it."

His voice dropped. "This man is my idol all my life. I have taken his name in his honor. *Manchmal*," he said gutturally, "sometimes I think I am his *weiderfleischwerdung*, you would say, his incarnation repeated." He turned toward Jewel again. He was almost drooling.

She goggled at the monitor. "Green. Is that bad?"

He said, "Your symptoms. I must know everything. Let me guess! At first euphoria, satisfaction at being the object of attention. Then, perhaps, a little alarm, yes? Shyness? It is not so pleasant to be under so much close observation."

She shuddered. "It sucks."

"I have studied original source material," Kauz said, nodding. "A delicately nurtured *mädchen* is unprepared for so much scrutiny. Perhaps she shrinks from the spotlight. One must have, I think, the soul of a circus performer to enjoy it. Let me print this reading—" he pressed a button and the image on the monitor froze. Then he pleaded, "If I could work with you. Your test is so remarkable. Your symptoms—if I could help in any way—I am familiar with Katterfelto's theories—"

"We ought to show him the Venus Machine, don't you think?" Griffy said to Sovay. "Do you mind? It's your machine."

Sovay rolled her eyes.

Kauz placed his hands together as if in prayer and

bowed to Sovay. "If I can examine the machine, perhaps I can find a way to cure this unfortunate woman's unbalanced aura. *Madame*, I beg you, be merciful."

Sovay jerked her shoulder. "Oh, why not? And bring that thing with you. I'm sure Virgil would love to see it," she said, sending an unpleasant look at Griffy.

"Of course," Kauz said.

"I'm going out for some air." Sovay slouched out of the room, and Randy followed.

And bang, Jewel's cases were as commingled as a laundry-load full of pantyhose. "I think I'll, uh, visit the locker room." She blundered out past Kauz's adoring gaze.

In the locker room she phoned Clay's cell. "Listen," she hissed, "I've got the spa guy coming to Virgil's house later this afternoon. He's in love with my green tones and he's got a hard-on for the Venus Machine. This is our chance to open him up."

"Did he say anything about the election?"

"No. Not a word. Though I picked up a scary pamphlet about magic in the waiting room. So, listen, what I want to know is, can you get Virgil Thompson to invite him to stay for a few days?"

"What are you hoping to accomplish?" Clay said in a guarded voice. "I thought you didn't want to commingle the cases."

"I didn't, but now I've messed up here and they're all tangled together," she confessed. "Will Virgil co-operate?"

"No problem. The guy's got a bunch of money for his campaign fund, but he needs more. And Virgil is rich and crazy about magic. Only question is, who'll be gladder to see whom."

"Groovy. I need to hear him talking about his platform. Also I hope to establish a link between him and Buzz. Buzz is distributing a concoction for Kauz, I'm sure of it. Maybe he'll have Buzz meet him at Virgil's house."

"Surely Buzz will cooperate if charges can be laid against him," Clay said.

She sighed. "You don't know Buzz." The locker room door opened. Sovay and Griffy came in. "I gotta go." She hung up.

Clay seemed mighty sure of Kauz's welcome. And very interested in Kauz's campaign money.

Great. She was unleashing one con artist on another. Three, if you counted Clay. No, four, she was forgetting Sovay the Snake. Was that ethical? Did she get to bend the rules when she was undercover? How much? When would the whole thing blow up in her face and leave her covered in anti-glory and federal violations?

She'd already had three showers but, now that Kauz had slathered her with his icky admiration, she felt a little less than fresh. She took another.

CHAPTER 12

While the others ferried Kauz and his psychespectrometer to Virgil's house in Griffy's limousine, Jewel took a cab, the better to get something through Randy's head.

He seemed totally not embarrassed. "Why should I feel shame? Men follow you down the street like dogs."

"Well, I'm embarrassed. I don't do men in public!"

"Except for Nathan the Napkinfucker."

Jewel goggled. "Where did you hear about that?"

"Nina mentioned him at dinner on Sunday. Don't you recall?"

My best friend Nina. Think I'll kill her. Jewel licked dry lips. "That was eight months ago. And we never got caught. And I dumped him. I wish I could dump you!"

"All you need do is to forget I am there."

"Forget you're in my bed? When you're sneaking into my *head*, into my *dreams*?"

"Next time I vanish into a bed—or a massage table." With a gesture he indicated the cab seat between them. "Or an automobile. Simply forget where I have gone."

He didn't have to add the rest of it. If he couldn't give her an orgasm, he couldn't get out of the trap by himself. Ever.

She bit her lip. "You could have told me you were in the massage table, somehow. I could have come back later."

"Would you have returned? You seem dissatisfied with my services of late."

So he *had* heard what she said to Griffy! Oh, gosh. *But girl talk is a necessity. I can't cope without girl talk.*

She avoided his eyes. "Well, you've been annoying me."

"I, on the other hand, cannot afford to be angry with you."

That annoyed her even more. He knew darned well that she knew that he couldn't afford to make her too mad. She was number one hundred on his magic list of stealth fucks. Until he'd given her an orgasm, he'd been a sex slave for two centuries.

And now he was her slave.

Funny how it felt like she was his.

If only she could figure out how she felt about that.

Her embarrassment was easing. "Look, this is not about my sex life, or even yours. You have to be careful. You can't be," she lowered her voice, "magical. There's very low tolerance. You're lucky you got sprung from that brass bed in Chicago. The Policy here is 'Don't ask, don't tell, cope.' It could have happened in Pittsburgh. Or D.C. I shudder to think what the feds would do with you."

"But in only three weeks I have seen magic everywhere—"

She interrupted him. "You have not seen magic. Not. You've observed a few anomalies that can happen in any densely populated community. When diverse peoples rub together, they naturally imagine that their experience is reality and everyone else's is weird. A city is a confusing place." She looked him in the eye with all her force of will. "People imagine they see all kinds of stuff. The world keeps on spinning, whether they decide to cope, or have hysterics over nothing. Why have a cow?"

"You care for your city," he said, the lightbulb going on.

"Duh. It's my home and it's my job. There is no magic," she repeated. Why should he believe her? She didn't believe herself. "Only a little inconvenience."

"Or a large one."

Scanning his big body she agreed. "Or a large one."

He looked miffed. "Then I must be more convenient."

Jewel knew this was as good as it got, Randy-polite-wise.

She drew a shuddering sigh. "Thank you."

At Virgil's mansion, Jewel saw that her humiliations had just begun. The newest addition to the loonybin, Dr. Kauz, was introduced to Virgil.

Then Griffy told them how Jewel had attracted all eyes at the Hancock Tower. "You should have seen it! I think that machine works. Of course Julia's already beautiful." She smiled at Jewel.

Jewel wondered if anyone could be that nice. "What I want to know is, does the Venus Machine have a reverse setting? Because I'm sick of this."

"But you said the Venus Machine was a fraud," Randy said with malice. "You said there is no magic."

"My, my," Sovay murmured. "The skeptic recants."

Jewel felt hunted. "You try it and see how you like it."

"Perhaps I shall," Sovay said. "But you haven't told them the most exciting part of your day." Jewel sent her a glare that would have decapitated a lesser bitch. Sovay shrugged her pretty shoulders. "Dr. Kauz, perhaps you could describe it."

"Of course, of course," Kauz said, whipping pictures out of a folder, and Jewel cringed. Did he have pix of her seaweed mummy-wrap dripping off the ceiling? "I have caused my psychespectrometer to be brought here so Herr Thompson can witness phenomenon of Ms. Hess and her powerful green tones." She thanked God for Kauz's one-track mind. "Perhaps if strong young backs can bring my psychespectrometer to a room where we can all observe—?" He looked from Clay to Randy.

"My collection room is at the top of the house," Virgil said, managing to look ninety years old, sitting still.

Randy looked snooty. "The servants perhaps?"

So of course Clay sprang forward. "We'd be delighted to help. Lord Darner, would you care to don a pair of gloves to protect your hands while we lug this thing inside?"

Randy sniffed, but he followed Clay and Dr. Kauz.

"I understand that your skepticism has suffered, Ms. Hess," Virgil said as he led the house party upstairs.

She mumbled, "It's sprung a leak."

"I think you should keep an open mind," Griffy said.

"I'm not paid to keep an open mind." Jewel hated to admit it, but she was scared. "I want that Venus Machine effect reversed. Even if it's fake."

Virgil smiled at Jewel, and she thought she saw Griffy look away. *Great, now I'm making her jealous.* He said, "I'm sure you cannot be more charming than you were already."

"It seems she can," Sovay said in a silky voice.

Jewel threw her a fuck-you glance. "You got a problem?"

Sovay raised her manicured hands.

"I didn't ask for all this attention," Jewel said tightly.

"I'm sure you didn't. When one has given up hope—" Sovay patted a yawn.

"I don't think Julia was ever hopeless with men," Griffy said, defending her again. "Besides, it can't be very pleasant to have *every* man's attention *all* the time.

Sovay coiled her arm through Virgil's. "One manages."

Virgil gave a senile simper.

To make trouble, Jewel said, "Once you fix me, maybe we should try putting Griffy through the Venus Machine."

As he opened the collection-room door, Virgil snorted. Or it might have been Sovay beside him.

Griffy stiffened. "Thank you, Julia," she said with trembling dignity. "I just might do that."

They found Clay and Randy had brought Dr. Kauz's machine to the collection room in a service elevator. They assembled it while the doctor made things beep.

When Jewel walked in, all three men turned toward her like flowers facing the sun.

She could feel Sovay's glare, hot on the back of her neck.

"Fix me!" she blurted.

After that things got noisy.

Dr. Kauz and Virgil went into a huddle, twiddling, clanking, and speaking newage.

Then she stood in front of the psychespectrometer. Then she had her Kirlian picture taken. To Virgil's painfully obvious sneers, Griffy went through the same process.

Then the mad scientists fooled with the Venus Machine.

Those less technical got out of the way. Randy drifted over to Sovay. The butler rolled in the liquor cart. Clay brought wine to Griffy and a Scotch to Jewel.

"I can't believe you want to reverse the machinkusization," Griffy said to Jewel.

"It sucks," Jewel said. "Like, uh, Lord Darner said, men follow me like dogs. I feel like Julia Roberts on a bad hair day. I've had enough."

"See anything good at the spa?" Clay said to Jewel.

"Oh, yes, they have everything," Griffy said. "And Julia had her chakras cleaned!"

"Was that fun?" Clay smiled at Jewel.

She sent him a silent *shh!* She was trying to eavesdrop on Sovay, who was chatting up her sex demon.

"This little scar on your jaw," Sovay said, drawing her finger down Randy's face. "How did it happen?"

"Hunting accident."

"A hunting accident!" Sovay echoed in a throbbing voice. "How terrifying!"

"A mere scratch, dear lady." Randy smirked.

Meanwhile Griffy was spilling the beans with a firm hand. "The green goo got everywhere! And the seaweed stuck on the ceiling."

Clay swigged his beer. "No!"

Jewel avoided Clay's eye. "What are they doing? I want to get this over with."

At that point, the mad scientist symposium broke up.

Dr. Kauz said, "Ms. Hess, if you would be so good as to be seated in the Venus *Apparat*."

Jewel sat in the green velvet chair. "This better work."

Dr. Kauz moved her feet. "Don't vorry. Be happy." He strapped her ankles in.

"What th—"

Virgil moved her head. "Try to envision a complete cure. We're not convinced this isn't a placebo effect, which is also fascinating. Here—" He lowered a big metal cap over her head.

She rolled her eyes up at the cap. "Did we do all this last night? Because I don't remember any straps."

"You were in a pretty good mood last night," Clay murmured.

Virgil strapped her wrists down. Then he took her pulse. Then he peeled back her right eyelid. "Hm. Still green."

By now she was rigid. *Bunch of clowns.*

Randy stepped forward and laid his hand on one of her fettered wrists. "Are you certain this is what you wish?"

"*Yes*, I'm certain. Cripes, you were there today."

He glanced from Virgil to Clay to Kauz. "You cannot know what is in their minds."

She let her eyes glitter up at him. He was so transparent. *Flirts with Sovay and then tells me what to do.* "Maybe I can."

Randy heaved a sigh and walked over to Sovay. "I can't watch this," she heard him say.

Dr. Kauz struck a pose at the big knifeswitch. "Stand back, everyone, please! Now, Ms. Hess, you must relax. Think of something beautiful. Are you ready? Oops! No, wait." Jewel groaned. He twiddled with her straps. "Okay, now we are ready. Relaaaaaxinnnnng—" Out of the corner of her eye she saw him throw the switch.

Nothing happened.

"Wonderful!" Dr. Kauz seemed delighted.

Jewel felt a cautious glow of satisfaction.

A little tingle started up in her scalp. It was sort of like the tingle she'd got when she found Randy in the bed.

Uh-oh.

She looked around for Randy and saw him leaning over Sovay.

"Okay, let's see the aura," Virgil said. "Both ways."

"Uh, wait a minute, guys," Jewel began, "I think something's happening," and the tingle turned into a buzz and the buzz spread over her body and then the buzz became a roar that rattled her teeth and shook her fingerprints loose. "*YeeeeeOW!*"

Dr. Kauz hurried to pull the cap off and unstrap her.

"You all right?" Clay said.

She shook her head, trying to clear it. "I think so."

"I don't think it worked," Griffy said with a worried frown.

"She still has a certain glow," Virgil said.

"I never saw a difference before," Sovay said, patting

a yawn, "but now she looks much worse. It could be her hair."

"Is there any pain?" Dr. Kauz said. "Odd sensation in the extremities? Nausea? Dizziness? Double vision? Bowels move?"

"That's enough!" Jewel struggled out of the machine. "For Pete's sake, leave me alone!"

"*Natürlich*. As soon as we perform colorimetry." Dr. Kauz grabbed her elbow.

She thrust him away. "Just because I made a mistake and let you do that Venus Machine thing to me, it doesn't mean I buy into your bogus ideas."

Shaken, she elbowed a path to the cart and poured herself a drink with trembling hands.

Kauz and Virgil watched her suck down Scotch for a moment and then turned to the Venus Machine. "Maybe there's an accidental ground somewhere," Virgil said.

She stopped listening.

Clay put his arm around her. "You don't look so good."

"That's right, rub it in." She drank Scotch, feeling its fire spread, and leaned into him. "Do me a favor and don't let me get drunk here again. This all started last night when I let Virgil make me drink and play poker."

"Uh, shouldn't that be coffee, then?"

"Oh." She handed him her glass. "Yeah." No one was looking. "Would it," she whispered, "be out of character for you to take me to my room?"

He pursed his lips at her. "A little nap before dinner?"

She peered into his eyes.

And saw a split-level Colonial-style house with a white picket fence and a golden retriever frolicking on the lawn. *What the heck?* She blinked.

"A nap alone, of course," he murmured. The picture faded.

I must be drunk again. Already.

Virgil had called the men over to his workbench. Sovay was at his elbow, handing him wrenches and voltmeters, touching his back, smiling at everything he said. Randy smiled at Sovay, looking suave and dangerous.

Griffy was looking at the Venus Machine, biting her lower lip, like a kibble-fed hound drooling at the Thanksgiving turkey.

Jewel joined her by the Venus Machine. "Listen, I don't know if I would recommend that you try this. They've done something to it. I don't remember much, but I'm sure it didn't zap me that way before."

"I can't afford not to." Griffy gulped. "I told you, *he* won't change. *I'll* have to change."

Jewel bit her tongue. "Then you'd better slip in and get your dose now, if you want to go through with it."

"I want to."

Jewel towed her to the green velvet chair, strapped her in, and set the cap on her head. *The poor sweet dumbass.* Nicest person in the world, but she was looking for the wrong thing if she hoped to get that old turtle to stop smirking at Sovay.

The last buckle clicked. Jewel stuck her thumb in the air.

Griffy smiled tremulously and jerked up her thumb.

Oh well. I guess it can't hurt her.

"Griffy, you idiot," Virgil called from the workbench. "That's not for you!"

Griffy scowled at him. "Do it," she told Jewel.

Jewel threw the switch with a clunk.

For a long moment Griffy sat there. "Am I supposed to feel anything?" There was a new sparkle in her eye.

Jewel shrugged.

Clay appeared at Jewel's elbow. "Girlfriend," he said with extra warmth in his voice. Jewel turned toward him. He was holding out his hand and looking past her at Griffy.

Griffy took the metal cap off her head. "Did it muss my hair?" She let Clay hand her out of the Venus Machine.

Wow.

Jewel was reminded of Lady Diana exiting a limo. Clay lifted Griffy's hand into the air, wolf-whistling, and she pirouetted for him.

The butler, clearing away dirty coffeecups, looked up at his mistress and let a spoon slide, tinkling, to the floor.

"Your hair's fine," Jewel said.

In fact Griffy looked dynamite. In her going-to-spa clothes and all her jewels, she looked like a movie star. She seemed younger. All her movements slowed down somehow, so you could notice how everything about her was perfect.

Dr. Kauz came away from the workbench like a sleep-walker.

Virgil followed, looking thunderous.

Sovay took one look, seized Randy by the arm, and swanned out of the collection room with her nose in a sling.

Griffy turned under Clay's hand like a ballerina on a music box, and Jewel realized that under all that nice-ness and self-effacement was a beautiful woman. She smiled on everyone as she turned, and the air smelled sweeter.

One must have, I think, the soul of a circus performer to enjoy it, old Kauz had said.

Clay bowed to Griffy. She curtseyed to him. In silence, they started waltzing.

It didn't look silly at all.

Kauz, the butler, and even Virgil stared as if dumb-struck.

Jewel swallowed a lump. Watching Griffy, she realized how very dangerous people like Clay and Dr. Kauz were. They knew what suggestion could do. And Randy, hell, he must be better at it than any of them. Two hundred years with nothing but a demonic ability to read thoughts, and the impossible goal of learning what women really want.

This, Jewel thought, watching Griffy. *We want this. To be loved, to feel lovable.*

CHAPTER 13

At dinnertime, Jewel had to ask the butler where her room was. *Man, I was drunk last night*. She sorted through the clothes Nina had brought. Randy's things were there; oh yeah, Lord Possessive had asked for one bedroom. His dark suit hung on the door, clashing with the Michigan B&B Cute decor.

Where the hell was Randy? Horndogging after Sovay, to punish her for spending last night in Clay's room?

Fine. Let him teach her a lesson. It'd keep him occupied. She could play with Clay.

She didn't want either of them all that much. What she wanted—what had Griffy said? About men having us figured out. Weirdly, she felt more uneasy about Clay's motives than she did about Randy sleeping with the enemy or reading her mind.

Her partner was a con man. Who could she trust?

Clay was ruthless. Sovay was a gold digger and an utter snake. Kauz could manipulate people's feelings, yet he believed his own bullshit, which was scary right there. And Virgil, causing Griffy so much grief—

—was Clay's father. Too late, Jewel remembered something Clay'd once said to her. *My father's in the same business, only he's ten times better*.

Virgil was a con artist, too.

This mansion, the money, the diamonds all over

Griffy, the collection room full of expensive toys—all were the fruit of his ill-gotten gains.

Jewel felt cold.

His doddering new ager act had sucked her in.

I bet he fiddled the card game last night, too. Got her drunk and high on his charm, let her win at poker to make her stupid, so she would submit to that horrible Venus Machine. What the hell did *he* want?

Virgil might be just as interested in taking Kauz for his campaign money as Clay was. He was up to something with Sovay. She bit her lip.

I am totally out of my league.

And still fatally attractive.

Standing in her bra and panties, Jewel looked in the mirror. Her fair hair, freshly washed and free of green goo, hung past her shoulders. She was six inches taller than Griffy, thirty pounds heavier than Sovay, and her white cotton underwear said Hometown Girl, even after college and five years in the big city and countless men, most of whom hadn't noticed her underwear since she'd been in such a hurry to take it off.

I need to figure myself out.

She looked into her own eyes. *What do you want?*

The mirror vanished for a moment, and all she could see was Griffy waltzing with Clay. *To be loved, to feel lovable.*

She blinked and took a step back from the mirror. *Who am I to want such a thing?*

The big blond dairy-farmer's daughter in the mirror stared back at her, uncompromising in her white cotton, with a solidness that made the froufrou room shrink around her.

Wearing her little black cocktail dress, Jewel joined the dinner party in the card room in time to hear Sovay say, "—That pink fog on the highway looks alarming."

"Merely a product of road rage," Clay said. "Control your temper behind the wheel and you won't even notice it."

Good boy. That's how you administer Policy.

"And the pigeons have the filthy habit," Randy said. Jewel sighed. Now she had to teach *him* to administer Policy.

"I haven't heard smoking called 'the filthy habit' for fifty years," Virgil said, eyeing Randy.

"We're a bad example to animals, aren't we?" Griffy said.

"Maybe they'll smoke some hemp and get too high to poop on my car," Virgil suggested. "Get it? Pigeons getting too *high*?" He cackled senilely. Jewel thought he laid on the brainless-old-fart thing too thick. Now that she knew he was Clay's father and mentor-con, she felt less vulnerable to his manipulations.

Sovay gave Virgil a full-frontal of her cleavage. "This wine is wonderful."

Virgil peered down her dress through his wineglass. "It does great things for you." He turned the wineglass toward Jewel and his eye appeared, magnified hideously through the wine. "I see we failed to reverse the Venus Machine," he chortled.

Sovay scowled.

Jewel grinned at him. "I'm holding back."

He toasted her. You couldn't help liking the old turtle. If he was playing her off against Sovay and Griffy, at least he was trying to make her feel good, too.

She noticed Mellish, the butler, standing behind Virgil, looking down on his employer's bald head with a puzzled expression. When he caught her eye, his face smoothed out. In that moment an image flashed across her mind of the butler doing her doggy-style on top of the tablecloth amid the crystal.

Jewel spilled her wine.

The butler lifted his chin and shifted his gaze over her head, his thick neck and ears turning pink.

Did he just think that, or did I? she wondered. *Look at him blush!* Holy crap, she was reading his mind!

Griffy was showing off her rings to Randy. "Virgil gave me that one for my birthday." She wore a tailored white silk dress, higher-cut but classier than the showstopper displaying Sovay's frontal assets. Her chin was up and her eyes sparkled.

Sovay craned her neck. "Nice. For your fortieth?"

Griffy looked her straight in the eye. "My forty-third."

Randy caressed Griffy's palm and turned it over to examine the ring. "Diamonds signify permanence. Rubies mean passion."

Griffy giggled.

Kauz told Jewel, "Men talk themselves out of much wisdom and into much foolishness."

"I agree," Jewel said. "When people believe in magic, they get nothing but trouble." *Back in character, whew.*

"That is because magic and science haff diverged." Kauz put his forefingers together and drew a "Y" in the air. "A scientist has from magic nothing to fear, and much to learn."

Jewel sent a look at Clay. *Get him talking.*

Clay seemed to catch on. "I've always said so."

"Why's that?" Jewel said to Kauz. "I'd think a real scientist wouldn't bother with magic. That's the definition of magic, isn't it? It's not true, so it's not science."

Kauz swelled. "On the contrary, the terms *ars magia* and *scientia* were once interchangeably used. Distinction was created in early eighteenth century by magicians—scientists—who didn't vant to burn for witchcraft."

"Burning!" Sovay shuddered. "So uncivilized!"

He gestured at Randy. "Your English Lord Bacon says

this, that magic intervenes in God's work, but science is the work of man upon nature."

"I thought Bacon wrote Shakespeare," Clay said.

"Is other Bacon, much later. This Bacon is a great thinker, great divider of hairs," Kauz said, forking up prime rib.

Clay said, "So the witch hunters come sniffing around your magician and he says, 'Back off, man, I'm a scientist'?"

"Is all context." Kauz waved his fork. "Before big heresy crackdown, your old-time magician wants to wooo nature, to looove nature, to maaarry her. Highly suspicious to witch hunters."

"Suspicious is right," Jewel muttered.

"New Baconian scientist says, God gave Nature to Man for his uses—" Kauz dug his fork into the air at every word "—to *own* her, to *plow* her, to *enslave* her. So is modern technology born."

Every woman at the table stiffened.

Virgil let out a crack of laughter.

Kauz smiled. "But, of course, that is also how a great deal of evil is born, for woman as well as for nature. You ladies glare at me! Come, a man who runs a spa respects both nature and woman. My life work is to defeat the patriarchal mechanisms that subject women."

"With beauty treatments," Jewel said with scorn.

"With treatments that convince every woman she is a beauty. For so she is," Kauz said forcefully. "Every woman." He gestured at Jewel, then at Griffy. "Behold the successful application of science to this, the *correct* problem—how the woman sees herself."

In other words, I'm cheating you for your own good.
"Using science," Jewel said.

"Even so. As did Katterfelto, my hero."

"Using magic, too?" she said with challenge.

He swiveled to face her. "By whatever means necessary."

They made eye contact, and she had a flash of the good doctor sticking a needle into her arm, drawing out a big vialful of her blood, and gloating over it.

Eeeuw! That was a nine-point-oh on her ick-o-meter.

He meant business. He could talk himself into trouble and charm his way out of it. And he was nuts enough to take this cockamamie philosophy to the media and spread it all over a vulnerable city, a city already struggling to cope with an assault on reality that might take it down.

"The power of suggestion," Virgil said, breaking the silence, "must be very important in your business."

"*Natürlich*. A man is seen as powerful if he has money. A woman, if she is beautiful. Money, this is a tangible thing, but beauty is an illusion, an idea, a mood, a whim. I can give a woman power by suggesting that she is beautiful."

"There are money illusionists, too," Clay remarked, glancing around the table.

You're all crooks and con men. Jewel felt a cold rage building. "If I were a cynical person, I'd say you're getting rich on your customers' fears. The older a woman gets, the more vulnerable she is to being fooled by a lot of razzle-dazzle."

Kauz shook his head. "My older customers are wiser, not more foolish. They know how old they are. They know quite well that beauty is an illusion. Merely, I must convince them. I teach them to use the power of suggestion to project the illusion of beauty, *und* lo, the illusion becomes reality. They become powerful women again. They use their power more wisely than when they were young and easily duped."

"That's corkscrew logic if I ever heard it." And yet it made a goofy sort of sense. Con artist sense.

"Primitive tribesmen," Virgil said, "use something similar."

"Sympathetic magic," Clay said. "Well-known phenomenon."

Yeah, you two are out of the same workshop. "Bunch of baloney," Jewel harrumphed.

Griffy was looking puzzled and distressed. "But the Venus Machine works. You didn't do anything to Julia to—to convince her," she protested.

Jewel's heart bled for her. The magic of her transformation was being exposed, and might crumble at any moment.

"No, she duped herself," Sovay murmured to Virgil, eyeing Jewel. Jewel saw Randy flash her a brief, ugly look.

Griffy's voice rose. "So is the Venus Machine real or isn't it? It worked for both Julia and me, but it worked different."

Randy smiled at her. "That is because you are different women. It's like the fairy tale about roses and jewels."

"Ooh, do tell us a fairy tale," Sovay cooed.

Virgil clapped his hands. "I love fairy tales!"

Randy looked from Jewel to Griffy to Sovay. "There once were three sisters, two sweet and one sour. The first sister went to the well for water and met an old woman, who asked her to draw water for her. The first sister drew her water and spoke courteously to her, and in return the old woman bespelled her. When she returned home, every word she spoke became a rose."

Randy leaned forward. "The second sister went for water, met the old woman, gave her courtesy, and drew her water. When she returned home, every word she spoke became a ruby."

Randy smiled and narrowed his eyes. "The third sister hunted down the old woman, and cried, 'Bespell me as you did my sisters, and do it now!' The old woman said, 'You are not so sweet as your sisters.' The third sister hit her with a stick, and the old woman said, 'Go home, for you are bespelled.' "

Randy paused to look around the table. "From that day forward, with every cruelty the third sister uttered, a live toad or a snake jumped out of her mouth."

Griffy gasped. "That's mean!"

Virgil said, "It's not nice, but it works."

"It is justice," remarked Kauz.

"Real justice is a lot slower," Jewel said darkly.

"And so often it misses the mark," Sovay said.

Hearing the word "mark" in Sovay's silky voice made Jewel flinch. *I've got con artists on the brain.*

This whole table was a minefield.

CHAPTER
14

Pleading tiredness, Jewel escaped the postprandial poker game. Randy followed her upstairs. Uh-oh.

"What was with the roses and jewels?" she said. "Should I have gotten something subtle out of that?"

"She is insolent to you," he said coolly. "That is not permitted." Jewel blinked. "I pointed the moral."

"You're sweet" was all Jewel could say. "But I thought you were trying to get into her pants."

"That, too. That way I can read her mind."

"I *know* that. But I thought you were going to, like, stay in character here."

"Perhaps my character would seduce Sovay. If she means to seduce Mr. Thompson, she's foolish to flutter toward me."

"So you're egging her on?" Jewel said, her voice rising.

"Surely you do not object if she turns from Mr. Thompson to me," he drawled. The madder she felt, the cooler he sounded. "Mr. Thompson may take offense. This would harm her schemes."

"I—uh." Jewel wanted to strangle Sovay for being mean to Griffy. It had completely escaped her mind that Sovay was out to take Virgil for money, too.

"In addition, the suspect may make a misstep. Or I may seduce her and bare her thoughts."

"And you don't feel that's kind of slutty?" Jewel blurted.

"No." He seemed pleased to get a rise out of her. "Why?"

She couldn't think of one single reason why she could object. Unless she was jealous, which was absurd. "What else?"

He took off his shoes. "Something's amiss with the butler."

"Mellish? He's a bit thick-necked. I think he pretends to be stupid sometimes."

"No, that's customary. In fact, he is the one servant I've observed here who seems to know his work."

"Griffy explained that. He's new." She remembered that unbidden fantasy of doing the butler doggy-style among the wineglasses. "What's the matter with the butler?"

"I don't know. In my own century, I could say. I've not known servants here. Perhaps I mistake. I will consult Clay."

"That reminds me, guess what? Virgil is Clay's father."

Randy stripped off his shirt. "So I suspected."

"Oh, you did not."

"There is subtle scorn in Virgil's manner toward Clay. Of course Griffy is his paramour, soon to be cast off, and Clay resents the change, perhaps out of sentimentality, perhaps because the new mistress is not under his influence." Randy's very correct undershirt came off next. At the sight of his naked torso Jewel forgot what she was going to say. "One cannot but observe that Ms. Sacheverell will be an improvement."

Jewel's gaze moved to his face. "What?"

Randy shrugged those beautiful naked shoulders. "She's younger, better bred, more discreet. She deals well with servants, unlike the lowborn paramour. She's better spoken, though she is not English and counterfeits an English accent."

"You're such a snob!"

"She also has a brain. She partakes of his interests intelligently. At his age this becomes more important, perhaps, than it was when he acquired Griffy."

Jewel snarled, "Doesn't 'bitch' count for anything?"

"And she comes with money of her own."

"So she's a good tradeup," Jewel said with sarcasm.

"Precisely."

Steamed, she slipped out of her black cocktail dress and hung it up. "Well, try this on your well-bred pianola, asshole. Sovay's also after his money."

"Of course. It's a mercenary arrangement."

"The hell it is!" Jewel protested. "Griffy loves that old turtle! She told me at the spa she's been with him for eighteen years. Nobody could have stood him that long without affection."

"That also is manifest," Randy said unpleasantly, "from your conversation with him."

Oh, now her sex demon was jealous of Turtlehead Thompson! "He's a mean old geezer in some ways, but I like him." She smiled. "He reminds me of somebody I used to date."

"'Date,'" he sneered. "This is your *politesse* for 'someone you used to fornicate with.'" He raised his brows. "Have you fornicated with a septuagenarian before?"

"I do not discuss my sex life with you!"

"But you discuss it with everyone else. With the castoff mistress, for example." He looked dark with anger.

"She isn't castoff yet." But Jewel knew that sooner or later she'd have to face Randy over what she'd told Griffy about him. "Look, I'm sorry you overheard that stuff. But women talk. Don't follow me around and you won't get your feelings hurt."

"I have a stake in your behavior."

"You have a stake in my paycheck. You have a stake in my willingness to rescue you from random beds. But you bought and paid for the grief you got today."

"You, also, have earned your sufferings—if sufferings they were," Randy said snottily.

"I was getting to that." Jewel lost her cool. "Anytime you get in a snit, you take it out on me by zapping into some public reclinery and forcing me to make a spectacle of myself." She threw her shoes clattering into a corner. "After all that noble talk, 'Simply forget where I have gone,' you fix it so I *have* to let you out of your self-imposed prison! I was a *mummy*!"

He waved his arms. "I didn't know that would happen!"

She jabbed his bare chest with a forefinger. "*Self*-imposed. How many times have you had a hissy and got zapped? Let's see."

He looked so dangerous that she took the finger off his chest and held it up to count.

"You zapped into a bed in the home furnishings department of Marshall Field's. You didn't want me to arrest Clay and, when I insisted, zappo, straight into my bed. That was convenient, guess I ought to thank you for that." She gulped air. "Then you zapped into a sofa in Clay's hotel suite *while I was having sex with him on it*. Then that stinky old wrecked car in the dump that same night! And let's not forget the soot all over my bedroom. You knew damned well you'd end up in that massage table."

Randy literally danced with rage. "I am not a magician! I don't know why it happens!" he roared.

"Well, I think mine is a pretty good guess!" she yelled back.

They stood nose to nose. He panted and looked purple and she double-dare glared. His hands were fists, but they were at his sides.

Inside, Jewel was icy calm. *So this is how he loses his temper. Good to know.*

As she looked into his stormy black eyes she had a mental image of Randy's portrait in *Burke's Peerage*: handsome, bored, all dressed up in old-timey lord clothes, looking down on a curtseying woman—who looked like herself.

She frowned. *What the hell does that mean?*

His color faded to a dull red. "Do not enrage me."

"This is not about emotion," she said. "It's about a living arrangement that's fucking intolerable for both of us. You want to own me, I want total freedom." She paused, because this was the part she hated. "I acknowledge that you have reason to feel some—some separation anxiety if you don't always know where I am. That's backwards, but it's understandable."

"What does 'backwards' signify?"

"If I'm supposed to keep you safe from any residual whammy that might be, like, left over from that curse, then you should be the one wearing an anklet, not me." To his frown she said, "Tracer anklet. It's a LoJack for people."

"LoJack?"

"Oh, forget it. Although that's not a bad idea," she added, thinking of his habit of going AWOL in public places. Be a lot easier to pinpoint his location if and when he did disappear. "The point is—I forget what the point is."

"The point," he said in a low voice, "is that you want your freedom. Whereas I want my dignity. I am not accustomed—" He stopped and pressed his lips shut.

She said as gently as she could, "You're a sex slave prone, but a lord perpendicular. I know."

"I'm not accustomed to women complaining about my services. Not in this century."

And back they were again at the part she couldn't talk about. "That was girl talk."

He glowered. "But presumably true."

His feelings must be hurt bad. She guessed that if you've lost everything to become good in bed, complaints stung.

"Look, I don't know you well enough to talk about—about that. Anyway, I'm not your target market. I'm not married to a lousy lay. I'm not lonely."

The little red blinking "liar" light went off in her head.

"I don't have trouble finding sex partners who satisfy me."

The damned "liar" light was still blinking. *Never mind. He can't see it—from here.*

"What I'm saying is, I'm not like the women you met in that bed. This is a different millennium. We have different problems. If I was some little old lady with a bad back, you would know how to deal with me, am I right?"

He stepped so close that his bare chest brushed her bra. "And were I some brainless twiddlepoop with pantaloons at perpetual cock-crow, you might use me and be rid of me."

She said breathlessly, "You're always horny."

"So are you." He looked big and dark and scrumptious and *dammit*, he'd done it to her again.

Another long night of magical sex stared her in the face.

She felt her insides melt. She relaxed. She smiled.

He bowed. "If I'm to learn self-control, there's no time like the present. Will you take the chaise, or shall I?"

He stepped away, leaving the front of her body to cool, and pulled blankets and pillows out of a closet.

Jewel gaped at him in astonishment. "What are you doing?"

"I will spend the night on the chaise. You sleep there." He pointed at the bed. "I shall not touch you in any way." With his gorgeous bare back to her, he made up the lame-ass wicker chaise with pillows and blankets, stripped his pants off, and wedged himself between the creaking arms of the chaise. "You may put out the light," he said with his back to her.

She realized she was taking little panting breaths. Her fingertips tingled. Way down in secret, her happyloola twitched.

She found her voice. "Oh. Okay. Thanks."

She felt light-headed and unbalanced. She sat down on the bed. "Unless you just want a quickie." *What am I saying?* She should be grateful he was cooperating.

He was silent. Punishing her.

She realized she was giving him the satisfaction he was after. So to speak.

She turned the light out, finished undressing, and slid between the sheets, which then heated up to scorching.

She lay as still as possible.

I could jerk off. That would drive him crazy.

But she was afraid to touch herself. She might moan or something. He would take that as a victory.

She was screwed.

But only metaphorically.

If I've got such a fabulous doggone sex life, how come I'm going to sleep horny the second night in a row?

CHAPTER 15

She couldn't sleep.

How ironic. Randy hadn't given her a full night's rest for two and a half weeks, and now she lay in bed, alone, staring at the ceiling, wide awake and horny.

Randy lay six feet away on the chaise, apparently dead to the world. The wicker creaked in time with his breathing.

Maybe she should, like, take up meditating.

The bed got too hot. At first she tried not to move, but sooner or later she ended up wriggling, and that made her think of wriggling on top of Randy, or under Randy, or *stop.*

She thought about the Thompson case instead. Sovay planned to sting Virgil, but how? Did she want to marry him, or would she settle for selling the Venus Machine to him for big bucks? Maybe she'd stolen it. Jewel had no sympathy for anyone who bought the Venus Machine. Did Virgil think it was stolen? What did he want from Sovay—besides the obvious? She wondered if Kauz had brought any contraband potions into the house. She wondered if Randy felt different about her since her double dose of the Venus Machine. She wondered if he was horny right now.

Stop, just stop!

She wondered if Clay noticed anything different about

her since her second dose. She could go to his room and ask.

And get rejected a second time tonight? No, thanks.

Besides, as fed up as she was with Randy, she felt that sneaking into Clay's bed would be pretty low.

The woman she used to be stood up and yelled in her head, *That's not fair! You don't owe him fidelity! This is not a "relationship," this is*—

She couldn't think what it was.

She only let Randy hang around because they never knew when the curse might kick in, and he would need his hundredth woman to fuck him free of some bed.

She let Randy hang around so she could get laid every single blessed night without fail, laid in a way no woman has ever got laid in the history of wild and wacko sex.

She let Randy hang around because he belonged to her, she owned him, he admitted it, and she loved it, and she hated that about herself.

But she didn't want him hanging around too close. Because clingy guys gave her hives.

It was too damned complicated, was what it was.

The wicker chaise creaked. A bolt of lightning shot through her lippetydip and Jewel made a disgusted noise and sat up.

In the dimness over there, Randy wasn't moving.

Maybe there was a bottle of that Scotch in the card room.

Oh, no. No more Scotch. But getting up would be good.

She breathed through pinched nostrils for a minute. Then she got into PJs, picked up her phone, and went out.

I'll wake Ed up and report. Share the misery.

"So, yow!" Ed said, and a lion's yawn came from the cellphone. "You got nothin' on the spa guy and nothin' on this gold digger with a magic machine."

"But a very fertile, creative nothing, with lots of potential. Plus I'd like some background checks."

"All right, all right, gimme a second, I gotta get a pen. Where the fuck does Nina keep pens around here?"

"Don't wake her up!"

"Got one. Okay, shoot."

"Butler. Name of Mellish. Age thirty, about six-two, big shoulders, thick neck, lantern jaw, I think brown eyes but who can tell behind the squint. He's from Household Temps. There's also a cook, at least one maid, and a chauffeur."

"Got it. What else?"

She bit her lip. She hated to do this. "Have we got a LoJack I can plant on somebody so I can follow them around?"

"Not without a warrant."

"It's for Buzz," she lied.

"Oh, okay." Ed's oft-publicized feeling was that Buzz had caused him so much grief, he would look the other way if somebody tied a rock around the kid's neck and tossed him into the river. "You want a tracer anklet."

"Make it two. I want one, uh, for his backpack and one for him." Hm, she wondered if the backpack ever stayed at the spa while Buzz scurried away. She doubted it. "How do I track him?"

"How the hell do I know? We don't do parolees in the DCS."

"I need those files yesterday."

"That all, Miss High and Mighty, or can I go back to sleep?"

"That's all. Nightsy-byesy-boodly-kins."

"Fuck you," her boss said, and rang off.

The air conditioning was icy in the upstairs hallway of Virgil's mansion. Jewel's bare feet chilled on the marble. The collection room was one floor up. She wondered what she could learn about the Venus Machine without mad scientists in the way.

But as she started up the big staircase, she heard a rustle.

Looking up, she saw Sovay descending the stairs, gripping the banister with both hands, looking slender and rich in an old, gold satin negligee set and matching marabou mules.

Jewel drew back too late.

Sovay spotted her. Half a word escaped her throat, and then she clapped her hand over her mouth and glared. On a scale of one to ten it was the juiciest glare she'd ever aimed at Jewel, who found it puzzling. *What've I done now?*

Behind her hand, the bitch heaved, a childish, you-make-me-wanna-hurl gesture.

Jewel stared. *I know she hates me, but jeez.*

Somewhere in the echoey stairwell, a faint creaking started.

She admitted now that Randy had a point. If he slept with the snake, he might learn something useful.

Sovay passed Jewel as if she didn't exist.

Jewel decided not to inspect the Venus Machine. Today had been too exciting.

Besides, Randy might have changed his mind.

He hadn't.

"We need to talk," Jewel muttered to Clay at breakfast.

"Don't be friendly with me," Clay muttered back. "It's not in your cover."

"Screw my cover," she hissed. She had tough questions for him. Plus she would need his help getting the tracer anklet onto Randy. "You have some explaining to do."

"Meet me out back in the alley," Clay muttered. "One hour."

"Meet me in my room," she countered. "*Now*."

Randy looked up from flattering Griffy. His face darkened.

Jewel's head filled with a picture of Randy locking her in a chastity belt and chaining it to a bed. She felt her eyes widen.

Randy dropped Griffy like a hot coal. He turned and cooed, "More coffee, Miss Sacheverell? Perhaps a slice of ham?"

Sovay smiled like a snake. "You are too kind, Lord Darner."

Jewel's phone rang. She checked the number. Ed.

"I'll talk to you in a minute," she hissed to Clay, and went out of the room to take the call.

"What is it? I'm undercover!"

"Go get that Buzz kid. Somebody's phoned in a complaint."

"Who?" What she went through to keep Buzz out of jail.

"George Dopposomethingpopolopolis, proprietor of a beauty salon up on The Mile." Ed read off the address. "Says the kid was hanging around his place of business this morning, selling unlicensed beauty products and driving away customers."

Jewel wrote down the address. "That's Giorgio lo Gigolo." She remembered Leo over at Spa On The Mile complaining about a bad peddler selling his customers love potions. "I'm on it."

"Do it now. I'd-a given it to the Health Department, but you got a soft spot for the little shit."

She didn't bother trying to defend poor Buzz. "Believe me, I'm on it." She snapped the phone shut. She needed Clay. Bring him with her on a Buzz hunt and she could discuss things with him at the same time.

But when she got back to the breakfast room, Clay and his father were nowhere to be found.

"Where's Virgil? And where's Clay?" Jewel sent Sovay a nasty look. *Shouldn't you be sucking up to the meal ticket?*

"Experiments are in train in the collection room," Randy said loftily, "to compare psychespectrometric readings with Kirlian photographs. Mr. Thompson and Dr. Kauz are there."

"And you're not?" Randy seemed to be blowing off his cover, too.

"I have been telling Miss Sacheverell about the family ghost at Llew's Howe. Mr. Dawes," he said with distaste, "went shopping with Miss Griffin."

Jewel rolled her eyes. "Okay. Well, *Lord Darner*, I've got a lead on that, uh, street practitioner we were talking to the other day. We should go find him. Right now."

Randy stared at her. For a moment she saw him in a plaid, earflappy cap with a curvy pipe in his mouth. *Is that what he's thinking?* That was the trouble with magic, you never knew how the darned stuff was supposed to work. *Or is it what he wants?* Jewel licked her lips. "You can play detective again."

He almost leaped out of his chair. "Very well." Randy bowed over Sovay's hand. "Another day, dear lady."

Sovay smiled up at him. "Any time, my lord," she said in a throaty voice. She turned the smile on Jewel, where it soured, and her lips made the word *cow* but nothing came out.

Jewel said, "Let's go."

Behind them, as they left the breakfast room, Jewel heard Sovay gagging into a napkin.

Taking this joke a little far, aren't you, bitch?

In the car Jewel said, "So you want to play Sherlock Holmes? I thought he was after your time."

"I want what?"

"I saw what you were thinking just now. Had me stumped for a minute, but I figured it out. You want to play investigator."

He flushed. "You cannot know what I am thinking."

"I can." The light changed. "Remember that argument we had the other morning? You didn't like me flirting with guys. You said, 'I wish you could see what's in their minds before you open your thighs to them.' "

"That stung, did it?" There was a smile in his voice.

"Well, ever since my second ride in the Venus Machine, every time I make eye contact with a guy, I see what he wants."

"Indeed." Randy sounded pleased. "I did not realize the Venus Machine dispensed justice as well as beauty."

"Neither did I. But what you didn't think about is that I can see what *you* want."

Silence from Radio Randy.

She risked a peek at him. He sat still, staring out the windshield. Then he faced her, and their eyes met, and she had a mental image of him in his lord costume, bowing to her.

Horns blared. She looked ahead in time to jam on the brakes and avoid broadsiding a taxi.

Important safety tip. Don't make eye contact with Randy when you're driving.

She mimed, *Sorry, sorry,* to the cabbie as she turned past him, and he glared at her. She got a disturbing image of the cabbie jabbing her in the eye with something long and sharp and she almost swerved into a Mini crammed with tourists.

Don't make eye contact with ANYONE!

"What are we investigating today?" Randy said.

"It's Buzz. We find him, take his stash off him, and find out what he's been doing—who he sold it to, stuff like that. Get a statement from him. With luck, we can get him free of prosecution, if he'll sing."

"Sing?"

"Testify against Kauz. Depends how dangerous the doctor's little potion turns out. Which reminds me." She rummaged in her purse and the Tercel swerved.

Randy took the purse from her. "I will find the potion."

"Later." She gnawed her lip. "I wish I could send you to the lab with it. Clay could do it if he wasn't being a moron."

"He wants to save his faux stepmother from being abandoned. Why not send me to the lab?"

She pulled the Tercel over to the curb. "I want to, I really do," she said from the heart. "But what if you, like, zap into some bed somewhere? As much as it drives me crazy having you glued to my side twenty-four-seven, I can't risk that."

"Don't dissemble. You want my mojo," he said in his precise English voice, and she choked on a laugh, partly because of the accent and partly because he looked so conflicted.

She put her hand over his. "Even if I knew it would be the last time ever, Randy, I couldn't leave you stuck. You said that the other morning, too. Like, why don't I leave you stuck somewhere if I'm sick of you. I won't do that."

He looked long into her eyes, and all she could think of was him looking into her eyes.

"I mean it," she said. A picture of a cellphone popped into her head and she added, "No, I don't think a cellphone is a good idea." His eyes widened and he jerked his face away. "Like I said, you always pull a zapper when we're having an argument. If we have a fight over the phone, I can't afford to search every bed in Chicago. Look at me."

He stared out his side window instead.

She whispered, "Now you know how I feel when

you're in my head, when we're in demonspace, when I'm dreaming."

"I see." He pulled his hand out of hers.

She felt sorry for him, and a little hurt. "People get real used to their privacy. You've had, what, two hundred years of it? That's a long time to be alone in your head."

She thought of the tracer anklet. He would never be in a better frame of mind to agree to it.

"Um, I have an idea. Instead of the cellphone. Or even plus the cellphone. You're right, you ought to have one."

He looked back with caution and hope in his eyes.

"There's this device, I mentioned it before. It's um, a magic anklet. It can tell me where you are. So say you're out somewhere buying groceries or at work—" *there* was a golden idea, Randy working and bringing in some money "—and you get in trouble? The anklet tells me. I can find out where you parted company with it. I assume it wouldn't stay stuck to your ankle in demonspace. It should fall off like your clothes do."

He looked intrigued. "I see."

"And then I would have a strong idea where, geographically, you've wound up stuck."

"That could work," he said. He put his hand over hers and curled his long fingers into her palm. Their eyes met again. She forgot to wonder what he was thinking. His long upper lip twitched, as if he had stiffened it against trembling. "Thank you. That would be—that would be wonderful."

Parolees all over the country cursed that anklet, and here he was thanking her for it.

Damn, I'm good.

Then she realized how much he must hate being her Siamese twin. He was her slave. And he didn't like it.

She squeezed his hand remorsefully. "You're a good guy, Randy."

"I will remind you that you said so." He smiled. "On the occasion of our next disagreement."

He looked so grateful that something twisted in her chest, and she pulled her hand free. "Time to kick some Buzz butt."

chapter 16

Jewel turned down Michigan Avenue, remembering how Buzz favored the Magnificent Mile, and had the luck to see his bicycle propped against a planter by Water Tower Place.

"Groovy," she groaned. Buzz in a mall, where he could do maximum damage. Plus, she didn't relish the notion of seeing a jillion male mall-goers' fantasies about her.

She parked in a short-term zone next to the old water tower on Chestnut, grabbed sunglasses out of her glove box, and slapped her Official Business tag on the windshield. A harness bull strolled over. She flipped open her badge.

"Hot pursuit, officer. Oh, hi, Petey." She donned her sunglasses. *One date, four years ago.* If he remembered, she didn't want to know.

"Hey, Jewel. Heard you were out of circulation. This the guy?" Officer Petey looked Randy over with approval.

"One of them," Randy said.

"No time for chitchat, Petey, gotta uphold the law, bye!" She attached herself to Randy's wrist. "Shut up about my personal business," she said out of the side of her mouth.

On the up escalator in Water Tower Place, he said, "I

believe I am your personal business. Have I not the right to free speech in the United States of America?"

Brother, did he catch on fast. "Not under this administration. Besides, you're not a citizen."

The conversation was going to hell fast, which made it doubly lucky that she saw Buzz at the first escalator stop, and, halleluia, he was on the balcony, with no store entrances or escalator exits for twenty yards in either direction.

"There he is! See him? He's with that woman."

"I see him." Randy was all business.

"Don't look straight at him. When we get up there, you break left and I'll go right. Don't move fast. Make sure he's bottled up in that cul-de-sac. He'll run away from me, so I'll keep facing forward. Even if he sees me, maybe he'll think I don't see him. And Randy—" She lifted her sunglasses so she could looked him in the eye. "Try not to hurt anyone or break anything. You are not covered by department liability insurance. We don't want to arrest him, just talk to him. Dig?"

"I apprehend your meaning," he said. On the wide-screen TV in her mind, she saw a muddy field with a dozen beagles baying, running after a rusty streak.

"Yeah, right, whatever. No bloodshed."

They split at the top of the escalator, Randy walking fast, looking taut and alive and happy. Damn. She needed to get him a job. One where his ignorance of American laws and customs wouldn't get him fired on day one. She turned to the right and saw that Buzz was still engaged with his customer, a rather mussed-looking older shopper who talked with her hands. Buzz glanced over the shopper's shoulder, saw Jewel, and bolted in the other direction, straight into Randy's arms.

Of course that couldn't be enough. He struggled and socked Randy, who was a head and a half taller, and

Randy grabbed his shoulders and shook him like a ter-
rier shaking a rat until the backpack slid down his arms
and little bottles rained out of it. Buzz slipped on a bottle and fell to the floor, bringing Randy down on top
of him. While they grappled there, Buzz's customer
dropped all her shopping bags, ran up, and started
kicking Randy in the head with her two-hundred-dollar
sneaker.

Jewel flipped open her badge and shoved it in the face
of Buzz's protector. "Consumer Services, ma'am, please
step away."

His customer jumped back as if she'd been bitten.
"Are you a police officer? Young man!" She bent and
whapped at Randy. "Stop him," she said to Jewel. "He's
hurting my friend!"

"You'll be sorry you kicked my partner," Jewel said.
Randy was now sitting on Buzz's head, a thing she'd only
read about in books. Seemed to work, though. The backpack and its contents were scattered all over. "Randy,
that's enough."

"*I'll* be sorry?" The shopper bristled. "Why? Are you
trying to arrest me? My husband is an attorney!"

"No, he's English and he'll make you apologize."

Jewel bent and picked up all the little bottles and put
them back in the backpack. Even the ones Randy had
fallen on were too small and hard to smash, thank
goodness.

Randy got up off Buzz, keeping his hand on the scruff
of the kid's neck. His eyes sparkled.

Maybe he can play football.

Huffily, Buzz brushed himself off. One of his zits had
popped open when Randy had rubbed his face against
the floor, but otherwise he seemed damage-free. "That's
mine," he said, looking at the backpack.

"And you'll get it back when I can find a bag for the
contents," Jewel said. "Buzz, you know darned well

your peddler's license doesn't cover consumables. You need a Health Department certificate for that."

"My husband can help him get one," said the loyal shopper.

"I could help him get one myself, if I trusted him not to stock up on white lightning and snake oil. Please, ma'am. We're just going to talk to him."

But the shopper wouldn't take a hint. "You were hurting him," she said fiercely to Randy.

"Your concern does you great credit, madam," Randy said with a bow. He flicked mall scuzz off his sleeve and looked down at the shopper with a bored-lord look.

The shopper blinked and simpered. "Did I hurt your head?"

Randy smiled. "It was only moderately painful. Think nothing of it."

"I'm so sorry," the shopper said.

"Bingo," Jewel said. "I don't know how he does it. Now, if you don't mind?"

"I'm not leaving," the shopper snapped. "This boy changed my life. I'll pay his legal fees!"

"He's not under arrest," Jewel said tiredly. "Buzz. This stuff you've been selling has been raising Cain all over town, I have no idea how. Giorgio lo Gigolo has filed a complaint against you, says you're hurting his business. Plus—and I guess I have to keep telling you this until you get the message—this stuff is a food or a drug or something. Consumable. If you can put it in your mouth?" She pointed down her throat. "You can't sell it. That can get you arrested and maybe jailed if anyone comes forward to complain about ill effects." She put her hand on his arm. "Work with me, will ya, buddy?"

Buzz didn't take his eyes off the backpack. "I want my stuff."

Jewel rolled her eyes. "Randy, can you scare up a bag?"

"Here," the shopper said. She selected a small, elegant, handled bag from her pile of shopping bags and dumped its contents into another, larger, elegant, handled bag.

They transferred all the little bottles into the new bag and Jewel gave the backpack back to Buzz. He wrapped both arms around it, looking calmer. Jewel sat him on a bench, Randy on one side and herself on the other. The shopper hovered. Her lipstick was on crooked, Jewel noticed. And her sneakers were missing their laces.

To Buzz, Jewel said, "We need to find out who's bought this stuff and what it did to them. So we go to every place around town where you've sold it and talk to people. And you have to help because, if you don't, I gotta let the cops have you."

Buzz looked scared. He whined, "Please, officer. I'll be good."

The shopper butted in again. "I can tell you right now that I bought some and it was wonderful. It changed my life. I haven't been to Elizabeth Arden in a month. I feel fabulous and I don't care how I look," she said proudly.

Jewel remembered Leo at Spa On The Mile complaining about his renegade hair client. Even Jewel could tell it had been ages since this woman had seen the inside of a salon.

"So what did this—this potion do to you?"

"I told you, it made me feel gorgeous." The shopper shrugged. "It doesn't taste bad. I only had one dose. God knows, if it ever wears off, I'll want more," she added with determination. "So you better find out where this young man is getting his supply. Otherwise a lot of very unhappy women will be looking for him."

"I bought a djinn in a bottle from him," Randy said. "It was drunk."

"Genie," Jewel said and bit her tongue. *Policy, remember?*

The shopper blinked. "Was there a genie in the bottle?"

"There was," Randy said. "It smashed a hansom into a bridge abutment and then set the hansom on fire."

"Heavens!" The shopper clucked as Randy described with relish how the fire had held up a five-way intersection at Lake Shore and Navy Pier.

Jewel thought hard. Dr. Kauz was hawking this stuff through Buzz. It made the victim feel great about herself. Kind of like the Venus Machine, she realized, which made you irresistible to men whether you wanted to be or not. *Holy crap.* She'd turned Kauz loose in a house with that machine. He already had this potion that women wanted. What could he do if he had both?

That must be why he was so hot to come to Virgil's. To get the Venus Machine. *Plus Virgil has money and he's a woo-woo fan.* Maybe Kauz hoped to get campaign funding out of Virgil.

It didn't add up yet, but she could feel it out there, some wackadoodle plan in Kauz's noggin that would combine magic and defrauding aging women and running for mayor into something that would make the Fifth Floor unhappy.

She just didn't know what.

Yeah, but I've got him cold on manufacturing and distributing an unlicensed drug.

That could stop him. She gnawed her lip.

She would have to put the case together carefully.

And she would have to find at least one unsatisfied customer of Dr. Kauz's potion. She turned to Kauz's beta distributor.

"Buzz, I can keep you out of jail if you cooperate. Will you help me? I don't have time to chase all over town when I need you, and Randy doesn't like getting kicked in the head."

Buzz nodded convulsively.

She framed her next question with care. "Ma'am, would you be willing to testify on his behalf?"

"Of course. I'm Mrs. Noah Butt. My husband is Noah Butt, Esquire, of Butt, Baron, Fessley and Queeg."

"If I could talk to one or two other people who would concur with your testimony—" Jewel paused.

"Of course!" Mrs. Butt beamed. "I've given samples to all my friends. I meet Buzz here every week, just so I can share his potion with other women. It changes our lives! We no longer waste our time and money on our appearance. A few of us have even gone to stay at ashrams."

Jewel fought an eyeroll. "You haven't given up shopping."

"There was a shoe sale at Lord & Taylor."

Oh, well, shoes.

"Ma'am, do you, or did you, used to patronize any other businesses besides Elizabeth Arden? Places that sell, oh, makeup and stuff?" Jewel was weak on that sector of retail that catered to women's insecurities. "You must be saving a lot of money since you stopped buying that stuff."

"Goodness, yes. My Arden bill alone was two thousand a month. I got my makeup there, except for lip color, which I got from Neiman's or Lord & Taylor, and I saw Giorgio lo Gigolo once a month for a pedicure. And I tried that new place in the Hancock Tower, Institute something, and then I met Buzz and all that was over. Come to think of it, that's where I met Buzz. He was on the plaza outside, selling samples."

Jewel hesitated while she had a sudden evil thought. "You've been a great help, ma'am. If I find the source of the potion and it turns out you can get it legally—if it's safe—would you like me to phone you?" She'd die first, but if she didn't make the offer, Mrs. Noah Butt would smell a rat. *I'm turning into a con artist!* Clay would be so proud.

"How thoughtful! That would be darling of you." Mrs. Butt glowed. "Take my card."

Jewel realized that Kauz must not be ready to reveal himself as the inventor of this stuff. Maybe he planned to stay in the background. The potion might be full of cocaine or something. *I only had one dose*, Mrs. Noah Butt had said. So it was nonaddictive. *God knows, if it ever wears off, I'll want more.* Okay, nonaddictive so far.

Hm. There was an idea. Let a herd of raging lipstick-o-holics come banging on his spa door demanding an illegal drug, and watch his campaign come tumbling down. She'd have to figure out how to orchestrate that. Which gave her an idea.

"Mrs. Butt, I'd still like to be sure that no one has been harmed by this potion. Here's my card. If you remember the names of anyone you've given it to, would you call me? We may ask you to make a statement."

Mrs. Butt flushed. "Lord Pontarsais has only to ask." She languished in Randy's direction, tucked two cards into her purse, and headed for the elevator in her expensive, laceless sneakers.

Two cards?

Jewel sighed. "Thank God she's gone. Let's take a walk down Michigan, the three of us, and visit Buzz's pitches." On the down escalator she hissed to Randy, "Did you give her one of those bogus lord cards?"

Randy raised his eyebrows. "I could introduce myself as your fellow investigator instead."

"No!"

With his hand on the back of Buzz's collar, Randy spoke quietly. "I must be someone, Jewel."

He was right. He couldn't get by much longer before he got challenged for real ID. And it was her responsibility to provide it, if she ever hoped to get him out of pajamas and into a job.

In the end, she'd wind up asking Clay to get him fake papers. Which would put her in Clay's crooked debt again.

Wasn't there a curse about this? You saved somebody's life, and then you were stuck with them for the rest of yours?

CHAPTER 17

Jewel stopped in at Arden, then at Neiman's, then Giorgio lo Gigolo. She didn't meet any more of Buzz's potion customers but she found plenty of unhappy beauty-industry professionals. Randy kept Buzz out of sight at each stop.

"I'm Jewel Heiss of the Department of Consumer Services, and I'm doing a survey on consumer buying patterns on the Mile," she said over and over. "How's business these days?"

"Business sucks," said the manager at Elizabeth Arden, a lacquer-finish brunette of forty. "We get plenty of tourists, but our regulars have fallen way off."

"Have any of these regulars disappeared for a while and then come back?" *Don't lead the witness, Jewel.* "I mean, have you talked to them about why they left?"

The manager stared out the window onto Michigan Avenue. "We're not a dentist. We send reminder cards, but we don't pester our clients by phone." Her eyes turned to Jewel. "How come Consumer Services cares about my business?"

"You aren't the only sufferer," Jewel said, trying to look official and inscrutable. "We're seeking a pattern to explain the trouble you're experiencing."

The manager nodded. "Good luck."

The perfumes and makeup counter at Neiman's had

the same story. "It's like they all dialed 1-800-GIVE-A-SHIT and then got tired of waiting on hold," said a glossy girl with long legs.

"I saw one of my regulars at the Galaxy Theatre last night," said a metrosexual wearing thumb rings. "She smelled. I mean she smelled *bad*."

This sounded promising. "Do you have her name and address?"

The clerks looked at each other. "It's on her checks, but she hasn't come here for, like, two or three months," he said.

Two or three months! Buzz had some explaining to do.

"I think her name's Eunice. Or Beulah or something like that," said Metrosexual.

"Beulah!" the leggy girl exclaimed. "It's in diamonds in loopy script on this huge-ass brooch. She always wears it."

"You've been very helpful." Jewel's phone rang. "If you remember anything else, call me?" She handed over her card with her left hand and flipped open the phone with her right. "Hello?" Her eye rolled, seeking Buzz. Whew, Randy had him by the elbow, waiting outside. She joined them, phone-to-ear.

"Are you working this case or not?" Clay's voice said querulously. "I'm all alone here with two slavering mad scientists and two women who hate each other's guts and I can't get anything done without you."

"Where," Jewel said, lowering her voice, "the hell were *you* this morning? You knew I needed to talk to you, Clay Dawes. Or should I say Clay *Thompson*? And another thing. Randy needs some ID, stat. Something solid. A crook like you should know where to get it."

"Piece of cake," he said. "When can you get back here?"

She eyed Buzz. He seemed docile enough. "Ten minutes. Hey, did a package come for me from the office?"

Clay paused. "Yeah."

What was *that* tone about? "Oh. You opened it. It was addressed to me."

"It was addressed to Jewel Heiss. I got to the door before Himmler did, that butler, so no damage done. I had to open it to find out who was dumb enough to break your cover."

That would have been me. She should have told Ed she was working under an alias. No point mentioning that.

"Well, if you haven't done anything creative with the contents, meet me at the Thompsons' back gate in about ten minutes." *Oh, duh. Clay must think I want to anklet him! Well, let him sweat.* "I am so pissed at you."

"Be pissed, but get here." Clay hung up.

"You don't hang up on your senior partner!" she yelled at the dead phone, then turned to her companions. "Buzz, we're going for a little ride, and you'll tell me some more about how long you've been at this, and this time don't lie."

"Are you taking me to a back room with rubber hoses?" he squeaked.

"I wouldn't know what to do with a rubber hose. We'll ask you some questions and then we'll turn you loose. And when I phone you—you have a cell, right?—you'll answer and you'll meet me when and where I want to see you."

Buzz relaxed. "Sure."

Sure is right. She loved him like a kid brother but she wouldn't trust him farther than she could shotput his bicycle. Which reminded her. "We gotta swing by Water Tower and pick up your piece-of-shit bike."

"If it's still there," Buzz said glumly.

The bike was still there. Randy put the bike on the roof of the Tercel and tied it down with some string Buzz had in the bottom of his backpack.

While he was doing this, a garbage truck stopped in front of them. Quick as thought, Buzz grabbed the bagful of teeny potion bottles out of the Tercel's front seat and hurled it into the truck's maw as the compactor blade came down. The bottles popped like firecrackers.

Randy had him by the arms in the next moment. Too late. Jewel stared into the garbage truck.

A keen investigator would be, like, sorting through all the pooper-scooper bags and spilled pop cans to find one intact potion bottle.

Euw.

"I still have a sample from yesterday," she said feebly.

Buzz looked crestfallen, then brightened. "Yeah, but your fingerprints are smearing mine."

"Smarty-pants." She put him in the back seat with Randy, drove to within a block of Virgil's place, then turned up the alley behind it.

Clay was lurking by the garbage cans, holding a cardboard box and looking pained.

Jewel parked, shielded from view by Virgil's back garden wall. "Lemme see the package."

The office had included instructions, which she read while Randy took Buzz's bike off the car. No tracking unit. A note from the office read, *Still adjusting tracker to track two anklets. Sending tomorrow.* The anklets didn't look like much, plain black rubbery bands, each with a little box on it.

"Okay, Buzz, c'mere."

Buzz approached cautiously, Randy herding him like a sheepdog. When he saw the anklet, he tried to bolt. Randy caught him and pushed his face to the alley wall.

"No, no, nonono!" Buzz beat the wall with his fists.

"Oh, hush. Shut up! Buzz, shut up and listen!"

He turned his head against the bricks and rolled one eye toward Jewel. "I'm a free citizen. You can't do this to me."

"You're about to go to jail for selling a dangerous drug without a license. Work with me." She laid her hand on his shoulder. "Buddy, this is what I keep warning you," she said in a softer voice. "This is why I want you to go to high school like a normal kid. Join society. You mess around on the fringe, you get in trouble. You're a very creative person and I admire that, but this is a stupid way to live."

"I like the fringe. Society doesn't like me."

She sighed. "Hold him." While Randy tightened his grip, she clipped the anklet around Buzz's ankle. All the fight went out of the kid. When she stood up she said, "I'll take it off when this case is over. That means, if we need you to testify, you are still wearing it."

Buzz tried to bolt past her, pushing her aside. Clay caught him by the tee-shirt collar. He made the kid face Jewel again.

"No judge is gonna believe nothin' a homeless person says," Buzz growled. "Not if he's wearing a illegal tracer anklet."

Jewel smiled a tight smile. "You're so sharp, you'll cut yourself. It stays. Now, what's your cell number?"

He looked sulky, but he gave her the number, which she tested then and there with her own phone. His phone rang in his pocket.

"Good boy. I'll call you when I need you. Give him his backpack, Randy."

Buzz grabbed the backpack, sent her one embittered glance, threw his leg over the bike, and pedaled off.

"Go inside, Randy. I have to talk to Clay. No, wait a minute, come here."

Clay and Randy exchanged glances.

"Bossy," Clay said.

"She does her duty," Randy said.

"Knock it off," she pleaded, and showed Randy the anklet. "This is what I was talking about. It has a teeny

GPS device in it that's always talking to the tracking unit. Which reminds me, you do need a cellphone. That way, if you're out and about somewhere, say you're late coming home, and the unit stops moving for a long time, the tracker knows. I can call you. If you're still connected to the anklet, you can tell me where you are, and that'll tie in with the signal. If you don't answer, I'll know it's time to go look for you, and I'll have a good idea where."

Randy eyed the anklet with mistrust. "Buzz recognized it."

"He watches more TV than you do." She bent and locked it around Randy's ankle.

"But why should he object?"

Straightening, she sighed. "He's a free spirit. He's a runaway, probably from some horrible home we know nothing about. He's underage and he knows he could be sent back to his family if he gets in trouble with the law."

"You didn't threaten him with his family."

"I'm not a total asshole." Jewel leafed through the manual provided by the office. "Battery good for five years. That's what I figured."

"I still don't understand why—" Randy's voice rose.

Clay blew the gaff wide open. "They put it on paroled convicts who can't be trusted to stay put."

Randy took this big. "What!"

Jewel looked up from the manual to see him swelling and glaring, headed for full snit.

She stepped as close to him as she could get without rubbing her breasts against him. "Easy. We discussed this, remember? We'll both be glad you have it someday."

"I'm branded a criminal! Even street urchins will know!"

She kept her voice calm. "Four hours ago, you wanted it."

"I am not a criminal! I may have no name, no employment, and no past, but you cannot *chain* me like a transportee!" He reached down and wrenched at the anklet. "I shall cut it off!"

"Not with conventional weapons," Clay said. "That's wire-reinforced. Try pulling your sock up over it."

Randy let go of his ankle and stood, panting and glaring at Jewel. "You know I am ignorant of the tools necessary to free myself. You take advantage of me."

"And you take advantage of me. Think of it as a flawed partnership. We're trying to work this out, okay?" she said when he still looked steamed. "Give it a chance?"

With a brief scowl at Clay, Randy flung away, strode through the back gate of the Thompson mansion, and slammed it behind him.

Jewel rubbed her temple. "That went well, I thought."

"Touchy."

"And you were so helpful." Jewel fixed Clay with a cold eye. "Clay *Thompson*. Come back here," she said as he sidled toward the gate. "With partners like this I don't need enemies. I can send you back to the office."

"I don't think so."

"I can get you fired."

"Bet?" He smiled his kissy-face con artist smile.

"Okay, I can whine and whimper to Ed and pull a Sayers, freak out, go on psych leave. Then see if Ed'll make you *any*body else's partner. What the fuck are you doing?" she burst out. "Is this whole case just a scam you're running so you can keep an eye on Griffy's crumbling relationship?"

Clay looked over his shoulder at the house. "Let's take a walk." She let him lead her around the corner onto Marine Drive. "First of all, I didn't know Griffy would call the department. She's usually not so creative or independent."

"Oh, that's insulting. I thought you cared about her!"

Clay walked, staring straight ahead. "I care about her a lot. She's been more of a mother to me than any other girlfriend Virgil's had." They crossed Marine Drive and walked down a ramp into a pedestrian tunnel under Lake Shore Drive. The tunnel was crowded with people headed for the beach. "If I had to, I would involve the whole department," he admitted, his voice hollow in the tunnel. "But I couldn't see how we could help, and I told her that. So Griffy phoned in the complaint over my head."

Jewel lengthened her stride to keep up. "Why didn't you tell me all this when Ed gave us the case?"

He was silent. They emerged from the tunnel into sunlight and into the park.

Jewel pulled him around to face her. "This isn't a game. This is my job. And it's the law. You're using it like a personal club you can bring down on people you don't like."

"You're being a little—"

"Sovay? Tell me you don't want to bust her."

He looked at her with no expression. "I can't tell you that." But she had a flash of Clay throttling Sovay until her tongue stuck out.

Jewel blinked. "Well, I'd love to. Only, being an officer of the law, I have to put that aside and look at the facts. The *fact* is, she may be putting moves on your father, but she hasn't yet tried to defraud anybody. I have reservations about Virgil and Herr Doktor Professor Gustavus Katterfelto Kauz, but Sovay, I fear, has done nothing but be a bitch. Unless," Jewel added, "she stole the Venus Machine from somebody."

Clay shook his head. "Sorry, no."

"You know this."

"Uh, a couple of files came with the anklets."

"And you were going to tell me when?"

He put his palms out. "You were in such a hurry with the anklets, I thought you'd rather deal with higher priorities." The relaxed, nasal whine was back in his voice, and she knew he'd recovered his balance.

"That reminds me, what have you done with the background checks *you* did on these people? Ed says he doesn't have them."

"Didn't you find those?" Clay asked in an innocent voice.

"Look me in the eye." *He* didn't know about the latest wrinkle from the Venus Machine.

He met her look with his blandest boy-next-door face.

"Are you worried that there's a warrant outstanding against Virgil?"

"No."

Looking deep into his baby blues, she could think of nothing but holding his hand. Then she realized he was holding her hand. He lifted it to his lips and kissed her knuckles.

"Jewel, I want Griffy to have what she wants."

"Is that all you want?" She searched his face. Again, she got a picture of a picket fence and a golden retriever on a lawn.

This new Venus Machine wrinkle was worthless. Like every other kind of magic she'd been forced to deal with.

"That's all," Clay said. "Oh, I also want to keep my job."

She pulled her hand free. "Then you'll remember who your senior partner is. You stick around for when I need you. And you cough up those files, including the ones that came today, as soon as we get back to the house."

"Absolutely." He was smooth, in control.

"And take this sample to the lab for me?" She rummaged in her purse. "Dammit, I had it here a minute ago." Then she remembered Buzz shoving her, trying to escape, and sighed.

"Can't find it?"

"He must have sneaked it out of my purse. That kid has way too many survival skills."

"I could chase after him."

"It's gone now. Sold or thrown in a Dumpster." She groaned in frustration.

Clay patted her shoulder. "What else can I do for you, partner?"

"You can get Randy a fake identity so I don't have to shit bricks every time he goes out in public."

Clay kissed her knuckles again. "For you, anything."

She threw up her hands and turned back toward Virgil's house. "Groovy. Get that sex demon to quit pouting, and we've almost got a team."

CHAPTER 18

Jewel sent Clay up to his room for the files and went in search of Randy.

She found a maid in the card room, vacuuming. No Randy.

She found Griffy in the kitchen with Mellish and the cook and a woman from a catering firm. No Randy.

She found Kauz in the collection room, taking pictures of things with his psychespectrometer. No Randy.

No Sovay, either, which put a sour taste in her mouth.

She even tried her own room, where "Lord Darner" might be sulking, lying in wait for her. Nope.

She did find Virgil standing in front of the bedroom door across the hall from hers, his knuckle raised to knock, and his ear cocked.

"Virgil, have you seen Lord Darner?"

"Lord Darner? Why, no, I haven't." There was the faintest tremor in Virgil's hand, and he smiled senilely. "I've been looking for Ms. Sacheverell, myself. This is her room."

Just then Jewel heard a rhythmic thump-and-squeak from inside Sovay's room. She felt herself blush. "Okay, guess I'll, uh, go to my room." *Randy and the snake!* The heat rose up her back, burning all the way to her ears. She blundered through her bedroom door across the hall.

On second thought, she closed the door, then opened it a fraction and laid her ear against the gap.

Knock knock knock. "Sovay, my dear? Are you in there?" *Knock knock knock.* Man, this guy had no tact. Or else he hoped to catch them at it. Virgil wasn't deaf, and he wasn't gaga.

Knock knock knock. "Sovay? We're almost ready for lunch. I've come to take you down."

Now there was a double entendre, if you chose to hear it.

Jewel heard a door open and Sovay's muffled voice. "Sorry, darling, I was napping." *I'll bet*, Jewel thought.

"Shall I come in?"

"No!" A rather artificial giggle followed this heart cry.

"I could help zip you up," Virgil chortled. Peeking, Jewel saw him start to push his way into Sovay's bedroom.

Sovay's hands appeared, shoving him back out into the hall.

Jewel ducked inside her room.

Sovay's door slammed. "Be right with you, darling!"

"Of course, of course. You look charming in that negligee, my dear."

"Naughty man!" Sovay said through the door.

Virgil chuckled. Footsteps sounded down the hall, and Jewel peeked out again to see him descending the stairs.

She felt steam coming out of her ears. *The witch!* She marched across the hall. *Let her think the sugar daddy's come back to pinch her again.* She rapped on Sovay's door.

"Coming!" Sovay trilled from inside.

Jewel had to knock twice. Then the door opened on a fully-dressed Sovay.

Sovay's face twisted into a silent snarl.

Jewel was glad she was two inches taller than the bitch.

"Hi, I wondered if you've seen Lord Darner any-where? He hasn't taken his afternoon penicillin. He's so careless." Jewel looked past Sovay at a rumpled bed. "About where he sleeps."

Sovay flipped her hair back and threw the door wide.

Jewel sauntered past, scanning the room for signs of Randy. No pile of empty Lord-Darnerwear. No anklet. A knotted pillowcase full of something tipped over and slid off the bed to the floor. Randy's clothes? Behind her, she could feel Sovay's glare like a red-hot slap on the back of her head.

No Randy.

It was a ninety-percent sure thing he was in that bed.

But Jewel had a huge advantage now. All she needed was the tracking unit and she would find him.

Stifling a sigh of relief, she swept past Sovay. "Lunchtime," she said brightly. "If you're not too full to eat."

She was startled to meet a glare of sizzling hatred. Not just you-bitch, but I-keel-you-feelthy.

Yow. Okay then.

At lunch, everyone but Sovay commented on Randy's absence.

"No clue," Jewel said more than once. "He just dis-appears from time to time. I wouldn't worry."

"Clay," she hissed when the meal ended an hour later. "I need to talk to you."

Of course he dawdled getting away from the table, and then Griffy wanted her opinion about the food she was ordering for a block party to be held on Virgil's birthday Saturday night, and then Kauz showed them fifty-seven pictures of the aura of a bowl of fruit. By two-thirty she was beside herself.

"What's up, officer?" Clay said when she had dragged him into her room.

"Where's the tracking unit that goes with those anklets? I need it. Now."

"It didn't come yet."

She grabbed him by the shirt and yanked him nose to nose. "Don't mess me around. This is urgent."

"Buzz can't have gotten in trouble alrea—" He stopped. "Randy?"

"Randy," she said through her teeth. "He was in Sovay's room before lunch, I'm positive. Virgil surprised them together."

"That must have been interesting," Clay drawled.

"Well, he didn't get the door open and see them. But if Randy heard his voice—"

"Catch Randy zapping into a bed because some guy walks in on him with his girlfriend? I doubt it." Clay looked thoughtful. "Unless he knew *you* were about to catch him."

"He might have. I was talking to Virgil by the door."

Clay nodded. "We have to get into that room."

"That's why I wanted you. You can watch while I, uh, look for Randy."

He blinked. "That's a real nice offer but I pass."

Jewel almost pasted him one. Then she realized what he meant and only socked his arm. "Watch the *hallway* for people who might catch us."

"Right. I'll get my tools."

Jewel followed him upstairs. When they got to his room, she found that Clay's tools were lock picks. "You brought burglar's tools with you?"

"Undercover one-oh-one. I take it you cut class that day." Clay leaned up against Sovay's door, looking left and right over his shoulder, and in two jifs he had them inside the room.

Jewel relocked the door.

"There you go," he said, gesturing at the bed.

The bed wasn't made. Jewel wrinkled her nose. "I

guess I have to." Now that she was here, she didn't want to do this. "Damn Randy," she muttered.

She sat down on the bed.

Clay wandered around, poking into drawers, going through the closet, fiddling with makeup on the dressing table. "You know, if I'd been more prepared I could do some real damage here."

"Stop snooping and go watch the door." Jewel closed her eyes and tried to concentrate, feeling for a tingle, a zing, some sign of her errant stealth fuck.

"Little stink juice in the perfume. Hair remover in the shampoo."

She sat up. "Could you please go outside? Like, lurk down the hall, and if she comes this way, you distract her. You're good at that."

"Hm. What if a maid comes to make the bed while I'm distracting her? Jeepers, how many shoes does a woman need?"

Jewel flopped back down. "At least keep quiet."

"Relax. She went shopping."

With an effort Jewel shut her eyes and relaxed. Time passed.

Clay puttered around the room.

Jewel prayed he wouldn't lift Sovay's jewelry.

He started humming. She jammed a pillow over her head.

Randy? Are you in here?

He had to be. The rhythmic thumping. The look on Sovay's face when she opened the door to Jewel was proof of that. Plus Virgil knock-knock-knocking and then taunting Sovay, since he was not a senile horndog but a razor-sharp con man on the hunt. Yep, she'd been banging Randy in here all right.

Jewel thought of Sovay's smug smile at lunch, rolled over, and punched the mattress. *I do not care who he fucks.*

Who was she kidding? She owned this guy. It was a dirty little secret that got bigger and messier every day, like a big old cow plop, spang in the middle of her conscience. She *hated* him screwing around. She herself did it with him every single day of her life. It was like sharing your toothbrush.

Except last night, when he'd been paying her back for the night before, when she also didn't fuck him. *Payback. Another excellent reason for avoiding a long-term relationship.*

She groaned and held still, trying to clear her mind.

In the silence she heard little clinks and rustles.

She lifted the pillow two inches off her face. "Quit searching her stuff. I mean it."

"You must have been a big sister—"

"I'm an orphan. No siblings."

"—in a past life. You're so bossy. Well, well, well. What have we here?"

Sweaty and annoyed, she sat up again. "I don't know, what? A class-one felony in progress?"

Clay was riffling through a mahogany-red jewelry box. "Checkbooks. Six of them. All in different names." He looked over at her. "How's it coming? Any sign of Lord Barenaked?"

She scowled. "No."

"Go to sleep. That'll fetch him," he said.

"I hope so. I think he's sulking. He was pretty mad at me."

Troubled, she lay back down and put the pillow over her head. Rustlings sounded, even through the pillow, so she wrapped her arms around it and squeezed it against her ears.

She tried to think about something sexy. Fancy underwear? She liked lingerie, but it seemed like a waste of money when she spent so much of her guy time naked.

Speaking of which, *where the fuck is that sex demon?* Concentration wasn't working.

What would draw him?

A horny woman.

What would make her horny?

About a million things, but she'd recently found a whole new side of herself, i.e., a girl too shy to come screaming and have her clothes explode all over the room in front of people.

In fact, the one time Clay had ever been nearby when she was doing Randy—

"Ah-hah." She sat up again.

Clay took his hand out of his pocket and turned around. "Ah-hah what?"

"I know what'll get him to stop sulking." She felt tongue-tied. She looked at Clay guiltily.

"What?" He drew near the bed. "You intrigue me, officer. What's that look about?"

She remembered how he had refused to have sex with her, two nights ago. *This will be fun.* She stared at the sheet. "Um, remember when we were in your hotel suite and Randy walked in?"

"Why, yes. Yes, I do."

Always so noncommittal. It was the con artist in him, making the mark do all the work. She set her teeth. "Well, he couldn't resist, um, showing up that time. I think it was more than knowing he had to, um, do something for me or he'd be stuck in that couch forever. It was like, there's a woman right here who wants it, so he *had* to, like. . . ."

Clay sat on the end of the bed. "Hm. I see what you mean."

"I mean, I realize you've sworn off sex. With me. Because of the partners thing. Which is wise, since you're insubordinate and in another minute I'm liable to phone in a green sheet for your file." She gasped and took a long, slow, calming breath.

"Ooo, a green sheet! I'm trembling. You catch more flies with honey than vinegar, partner," he drawled, not moving. Goddammit, he was always trying to get in her pants.

Until two nights ago.

She swallowed, not looking at him.

"You're not used to asking for it, are you?" he said with a smile in his voice, and she wanted to punch him so bad that her arm jerked by itself. "All you have to do is look at a guy and he sits up and begs. And that was before the Venus Machine kicked your green tones into high."

She looked up and said sharply, "I don't want to d-do anything with you any more than you do. But we do not leave our people trapped and alone."

"He won't be alone by tonight."

She eyed Clay. "Are you having fun?"

He crinkled his blue eyes at her. "Why yes, I'm having a ball. I haven't had so much fun since we hid under a thirteen-thousand-dollar sofa at Field's and then burgled the joint." She drew air across her clenched teeth. "But you're right. We don't leave our people trapped and alone. Very praiseworthy. So, uh."

He looked at her, looked at the space between them, looked at the bed, cleared his throat, and scooted a couple of inches closer to her. Hesitantly, he reached out with both arms, circled her in an awkward hug, then let his arms drop.

"Uh, I'm experiencing a little performance anxiety here."

If she killed him, she wouldn't have any way of flushing Randy out of his hiding place. "I can understand that." She heard embarrassment in her own voice.

"Let's hold hands until we think of something."

Gratefully, avoiding his face, she scooted over and he boosted himself onto the bed beside her. She put one hand out and he took it. They sat side by side, leaning against the headboard, holding hands, looking straight ahead.

She said, "Will we get caught? We're gonna get caught."

CHAPTER
19

"I pennied us in."

"Excuse me?"

"Didn't you do that in college? Tons of fun. You stick a penny in the door crack and it won't open."

She was touched. "That was thoughtful. Thank you."

They didn't say anything for a minute. *This is so awkward.*

"Now *I'm* having performance anxiety," she said.

"You can't expect me to do all the work here. You're the one who insists—"

"I know, I know!"

"I'd seduce you in a New York minute, if it was my idea."

"Well, it wasn't my idea to go to *your* room two nights ago!" she burst out and then bit her lip. "I mean," she said more quietly, "it wasn't. I was so drunk I couldn't think straight." She considered saying, *And I thought you were taking me to my room*, but decided it wasn't true.

He said, "Okay, you're right, I made a mistake there. I had this foolish plan to, I dunno, break the ice between us. Get you to loosen up a little."

"I do not need to get any looser," she stated.

He looked at her and she turned her head warily to meet his eyes. In a gentle tone he said, "You can get tense on the job."

"That's because it's a job, not a con or a game or a—"

He said hastily, "But I saw how wrong I was when you explained it. So I want to stay your partner."

He didn't say any more. She digested this. *He's not pushing for sex. He wants to stick with me.*

That felt weird. Weird, but good.

"Is that why you're . . . not helping me here?"

"I'll help you. I want to help you." He said with quiet sincerity, "I just don't want to wreck our working relationship."

She drew a deep, shaky breath. "Okay. Here's the thing. Once you can tell Randy's starting to, um, *manifest*, would you be willing to go outside and wait 'til we're done? He's not, like, solid until I, um. But maybe you can tell before, um. Because you don't like when he's between us, anyway, right?"

"Sure. I wouldn't want to be in the way," he said in a saintly boy-next-door voice.

She squeezed his hand. "Thanks, buddy."

Then he smiled.

"You booger! You are so yanking on me!" She dove at him and stuck wriggling fingers into his armpits.

He squirmed and ducked his head. "Hey! Quit!" He tried to cover his armpits with his hands.

"You're conning me and yanking on me and messing with my head!" When he tried to turn on his belly she threw a leg over him and pinned him between her thighs, going for his stomach, his sides, and the backs of his ears.

"I'm very ticklish! Help! Help, I'm being assaulted!"

"Shut up, do you want to get caught?" she said, laughing.

"Help!"

His belly was all muscle, which made it a lot easier to tickle him, and she threw herself down on him and stopped his mouth with hers. Those big poochy lips met her halfway. He stopped protecting his armpits and put his hands on either side of her face, so tenderly that she forgot to tickle him, and she thought, *Okay, I can do this*, and then he made a little happy sound in his throat. She settled over him so the banana in his pocket made contact at the right spot between her legs and then his kiss opened up and she forgot about other things.

She wondered if he was getting off on this the way she was.

I don't want to figure you out, she thought, *I want to get you hothothot*. If she could peel away his fake humility and his fake boy-next-door innocence—she popped the fly of his khakis and he pulled the red top over her shoulders—if she could make him be real for twenty minutes—she tossed away the top and then wriggled as he tickled her under the elbows and went for her bra.

She took her mouth off his to say, "In front."

"Ah." Their eyes met as he worked the front clasp on her bra and she realized with a start that she didn't have any pictures in her head at all.

All she saw was a humble, innocent boy next door. Huh. Was that the secret to being a great con artist? Be yourself?

That, and lie a lot.

He got her torso naked and she pulled off his khakis. She kicked her twisted panties and jeans down to her ankles. Then she snuggled down against him, still breathing hard. He patted her back. Her heartbeat slowed to a hard, hot thump. *Thump. Thump. Cuddling. Why have I never tried that?*

"You're being too nice," she murmured. "I think I've been ruined for nice men."

"Bet?" He kissed her forehead and her eyes closed. She moved against his smooth skin, enjoying his warmth and the uncomplicated way his big hands kneaded her buns, stroked up and down her back, squeezed her buns, and stroked back up again, as if he too loved the feel of acres of skin on skin.

Honestly, she wouldn't mind if he speeded up a little.

"Didn't you have something for me?" She bumped her pubic bone against his woodie, smiling at the way he squeezed her all over when they hit.

"No rush." He slid his hand up her side, warmly cupped her nipple, then cradled the side of her face. The look in his eyes made her breath catch.

I can't be feeling this, she thought in rising panic. *I don't know you. You're a crook. You're not my type. You—*

He kissed her and she shut her eyes against her own thoughts, clasping her thighs around him, willing him to enter so that she could stop feeling so close. One of Randy's favorite phrases came to her, unbidden: *Are you afraid because you are aroused, or aroused because you are afraid?* Caught in the paradox, she let Clay kiss her, kissed him back, *My God, I'm kissing him back*, like, duh, why was this scarier than the fifty-seven crazy things she'd done with Randy and fifty-seven guys before him?

But it was. And he kept doing it over and over, the kiss that made her hothothot, letting her squeeze tight against him but never squeezing too tightly in return, the skin-on-skin marathon of their hands all over each other, then the pullback and that look in his eyes, until she couldn't take any more and had to kiss him, so she could shut her eyes and not see it, not feel the rise of something bigger than fear inside her. Her heart heated up in her chest. *I know you.*

What a lie!

But panic couldn't talk louder than the things he made her feel.

She struggled for self-control. *So this is what being*

conned in bed is like. The haze was too pleasant, too confusing. She knew she was being conned. Her breath came short. She could let it happen, go along for the ride the way she did with every other man. Appreciate it.

So she appreciated it, wallowing in the slow kisses, marveling at their power, as wild as doing it under a restaurant tablecloth, as potent as sex with a fire-breathing dragon. Her lips swelled and grew so sensitive, she felt the pressure of his lips like a hot, firm thumb on her trigger, how did he *do* that? Was she going to come from kissing? Her whole body throbbed. For some reason she could barely breathe.

And then he pulled away and looked into her eyes again and she forgot to be afraid. Her heart thudded in her ears. She forgot her name.

"Don't think I don't know what you're doing." Her breath began to come in long, slow, deep pulls, and she knew she was one inch away from orgasm.

To her relief, he glanced at her mouth. "Thank goodness. I was hoping one of us did," and leaned in for another kiss as she started to laugh.

Technically, she came one half-second before their lips met. She forgot to shut her eyes. This close, his eyes were wild and white-rimmed as a panicking horse's and, at the thought that he, too, was scared, the throbbing spasm in her hoochiesnatchie bounded ahead, faster, harder, making her breathless. She waited it out, thinking, *I'm fine, this is okay, I'll breathe again later*, but when he pulled back for another look, another kiss, she shut her eyes and turned her head away, trembling, sucking air in great heaves. To her horror, she felt a tear leak out of one eye.

They held each other in silence.

She said, "Can we fuck now? I need to clear my head."

"Well, sure," he said, sounding as calm as ever, which

had to be a lie, she'd seen the panic in his eyes. She couldn't look.

She heard foil rustle. A moment later he was sliding into her, and she hooked her chin over his shoulder so he wouldn't see the tear, and they banged and banged and banged.

And that was good, too.

Ten minutes later Clay rolled his head on her bare shoulder and said, "I think he's embarrassed."

"Your dick? Whatever for?"

"Randy," Clay said.

"Ohmigod. What time is it?" She glanced at her wrist-watch. "Holy crap." She pushed him off her and sat up. "I think he's not here at all. No way could we have got away with all that and not a peep out of him."

Clay stretched. "Plan B then."

"What's plan B? Do this on every bed in the house?" She hunted around the bed for her clothes. This would not be a good place to leave anything behind. "I don't think so."

"We could get that tracking unit from Ed and see where the anklet is."

She dropped her bra on the floor in surprise. "Duh!"

"Ah, officer. I can see why you were celibate for six months. Sex clouds your mind."

"Who told you I'd been celibate for six months?"

"Your best friend, Nina."

"I'll kill her. Where's my goddam bra?"

"Think I'll keep these," he said. "In memory of a special occasion."

Standing up with her bra in her hand, she saw Clay with a pair of Sovay's underpants on his head. She burst out laughing.

The door opened.

Sovay stood in the doorway, both hands full of shopping bags, her mouth ajar.

Naked Jewel and naked Clay stared back at her.

"Oops," Clay said.

Sovay's jaw flapped as if she couldn't get words out. Then she backed up a step and slammed the door.

Scrambling into her jeans, Jewel said through her teeth, "I thought you pennied us in."

"I thought it would relax you to think we were pennied in," he said. "I'm sorry. You were so tense. It seemed like the decent thing to relieve your mind of at least some of your wor—"

She socked him on the arm with one hand, pulled up her jeans with the other hand, and stuffed her feet into her pumps. "Did I bring a purse in here?"

"No."

"Are you sure, or are you saying that to make me feel better? Wait a minute—" She snagged his arm as he was reaching for the bedroom door and yanked him close so she could hiss in his ear. "What did you steal while I had a pillow over my head?"

He widened his eyes at her and pooched his lips out. "Not a thing."

"If you stole *anything*, that's a green sheet in your file. I'm not kidding about this."

Rustling came from the other side of the door. Sovay, waiting.

Jewel said, "This screws our cover, you realize."

Clay shrugged. "So we change it. Now that your green tones are through the roof, you can't resist sexualis imaginarium, so we're having a little fling. It wasn't your fault."

"That's lame, but we're stuck with it." Jewel sent her eyes around the room. "I wish there was another exit."

"Why? She knows we're in here."

"I can't stand walking past that bitch. She'll needle me about this forever."

"Leave it to me. I've got a story cooked up already."

"Of course you do," she muttered, and let him open the door.

Jewel bolted past svelte, perfumed, lovely, seething Sovay as Clay said, "Sorry about that. Been trying to get into her pants since she got here. I found out she has a fetish for other people's beds." He winked and aimed a pistol-forefinger at Sovay. "I'll make it up to you."

Over her shoulder, fumbling at her own bedroom door across the hall, Jewel hissed, "Green sheet!"

chapter 20

Clay bowed his way out of Sovay's room and breezed down the hall, feeling brilliant. *Intense, our Jewel.* For an unsettling moment he wondered if he was up to her. *It's not like I have a gene for long-term relationships.*

On the other hand, neither had Jewel. Full of optimism, he ambled into the kitchen, where he found Griffy looking at a catalog amid a whirlwind of caterers. "Oh, Clay," she said, too familiarly for a hostess speaking to a relative stranger. "Have you seen Virgil? The crab cakes are six dollars! He loves them, but he's so mad about this birthday party, and they're so good I don't think people will take just one, but, so the crab cakes will cost about five hundred dollars, so I don't know whether—"

"How about we have some coffee?" Clay said, drawing her away from Caterer Central. They sat in the breakfast nook around the corner. The cook brought coffee and a grateful smile for Clay.

He didn't bother reminding Griffy that he was supposed to be a total stranger. "I thought this was a block party."

"He's seventy tomorrow," she said with determination. "He gets a birthday party."

"Maybe he's sensitive about getting old." He had thought she understood that. Her education was deficient in everything except makeup and male-ego management.

She lifted her chin. "Seventy is a milestone."

Clay abandoned tact. "Are you telling him he's too old for a new girlfriend? Virgil doesn't like people to notice his weaknesses. He's ruthless. He cuts his losses like lightning."

She flashed her eyes, looking superb, he had to admit. "So maybe I need to get ruthless, too."

He threw up his hands. "Fine. Whatever. Piss him off. I suppose it's good for his blood pressure."

She gave a merry laugh, and Clay blinked. She was in a good mood, he realized. She wasn't scared. She was enjoying the prospect of matching tempers with Virgil.

"You're not afraid of him, are you?"

"No, and you know something, I realized this yesterday, but I never have been. I act like I'm scared so he doesn't get all kerfluffly. You know what he's like." She fluttered her hands like a teenager.

He smiled at her in bemusement. "I've been scared of him all my life."

"I know. I've been scared for you sometimes. But his temper never bothered me." She stood up and grabbed the caterers' catalog. "Where is the old buzzard? It's time he made some decisions around here."

Brain spinning, Clay followed her in search of Virgil. At least he would be a witness if anything exploded.

Virgil was in the card room, playing solitaire with plenty of wristy follow-through, an ugly look on his face. Clay pretended to interest himself in the checking-account deposit slips he'd snitched from Sovay's room.

He wished Griffy would be more careful. The old man seemed to be on the edge of something. Clay could hear his tone, harsh and full of authority as usual, and Griffy's, cheerful yet defiant. That was bizarre—what could she be thinking?

But that was why Virgil had brought Griffy home in the first place. He didn't know what Griffy thought and he didn't care.

The lonely teenager, starved for mother love, had cared. Because his father brought home the most beautiful showgirl in the world, with the kindest heart.

He lifted his head and eavesdropped. He heard Griffy say, "So you needn't worry about the price because I'm giving you crab cakes for your birthday."

"You're feeding the whole block. How can you pay for it? You don't have any money."

"I'll sell my rhinestones. You never liked them because I got them before I met you."

"Rhinestones will buy crab cakes for forty people?" Virgil said, but Clay heard a different question in his voice.

Amazed, Clay turned to look at them.

"They're very collectible right now." She swooped forward and pecked Virgil on his bald dome. "So that's settled. I'll be in the kitchen if you need me."

And off she sailed, leaving Virgil and Clay gaping.

Virgil slumped in front of his solitaire game. "What," he said in a bewildered voice, "the *fuck* has got into that woman?"

Clay flinched. Virgil didn't swear often. When he did, bad things happened to small boys. He opened his mouth, and Virgil cut him off with a savage hand-chop.

"And what about this cop you're sleeping with? So help me, boy, if you've abused my hospitality so she can investigate me—"

"Can't you tell? I thought you knew everything about everybody."

Virgil looked daggers.

"We're not investigating you. For some strange reason, everybody thinks you're a nice person."

But Virgil veered away. "What's that noise?"

He listened. He heard a faint, high-pitched ringing noise, like a fan belt slipping. "Sounds like it's upstairs."

"I told her to call the air conditioning company." Virgil

seemed to be working himself up. "Rhinestones. Crab cakes. Block party! She's out of her frigging mind!"

I'm not a small boy anymore. "She's a good person. She's giving you a birthday present you don't deserve, and she's paying for it with her own jewelry."

"It's cheap trash." Virgil's lower lip worked, and Clay wondered if he was thinking about all the times he'd tried to stop Griffy from wearing the rhinestones. She was right, too, about his motive. The old man didn't like to be reminded that she had had other keepers before him. "Junk," Virgil muttered.

"It'll buy forty people crab cakes for your birthday."

"I don't want a birthday party!"

Clay leaned forward until he was nose to nose with his sire. "Well, you're getting one. That's a hell of a woman. She loves you, in spite of your rotten behavior. And you may not have noticed, but she is right on the edge. She's figured you out. She knows she's worth something. If you don't bother to figure her out, you'll be eating crab cakes by yourself."

Virgil gave him a puzzled look. "What's got into you, boy?"

"Better hire another food taster. You could be notch number six in Sovay's belt. Because it doesn't look like Griffy will stick around." Virgil stared at him, speechless, so Clay lobbed his last grenade. "My mother left you, and now you're going to lose Griffy. And it'll be your own fault."

On that last word Clay walked out, his skin sizzling with terror as his body caught up with what his mouth had done.

Mrs. Noah Butt was as good as her word. She arranged for nine of her fellow fugitives from the beauty salon to show up in the coffee shop at Chestnut and Michigan.

Jewel had got the idea to quiz them all at once, hear

them talk, get a sense of Dr. Kauz's popularity base, if he ever unmasked as the inventor of the Amazing Whatever Potion.

This turned out to be a bad idea.

"Shirley, you look wonderful!"

"How are you, Diane? That sweatshirt suits you! You're radiant!"

"So are you, darling. We all look wonderful now."

"Isn't it fun?" said Mrs. Butt, the only person in the coffee shop Jewel recognized. "Have you ever seen a room so full of happy women?"

"Not since Janine Dorchester's detective showed those pictures of her husband in divorce court."

This remark caused mass giggling. Jewel lifted her gaze to heaven. The smell wasn't nasty. Just not what she would have expected from a coffee shop full of Gold Coast matrons. Sort of sweat-socky. A little bit funky. She cleared her throat.

"Hi, I'm Jewel Heiss." She gave her job title and handed out cards. "The reason I asked you to come today—"

"Who's that?"

"That's the girl from the city."

"Is she a new convert?"

"Oh, she must be. Look how lovely she is."

"Yasmin, ask her how long ago she took the potion."

"Ahem!" Jewel raised her hand. "May I have your attention? I just have a few questions I wanted to ask you. I thought that if there were variations in your experience, a group discussion would bring them out, which will be helpful to my investigation."

"I thought you were going to find a legal source of the potion!" Mrs. Butt said, ruffling.

"Haven't found one yet, but I am on the track of the person who invented it. The first step is finding out what it does, and whether it's harmful. You wouldn't want to give a harmful substance to a friend, would you?"

"We got ours from Eileen Butt," someone said. "Didn't we?"

The ladies looked at one another. After loud consultation, it was agreed, they had all been supplied with potions by Mrs. Butt, who had her supply from Buzz.

"But he's just the retailer," Mrs. Butt said. "You said he wouldn't go to jail."

"Not unless the potion proves harmful. Can you describe your, uh, symptoms for me? Oh, and I'm passing around a sign-up sheet, so we can all, uh, stay in touch."

"What a good idea!" someone said. "Make two copies. One for Officer Heiss and one for us."

Another woman leaped to her feet. Her dark red hair was every which way, but at least she smelled more like soap and less like a jockstrap. "My name is Yasmin Sabra, that's Yasmin without an E, and I got my potion from Eileen two weeks ago. We were having lunch in that adorable little place up on Dearborn, or is it Oak Street—"

"Oak Street," Mrs. Butt said. "Hamburgers and Absinthe."

"Oh, I've been there," said another woman.

"Just the part about your symptoms, ma'am?" Jewel said.

"Of course. Well. I put it in my purse and went for a massage and that night Helmy came home with lipstick on his cuff *again*, and I was miserable, and I remembered the potion and after he went out, we had this huge fight but that's not important, anyway, I took it."

"And?" Jewel prompted. "How did you feel? What did it taste like?"

"Well, I didn't feel anything. It was minty."

"Yes, so was mine."

"I thought wintergreen."

"With cloves, maybe?"

"Can we let Yasmin finish, please?" Jewel said desperately.

"Well, I began to feel better right away. It's not as if I don't mind Helmy sleeping with that little tramp, because I do." Her whiny tone vanished. "But, well, I realized that it isn't about me, really, is it? I'm a good person. I'm lovable and beautiful." She stood straighter, and her eyes shone. "I don't have to work at making myself satisfactory to anyone. I'm satisfied. I love myself and I love my life." Her voice rang out, strong and confident. Jewel found herself smiling at Yasmin Sabra. "I even love my husband. Someday he'll understand, if I can get another dose of that potion for him. Then he might realize that he doesn't need to screw twentysomethings to be lovable." There was no censure in her voice, just sad, sweet pity and hope for a lovable guy.

The other ladies murmured, and one or two clapped.

"I have half a dose at home, if you want it," offered a woman wearing parts of two different track suits.

Yasmin clapped her hands. "You're the best! My marriage is saved!"

"Uh, maybe we should find out if it's harmful," Jewel put in, but she was pooh-poohed by all present.

Yasmin proclaimed, "If I ever meet the man who invented that potion, I'll give him a hundred thousand dollars to advance his research!" She sat down to applause.

"Me next!"

"Oh, me!"

Jewel covered her eyes with one hand.

"I hate this tankini," Jewel groused to Clay. She tugged at the bottom. It didn't budge. Her frontispiece felt like a battering ram: high, tight, hard, and huge. She felt like she could play football in this swimsuit. She could plow snow. "I don't want to go out in public like this."

Clay crinkled his eyes at her. "You're adorable."

The house party had gathered in the vestibule. Virgil was taking his guests to the beach for a picnic supper, and to view the kite show and the fireworks to follow. She didn't want to go. Randy was still back in the house. Her cavorting with Clay hadn't flushed him, and that filled her with worry.

Everyone wondered where Lord Darner was. Jewel made an excuse about a ghost hunter in Skokie who'd called in a hot tip.

"I told him it was impolite to leave in the middle of his visit, but he's such an enthusiast."

She wanted to get her hands around Lord Darner's throat and squeeze, but first she had to get over the recurring panic attacks, wondering where the heck his bed could be.

"Well, we can't wait for him!" Virgil said gaily.

Sovay looked fabulous, swanking in her teeny weeny red bikini and transparent beach robe.

Yet Griffy, though older and softer, got even more

wolf whistles for her trim blue one-piece. She smiled and waved, looking thrilled with her celebrity and comfortable with it.

Virgil and Kauz walked behind the women, presumably enjoying the view.

They entered the pedestrian tunnel under Lake Shore. Jewel felt like a Viking in her tankini. She drew whistles, hoots, and animal noises. *They follow you like dogs*, Randy had said. Too proud to cringe, she held her head high and avoided men's eyes, praying that nobody she knew—

"Jules! Baby!" came a shout behind her. "Where ya been?!"

She grabbed Clay's arm and squeezed it.

"Hey! Hey, Jules!" A volleyball team clogged the end of the pedestrian tunnel. Their leader, a sunburned hunk Jewel remembered from some years ago, frolicked up to her. "It's me, Fred, from the Katz Beer Tournament? Whoa, baby, you look hot!"

"Fred, this is Clay, my *partner*."

Fred's face fell. "You're kidding. You're out of circulation? Oh, man!"

Clay was a picture of huffy possessiveness. "Yeah, she is."

"Oh, man! Bummer! Man, nobody'll believe this." Fred turned to his teammates, who clustered around as if hoping Jewel's touch could cure them of scrofula. He bellowed, "She's out of circulation!" His voice echoed down the tunnel.

A chorus of groans greeted this announcement.

Griffy beckoned to Mellish, trailing the party with Mike the chauffeur and a load of picnic gear. Mellish put his load down and went back to the house.

"Jules, I still have a lock of your pube hair."

"Hey, Jules, is your number the same?"

"Yeah, if you ever dump this guy, like, call me!"

Sovay's lip curled. Jewel burned with humiliation. Clay put his arm around her and said, "Guys, can we clear the tunnel?"

"Okay, bye!" The team romped away in Fred's wake.

One minute later, Mellish appeared at her elbow. "Miss?" He held out a beach coverup and a pair of giant sunglasses. "Miss Griffy thought you might want these."

"Oh, thank God!" Avoiding his eye, Jewel wrapped herself up like Jackie O. She felt sweaty, but the parade behind her dispersed.

They made it to the beach. Among thousands, she felt less conspicuous.

The summer sun hung low in the sky. The beach crowd was in a festive mood, watching the water kites. Dogs peed, children wailed and threw sand at one another, and humanity sweated in their flip-flops and shorts and tank tops. Pink thunderheads lay far out on the horizon, making a nice backdrop for the kites. A stiff north breeze cooled the sand and filled the sails of boats on the choppy gray-blue water.

"We need to talk," Clay said, drawing her away from the party. "I'll buy you a Mexican ice cream bar."

"We do. I never say no to ice cream." She followed him up the battered concrete walk to where the pushcart stood. "But what about our cover?" she said around a rice-pudding-flavored paleta.

"Between you passing out in my room and Sovay catching us in her room, I don't think anybody's surprised," Clay said around a mango-flavored paleta.

"That's true, I guess," she said. "I'm so tired of this Venus Machine crap, I could scream. Remind me to stop jumping at undercover cases."

"We have to get back to the house and look at those background checks."

"And find Randy." She licked her finger. "But when?"

"In another hour it'll get dark enough for fireworks."

She nodded. "We'll sneak away then."

"You don't look happy," her partner said with concern.

"I'm having a panic attack. I can't breathe, worrying about Randy. Plus I think I screwed up big-time."

"Getting drunk and sleeping with me?" He was such a guy.

"No," she said, nettled. "But I called that woman I met through Buzz—you would have been there, only you were screwing around instead of working with your partner, remember? She got her friends together, and they worship Kauz's little pink socks, and if they ever meet him they'll give him a jillion dollars to further his research. They fucking love the potion."

"They loved it before. You didn't do that."

"No, but I brought them all together and that gave them the idea to, like, *organize*. If they find Kauz, we're toast. I may have single-handedly doubled his campaign funding."

"Don't worry about it yet." He leaned closer. "Notice anything about the fair Sovay?"

"Besides the teeny bikini?" she grumped.

"She's not being such a bitch."

Flash a bikini on a guy and his brain vanishes. "Sorry," Jewel said, not sorry. "I look at her, all I can see is five-nine-worth of bitch. Plus she probably stole the Venus Machine."

"No, she didn't. She bought it in an estate sale in France two months ago. I traced the sale. No, I mean, she's not talking trash on Griffy so much. Or on you."

Jewel eyed Sovay, sashaying beside Virgil like hired arm candy. "Her body language sure is chatty."

"Pay attention," he said sharply, and she looked at him in surprise. Clay was never ruffled.

"You okay, buddy?"

"I am not okay. Virgil is showing his teeth. He hates this birthday party. Griffy won't back down, and this Sovay woman is a—a menace, and heaven knows how Virgil will lash out if his stupid plan turns sour." He hesitated.

"What else?" Jewel mentally filed "Virgil's stupid plan."

"Listen," he said, and met her eye. "You won't like this, but the bed we, uh, found in Sovay's room? That's not the bed that was in there before."

She squinted. "What? Before when?"

"Somebody switched the bed from that room after Randy vanished and before we got in there. Virgil must have done it."

"Why?" She scowled. "Plus, he couldn't. He's seventy."

"He has servants. Nobody else knows why the bed matters."

Jewel stared blindly at acres of sunburned skin. "He knows Randy was in that bed?" She turned on her partner with razor eyes. "*How* does he know?"

Clay flinched. "I had to tell him."

"Why? Because he's your father?"

"He knows I work with you." Clay held up his hands. "Hey, hey, take it easy. Flirt. We're undercover." He slid an arm around her rigid back. "I told him about my job weeks ago."

"Randy and—and beds and things is not your job." She stumbled across the sand. "Oh. You mean your old job?" *As in, con artist.* She said with horror, "Do you think he wants to run another sex-therapy scam, like you did?"

"I doubt it. In spite of all the newage in that house, Virgil's a skeptic. I think he took it to mess with me."

"I don't get it."

Clay looked unhappy. "I don't either. But you don't see it coming, when it's Virgil."

"We have to find that bed," Jewel said, cold with fear for Randy in Virgil's clutches.

"First find the anklet. That should be a big help."

"Yeah." A nasty suspicion hit her and she narrowed her eyes. "When did you know that bed wasn't the right bed?"

Clay hesitated. "There's more. Kauz and the block party. He's talked Virgil into setting up the Venus Machine and his spectrometer in the alley, where he can give free shots to people at the party. If that doesn't scare you, it should."

Holy crap. Jewel imagined a whole neighborhood going through what she was suffering. "I'm scared, I'm scared."

"Then you'll love this part. Kauz has called in the society reporters to cover the party."

"Shit!" This was bad news.

"Lower your voice and flirt. The butler is watching us." That bothered her, too. Randy had suspected the butler. She wished Clay had let her see those background checks.

"This is not good. The Fifth Floor will notice. Ed will convulse."

Clay leaned over and licked the corner of her mouth. She drew back in shock.

"Ice cream face," he explained. "Can't help myself, it's the Venus Machine effect. Flirt with me, partner." He nuzzled her ear. "So why the big worry? Kauz wouldn't declare his candidacy to a bunch of society reporters, would he?"

She leaned her forehead against his. "He's building a media presence. The Gold Coast is a fancy neighborhood. The party will be full of somebodies. He'll get them giggly over the Venus Machine and pictures of their damned auras, and then he'll be in the news. Two things we can't afford."

"Two things?"

"Kauz in the media, and magic in the media." She thought. With media present, Kauz would be danger-ous, but he'd be vulnerable. "Huh. Maybe this can work to our advantage." Clay patted her butt. She twitched away. "Boy, you are grabby."

He grinned like a dope. "I'm drunk on your green aura."

They horsed around, following Virgil's party. Mellish and the chauffeur unrolled a huge grass rug on the sand. Then they set up a folding table. Then the beach chairs. The chauffeur faded back and Mellish unpacked the pic-nic baskets: candlesticks, wine, cloth napkins, fancy plas-tic stemware, gold-rimmed plastic plates. Everything was genteel except the noise level.

Kauz cut loose and ranted, and Jewel no longer won-dered if the case was as serious as the Fifth Floor feared.

"With your help, I will usher in new era of harmony!" he exclaimed into Virgil's ear. "Harmony between magic and science! This fool in office now, he would brush the mighty power of enchantment under the rug. He stands against progress! But he is wrong! Every citizen has a right to magic!"

"How's your campaign fund doing?" Virgil said.

Kauz's eyes gleamed. "I can always use more support."

"I wondered if you wanted to buy the Venus Machine from me."

Jewel and Clay whipped their heads around.

"But it belongs to Miss Sovay," Kauz said, licking his lips. "I offer to buy it from her already."

"She's selling it to me." Virgil snaked an arm around Sovay, who looked smug as an Egyptian cat. "I couldn't let her give it away."

Jewel met Clay's eyes. *You called that one.*

Griffy looked pale. "Will you have red wine or white?" she said to Sovay, as if Virgil were her brother.

From the circle of Virgil's arm, Sovay hesitated. "White, please. Thank you."

So Clay was right about something else. Hate Radio Sovay seemed to be off the air.

Virgil passed the glass, wrapping his fingers around the bitch's hand as he did so.

"Excuse me," Clay muttered to Jewel. "Don't take this personally." He moved his chair next to Griffy's. A moment later Griffy giggled and swatted his hand off her knee.

Virgil sent a dark look at Clay. "Fickle pup." He moved his chair next to Jewel's. "How's the investigation going? You got anything on that criminal yet?"

It took Jewel a minute to remember all the games they were playing. *But why bother? Virgil knows who Clay is.* "We almost have him where we want him, sir."

The cuddly old-turtle expression left his face as he watched Clay flirt with Griffy. "Put him behind bars," he commanded. "As soon as possible."

He moved his chair back to Sovay's side just as Clay tenderly wiped Griffy's mouth with a napkin. Then Virgil "accidentally" dropped a chicken leg into Sovay's lap.

Kauz leaped forward to brush off Sovay's beach robe with his napkin. Griffy noticed and her smile turned sad.

I need a scorecard for these meals, Jewel thought.

She looked out at the lake, where a man flew suspended under an oblong parachute, striped bright orange and blue, being towed through the sky by a motorboat. "Randy would love that. He's a flying nut."

Kauz looked up from dabbing at Sovay's lap. "Does he make you be flying?"

What kind of question was that? "I'm afraid of heights."

"The power of air! But you, Miss Julia, you are the power of fire. Air is your friend." Kauz waved theatrically. "The demons of air obey those of fire."

She flinched. "Demons?" The man with the blue-and-orange sail came to rest neatly on the back of his tow-boat.

Kauz hitched his chair closer to hers. "All the world is made up of four kinds of demons—air, water, fire, earth. Trillions upon trillions of them." He smirked and dug her with his elbow. "So much more magical than to call them atoms and molecules. Although the English speak of fairies as atomies."

"Demons," Jewel muttered, thinking of her AWOL incubus.

"Someday every man, woman, and child in Chicago will have dominion over these demons!" Kauz proclaimed.

What a bad idea.

"Speaking of the English—" Kauz said.

"Think I'll go look at the parasail," Jewel said.

"I'll come, too," Griffy said.

Virgil waved royally. The two women walked down to the breakwater where the parasail was being moored.

CHAPTER 22

How it happened, Jewel couldn't say. The parasail guy talked as she looked out at the endless water and the pinkening sky. She thought of Randy falling, falling through clouds, how much she'd loved having huge white wings, and how she was sick of being afraid of heights.

"Well, I think you should go for it," Griffy said.

So there she was, all harnessed up, standing on the butt of the boat, and thanking Griffy, whose credit card had appeared at the moment when she might have chickened out.

Then the motorboat started up and second thoughts became impossible. She held onto the cables as instructed, and the boat moved slowly forward. The sail filled. The seat came up under her butt. Once out on the choppy waves, the boat sped up.

The parasail lifted her off her feet, into the air.

She hung on for dear life as the boat towed her into the sky. The seat felt secure. Up here, she smelled cocoa butter, beer, burning charcoal, and the overpoweringly-fresh lake smell. She looked down, her heart in her mouth. The lake didn't scare her. If she fell, she knew she could swim like an otter.

Then the boat turned, swinging her around like a stick on a string. Jewel shrieked. They sped up, racing the wind south along the beach again. The lake rushed by and the human figures below looked up. Her heart filled. Far out on the lake, white sails leaned into the wind, the way she leaned. She heard only the wind.

Full of the hugeness of the sky, Jewel turned her face toward the sun and blessed herself.

Would Randy like this? Or would it be too real for him?

She leaned hard and the parasail dipped slightly. She didn't have control, but she wasn't helpless.

Lean. Dip.

Big lean, and a swoop that made her shriek.

It was kind of fun.

Somewhere under the fun, the amazement, and the raw whip of the wind cold and hot on her skin, Jewel felt fear, but it was a different kind of fear. Not fear of losing control, but a fear like galloping bareback across a meadowful of thistles, knowing the dangers but knowing she had the horsemanship to stay on. A fun fear.

The boat turned again, slower this time.

Under her she saw a floating mattress and, lying on her back, a chubby woman, a hat shading her face. The floating woman tipped back the hat. Jewel saw her smile with peaceful benediction. She smiled back.

As the boat slowed, the motor winched Jewel in, like a fisherman reeling in a fish, and she came down and stepped gracefully onto the launch deck.

"Okay?" said the grinning boatman.

"God, that was fun! That was *great*!"

As their boat chugged up, Griffy bounced with excitement on the breakwater. "I want to try!" She waved her credit card.

The instructor glanced at Jewel, but the glow in Griffy's face drew him back. *The Venus Machine effect,* Jewel thought. *We both have it, but it comes naturally to Griffy.*

While the instructor took Griffy's credit card, Griffy handed her little purse to Jewel. "Can you do me a huge favor? These are Virgil's birthday invitations. I need them delivered tonight." She didn't look at Jewel but at the blue-and-orange-striped sail. "I'd rather he didn't see me deliver them. They're addressed. It's the one block, both sides of the alley."

"If you're doing this because of Sovay—"

"I want to."

"But if he doesn't want a birthday party—"

Griffy stroked the edge of the parasail. "I want to fly."

Jewel gave up.

The instructor started his training spiel for Griffy. She was so comfortable being looked at.

I don't think it's being undercover I like. I like the idea that nobody knows who I am.

The woman with the peaceful smile paddled her mattress up to the sand and beached herself serenely amid the children and dogs. Jewel felt calm. It seemed for once as if her bare feet touched the ground by decision, not because she was some ground-bound land mammal.

She should sneak off and deliver Griffy's invitations. And look at those reports Clay had brought. Retreating up the beach, Jewel glanced over her shoulder.

On the sandy slope, Virgil's picnic sat like a tea party at a riot, Virgil pouring wine for Sovay, Kauz looking at something through field glasses, and Clay biting his lip, staring in the same direction without field glasses.

Virgil looked up. He tapped Kauz on the shoulder and Kauz handed over the field glasses.

Jewel looked where they were looking.

On the breakwater, Griffy was getting harnessed to the parasail. Her excitement lit all the faces nearby. She looked younger at this distance, or maybe it was the Venus Machine effect. She seemed like a little kid, full of bounce and glory.

Jewel couldn't help but smile.

In the pedestrian tunnel under Lake Shore Drive, she met the woman on the mattress. She was wearing a sparkling brooch again. The sun slanted through the city buildings and poured pink fire down the tunnel onto the brooch. The brooch said "Beulah" in script.

It was the Neiman's customer who smelled bad!

"You're the girl who flew," Beulah said. She didn't smell bad now. Of course, she'd been in the lake.

"That's me."

"Even from below I could see you're a convert," Beulah said.

"A convert to what?"

She smiled like a saint. "To Self Love."

Jewel pulled her coverup tighter around herself. "That's a religion?"

"I can tell you've tasted the potion. There's no mistaking your—" She broke off, wavering the edge of her hand in the air. "I can't explain how you look so—so—"

"Green. There's too much green in my aura."

Beulah conceded the point with a graceful turn of her wrist. "Whenever I see the prophet, I buy every bottle he has."

The prophet. That would be Buzz. "You drink them all?" It would explain why Beulah seemed crazy.

"Oh, no. Once is enough. I share them with women who still wander in the night of self-hatred. I've seen so many turn from the path of self-destruction to love, light, and joy."

Good grief, Kauz wasn't making potions. He was manufacturing a cult, and he hadn't even met his cultists yet.

"They no longer torment their bodies, their skins, their dead proteins," she said in a thrilling voice.

"Dead—?"

She indicated the rat's nest on her scalp. Self Love hair was not a selling point.

Jewel got a fiendish idea. "You like to talk about your, uh, Self Love experience, don't you?"

"Oh, yes!" Beulah frowned for the first time. "I wish I could interest the media. They're all blinded by the regimens of self-hatred. Since I stopped wearing makeup, no one sees me. Not that they saw me when I wore it," she said, descending from her Self Love cloud.

They walked out of the tunnel onto Marine Drive. "Well, I—wait, uh, hi, my name is Jewel—"

Beulah stuck her hand out and Jewel shook it. "So pleased. I'm Beulah."

"—I know how you can get some great media coverage. See that house over there?" Jewel pointed at Virgil's marble-fronted mansion. "A whole lot of important people will be in the alley behind that house tomorrow night for a block party. Reporters. Cameras. You should come. Tell them your message."

Beulah lit up. "I expect to see the prophet tomorrow." She might be as appealing as Griffy, if she would comb her hair. "Would you like a dose?"

"Don't bother, I have a supply," Jewel lied. *That little devil, Buzz. He never told me any of this.* "You should come, to be a living example for the—the benighted ones at this party."

"I would be honored," Beulah said superbly.

"Around eight. Bring all your friends. The ones who took the potion and converted to Self Love. Oh, and here—" She dug in her purse for Mrs. Noah Butt's card. "I know some people you would love to meet. Bring them, too."

"Thank you. I will." Beulah moved away, slow and serene.

Jewel delivered Griffy's invitations. Then she sneaked into Virgil's house and took the back stairs to her room. On her bed she found the anklet-tracking unit, which was about the size of a parking ticket book, and a pile of background reports. She settled down to read.

Nothing on the cook or the maid or the chauffeur. She opened the butler's report and was confounded by a blank page with the word "classified" stamped at a slant. "What the—?" A sticky note was stuck to the page. "*Couldn't get clearance for this,*" she read aloud. "What am I, chopped liver?" This guy could be a serial killer or a terrorist or something.

She stared at her flowery bedroom curtains, pondering, until she heard a soft footstep in the hall. *Maid?*

She flew to the door and locked it.

The footsteps passed.

Heart pounding, Jewel picked up the next report.

By comparison, Griffy's life was transparent as a martini glass. Until she was twenty-six she had stripped in Atlantic City, and accepted short-term protection from life's storms with various male philanthropists. At twenty-six, her employment record ceased and her profile became a catalog of increasingly expensive purchases. She did not seem to have been gainfully employed in a very long time.

Jewel tapped the report on her front teeth. If Virgil had kept her since she was twenty-six, at least he'd kept her well.

On to Virgil's report. His records were more complete. Birth in Utah sixty years ago, *that can't be right*, a year of junior college, a stint in the National Guard, an early killing in tech stocks, a lifelong interest in antiques related to swindling, and articles about same posted to the Internet. Back in the early 2000s he'd been on the board of an oil company that did an Enron-like scam on a small group of investors, but he was listed as a victim of the scammers, not a suspect. That was the sum total of his interactions with the law.

Jewel didn't believe a word of it. Griffy thought he was seventy and she was incapable of lying.

Tucked in the back of the report was a loose printout, a Google list of URLs. The names and data were all over the map, but the "search" box on top gave her a clue. *"Virgil Thompson" "Virgil Athabascan" "Virgil Marconi" "Virgil Dante NOT inferno" "Dante Virgil NOT inferno" "Inaeas O. Virgilius"*. In Clay's handwriting, two words: "still married!"

Now Jewel wondered if Griffy's lack of employment history might be due to a change of name. If Virgil changed his own name—she glanced from Virgil's background report to the Google printout. These were aliases the department didn't have.

On the other hand, going by this page, Google hadn't found much on those aliases, either. Only ten mentions for the list.

I should check AFIS for these aliases. She stuck the sheet into her purse.

On to Dr. Gustavus Katterfelto Kauz's file, the one sent over by the Fifth Floor. Jewel's eyes popped. Then she smiled.

Gustavus ("Gussie") Kauz had spent his childhood on a commune in western New Jersey. His parents were disciples of a severely crunchy demagogue—*maybe a role model for Kauz's persona?*—a good talker who peddled homegrown drugs and primitive applications of zen. After college and a business degree, Kauz did the commune's books for ten years. He then abandoned his Birky-wearing, yogurt-brewing, flea-ridden parents and converted their muddy-ankled mysticism into something that met the comforts—and sanitation standards—of a luxurious spa.

Hm, this could be good for something. Jewel knew all about coming from a small, muddy place to the big city. She might not be able to defeat Kauz with it, but with careful use of this information she could unnerve the shit out of him.

At the bottom of the pile she found Sovay's file. This included the department's skimpy findings and, again, Clay's printouts. Jewel licked her lips. This would be what had made Clay so hot to hide the whole case from her.

The first three pages were wedding pictures. Every bride was Sovay.

The next two pages were obituaries of the guys who had married her.

Holy crap. No wonder Clay was worried. His whole charade clicked into perspective.

CHAPTER
23

While Jewel had been risking her neck, Clay had been trying to find out what his father was up to. *He can't kill me for asking.* Over the shrieking of volleyball players, he yelled, "Where'd you put the bed, Dad?"

Virgil signed for silence, then jerked a thumb. He marched a few yards away from the picnic table, and, when Clay followed, he took off his sunglasses, a DefCon 4 act of aggression. His naked pale-blue eyes were something out of a nightmare.

"What have you been saying to Griffy about me?"

"We didn't talk, we had sex," Clay said airily, and enjoyed the old man's horrified double take. Wow, that got a bigger reaction than he'd hoped for. Virgil looked so taken aback that he pushed. "So she's old enough to be my mother, eh, well. She can do more with a twinkle than most women do naked."

His father's eyes narrowed. "You had a crush on her when you were a kid. Sticking up for a stupid bimbo all the time."

"Take her off your hands," Clay suggested. "Problem solved."

Virgil ruffled up like a scrawny turkey confronting a bear. "You can't afford her."

"She doesn't want money. She wants love. You've always confused the two."

"Good thing, since you can't make any money," Virgil hissed.

"Bet?" Clay smiled without humor. "Bet you I get Sovay's money before you do."

At that Virgil grabbed him by the arm with a strong claw and yanked him close. "I have videotape of you and your girlfriend doing the hokey-pokey on that bed."

Clay felt his skin shrink up cold. "You're bluffing."

"Try me."

Thinking fast, Clay sneered, "Videotape! How lame is that?" His heart was in his mouth. Then it occurred to him to ask what he should have asked in the first place. "What do you want?"

The old man laughed delightedly, as if he knew how off balance Clay was. "There's an investigation focused on my house. I want your girlfriend looking at someone besides me."

"You dope, she's watching Sovay."

Virgil waved a hand. "I don't give a hoot about your fool job. There's a real investigation, FBI, and they've put someone in my house, and I want you to find out who it is."

Clay was shocked. Virgil *never* got caught. "You sure?"

"Him or her. I heard about it through my own channels. I need the mole's name."

"You can't con the FBI, Dad."

"Leave that to me. Do this, or I'll play the tape where you least want it aired." He shuffled closer and lowered his voice. "Who'll hate it worse? The girl? Her boss? Anonymous gift in the mail, wonder what this is, pop in the cassette, looky!"

Jewel would hate it worse. Clay knew the pupils of his eyes had betrayed him. The old man was good. He fumbled for damage control. "The boyfriend's jealous. Lord Darner."

"Your rival, Lord Pontarsais?" Virgil corrected. "He's gone. Sneaked out the window when I caught him in bed with Sovay. If he dares to come back, I'll show him the tape, too."

Videotape. Cassette. Tape. At least it was ordinary video, not a digital file. Clay's eyes narrowed, hiding his relief. "You'll have trouble finding him. He's in that bed."

"*In* the bed."

"Yeah. He's a sex demon. He's possessing that bed now."

"Still believing your own fairy story. Well, then you should care as much as your partner cares. Make her co-operate." Virgil chuckled. "Magic is for marks, boy."

Clay flung away, trembling with fear and rage, trying to be calm. *Tape. Good.* If it had been digital, finding and destroying all copies would have been hopeless.

He waited for Jewel to come out of the sky. She would not be happy about any of this.

But she scrambled out of the parasail and walked away down the beach, looking behind her as she made her getaway.

Then, of all people, Griffy started harnessing up. Clay forgot his partner for a few minutes.

"I want twice the time you gave my friend," Griffy said.

"Costs more," the instructor said.

"I'll pay extra." Already high on anticipation, she checked the harness links and couplings, ran her hands over the lines of the parasail, lifted her head to sniff the lake breeze. The blood sang in her veins. "I want to fly before it gets dark."

It was just as glorious as she had hoped.

Pink light washed between the buildings to the west and flooded the beach, making the crowds look as happy as she felt. The wind lifted the parasail higher.

Through the harness lines, she could feel the sail as if it were part of her body. Below, the lake spun by like the ground under a roller coaster. Griffy let the wind carry her laughter away.

She passed gulls on the wing as if they were standing still.

Faces on the beach turned up to her. It was like stripping, only she didn't have to glue pasties on. She could just *be*.

She waved. Everybody waved back, and cheers flew up from the beach. She felt marvelous. Maybe she *could* start over. Sovay had been telling her that she had no future. *But I have.* She didn't have to feel trapped with Virgil, or lost without him. The wind carried her along. *I'm free.*

There was her picnic. Sovay was drinking, looking bored. Virgil and Clay were tussling over the field glasses. She blew them a kiss. How old and small Virgil looked down there, all by himself. No matter what she did, he never seemed to realize he wasn't alone. She never felt alone when he was there.

She felt alone now. It was glorious. She felt powerful and free and happy.

The boat slowed and the parasail dipped lower. Griffy sighed. That instructor must be reeling her in already. The boat whirled past the breakwater and began its turning arc. She sank lower still. The sail carried her smoothly over the pink and blue waves.

Down on the sand, Virgil stared up at her. Sovay came to his side, turned him to face her, and kissed him on the lips.

The sight struck Griffy over the heart. She slipped to the side in her seat, and the instructor, with a look of alarm, reeled her in to the flight deck. She fumbled out of her harness, blundered off the flight deck, tripped, and fell headfirst into the lake.

She sank, not caring.

She was thinking, *I can make it without him. It'll hurt, and I'll be lonely. But I'm not broke. I can make it.*

The instructor hauled her out of the water. "Are you okay?" he kept yelling.

Fierce, hot pain tore at her heart, though she was dripping and shivering. "I'm fine." *I've lost my old buzzard. But I'm going to live.* She hoped her tears wouldn't show.

Here came Clay, looking panicked.

Virgil took the towel out of Clay's hands and wrapped it around her shoulders. Then he pulled her into his arms.

Griffy blinked against his bony shoulder. "Virgil? I'm okay."

As he led her away from the breakwater, their eyes met for one moment. She almost tripped.

In eighteen years, Virgil had never looked at her like that. Like he wanted something from her. With his heart showing.

Her breath caught.

In the next instant he had handed her off to Clay, who sat her at the picnic table and poured her a glass of wine. Virgil sat across the table and turned his attention to Sovay.

And yet. For the next twenty minutes Virgil's knee touched hers under the table. He spoke to Sovay, but whenever Sovay's eye was off him, he smiled at Griffy. Griffy was so stunned she forgot to smile back. Sovay flirted with Dr. Kauz, with Clay, with Virgil, and Griffy sat like a mummy, wrapped in her loss.

Yet every now and then Virgil would look at her. It was a secret look that made her heart thump.

This wasn't the face he used for business. It seemed as if he wasn't thinking about his face, which couldn't be true, not Virgil. She studied him by the light of bursting red and yellow stars, feeling her heart jump around, feeling more noticed by him than she had since that first bottle of champagne eighteen years ago in the back of a limo in Atlantic City.

Halfway through the fireworks Dr. Kauz took Sovay for a walk. They hadn't returned by the time Mike the chauffeur came to pack up their baskets. In the dark, by colored starlight, Virgil squeezed her hand. Numbed between the thrill of hope and the ache of loss, Griffy felt as if her feet didn't touch the ground.

Behind her, Clay murmured to Mike. She walked homeward, ignoring them, her head high, her heart in turmoil.

It's just for one night, he'll be over it tomorrow, he'll have to tell me it's over sometime.

Then she stopped thinking, because there might never be another moment like this one.

Jewel fiddled with the tracking unit. The manual said it could find the anklet within twenty-five feet. She panned slowly around the room. A string of numbers appeared on the tiny screen. "Groovy. What does this mean?" She consulted the manual. Ah, that was her longitude and latitude.

Now she needed to determine which anklet was to be located.

Fudge. They hadn't bothered to check which anklet was which. Just snapped 'em on and let 'em run like they were freaking cheetah cubs. "Can you say 'half-assed'?" she muttered.

She shuffled out of her room, watching the screen. New numbers appeared. The first numbers changed as she moved, the last digits shifting slowly. "So that's me. And this number down here is the anklet I'm tracking."

The anklet was, she realized, only a few digits away from the coordinates representing her.

That must be Randy's anklet! It must be in the house!

She felt triumphant until she realized she already knew that.

All she had to do was move around until the numbers matched.

Keeping her eyes on the screen, she slipped out of her room and crept up the corridor.

The whole party stopped at the entrance to the pedestrian tunnel and looked back. A humongous fireworks star burst over the water, first a big red bang, then a smaller white star, then a yellow star that popped and sizzled, then an even larger green star that made Griffy think of the color of Jewel's aura in Dr. Kauz's pictures. Green light flashed on Clay, on the chauffeur with his arms full of chairs and baskets. The green lasted a long time before it faded.

Sovay still hadn't returned with Dr. Kauz.

She felt Virgil's arms slide around her from behind. He squeezed. "I'm going to be seventy tomorrow," he whispered.

Her breath caught. "Yes." She kept her eyes on the sky.

"I've missed you these past few weeks. Come upstairs?"

"Our guests," she choked out.

"Are grown-ups. Clay can take care of them."

She swallowed a lump. "Okay."

CHAPTER 24

Jewel tracked Randy to a door at the end of the corridor on the second floor. Pulse quickening, she turned off the tracking unit and tried the doorknob. It turned.

The room inside was lit by streetlight. Big paintings covered two walls. The windows bowed out, showing Marine Drive and the fireworks through many small panes. Master bedroom. Virgil's. Where else would he hide something the size of a bed?

She closed the door and ran to the bed, a high, queen-size sleigh model with a curving headboard and footboard, piled with pillows and covered with a patchwork quilt. Sovay's bed!

Jewel lay her hand on the quilt. *Randy?*

Her palm tingled.

She was about to hop up on the bed. Then she remembered the massage table and seaweed on the ceiling and ran back to lock the door. *My God, I'm shaking.* Better not tell Randy how much she had missed him. Wait, where was the anklet? Find that first.

She went over the bed until she located the anklet, wedged between the headboard and the frame. It was small and black and easily missed if you were, say, rolling the bed down the corridor to that so-convenient service elevator. She pocketed the anklet.

The floor creaked outside the door.

Jewel snatched up the tracking unit and slid under the bed.

The locked bedroom door opened and the light flashed on.

She held her breath. If the maid had come to vac under the bed, she was dead.

Not a sound but the faraway trilling of the air conditioner.

A pair of men's dress shoes with thick, soft, black soles approached the bed. Someone rummaged in the nightstand drawer. He opened and shut dresser drawers, then opened the walk-in closet. Jewel eased herself toward the footboard and peeked.

It was Mellish.

He looked big and scary in his dark butler clothes.

She scootched deeper under the bed and lay still, hugging the tracking unit and inhaling fluff.

What the hell?

A guy with Virgil's money, of course, must attract crooks.

Maybe Mellish was working with Sovay. She could find all Virgil's treasures, bump Virgil off when she was married to him, and then—get Mellish to burgle the place?

Too complicated. Successful crooks kept it simple.

Her legs were stiffening up, squished under the bed. Then she realized she felt another sensation, a familiar touch like a hand on her tush in the middle of the night, asking in Braille, *Are you awake?*

Randy. *Shit.* Not now!

Not now! she tried to tell him by ferocious telepathy.

A warm feeling flooded her, a big joyous-puppy welcome.

Not now! She squirmed to another spot under the bed.

From the closet, Mellish gave a satisfied-sounding

grunt. Jewel rolled closer to the edge to see what he'd found.

At that moment, voices sounded in the hall.

Mellish whisked into the closet and closed it.

A moment later the bedroom door opened.

"I'm not the first woman you ever got out of that strip joint," Griffy was saying with fond severity.

"No, but you're the best. You stuck with me, Griffy." Jewel peeked. Yikes. That syrupy, husky voice was Virgil's?

Their two sets of feet came close together and Jewel felt the hairs rise on the back of her neck.

Griffy made a little happy sighing sound. "Hey, is that the same bed we had?"

No! No, no, no! Distract her, Virgil! Jewel prayed, squinching her eyes shut and crossing all her fingers and toes.

There was a smooch sound. Virgil said, "I think I'd better shave," in a lewd tone. He went into the bathroom.

Whew! Jewel breathed again.

Griffy moved out of Jewel's sightline.

The closet door opened silently. Mellish's black shoes moved past the bed toward the bedroom door. The door opened.

Griffy squeaked.

"Will there be anything further, Miss Griffin?" Mellish said in a bored voice.

"I didn't hear you come in!"

"I am sorry, Miss. In the future, I will knock louder."

"Oh. Well, no, thank you. That will be all. That is, I don't know if Ms. Sacheverell and Dr. Kauz have come back—"

"Yes, Miss. Still no sign of Lord Darner, Miss," Mellish added, sounding disapproving.

Splashing noises came from the bathroom.

"What?" Griffy sounded distracted.

"Lord Darner. He has not returned to the house."

"I'm sure it's none of your business," Griffy snapped.

Attababy, Griffy! Jewel grinned under the bed.

"The cook, Miss, would like to know how many there will be for breakfast."

"The cook, *Mister*, can figure it out tomorrow morning. I might not come downstairs, myself. Or I might. You can go now."

"Yes, Miss." The door shut behind the burglar-butler, and Jewel prayed that Virgil would invite Griffy into the shower.

"What was that?" Virgil said, coming out of the bathroom.

"Mellish," Griffy said with loathing. "He gives me the heebie jeebies. I wish we could get rid of him!"

"Never mind, old girl." The lights clicked off. "They'll all be gone in a few days."

"You mean that?" Their feet shuffled within Jewel's view in the dimness. *Not again.* "You used to take me out for dinner. When the job would be over."

Silence for a moment. "No more jobs," Virgil said softly.

A longer silence. Jewel imagined she could hear kissing, which kind of icked her out, and then Griffy said, "Do you mean this job with Sovay is over?" and Jewel heard tension in her voice. "Or is this our last night?" She seemed in pain but under control.

Jewel's heart ached for her.

"Sweetheart," Virgil said in a breaking voice. "Give me just a little more time."

They sat down on the bed, making the springs creak over Jewel's head. She felt Randy's cloud of need trying to draw her up against the bottom of the bed like a big old horndog magnet.

"I've given you all the time I have," Griffy said.

"You've given me everything," Virgil said. "Come to me."

Their feet left the floor as they climbed onto the bed. Jewel felt Randy's power surge. In another minute he would be able to suck her into demonspace with him, whether she was on the bed or not. *That does it, I'm out of here.* She rolled quietly out from under the bed and crawled behind the footboard.

After a long interval, Griffy said, "Damn you, Virgil," in a voice that had no innocence left in it.

"Do you still love me?" Virgil sounded stripped.

No words, but more sounds came.

Jewel crawled behind a chair near the door and crouched there, her hands clamped over her ears, for a very long time. When at last the room was silent, she snuck out the bedroom door with the tracking unit under her arm.

Clay was sitting on Jewel's bed, reading background files and trying not to panic, when she walked into her room. "We got problems," he announced as she shut the door.

Her white swimsuit was smudged. "No shit. The butler is a burglar. Burglars don't cut people's throats, do they?"

"I wouldn't know," Clay said, feeling on edge. He tossed over the files on her bed. "There isn't much on anybody here."

"Except Sovay. Your father seems to have skated clear all right." Clay didn't rise to this barb. She sat down on the bed facing him. "Randy is in your father's bedroom."

That made Clay look up. "Doing what?"

"Doing Griffy, I'm afraid. Simultaneously with Virgil." When he made an "ick" face she said, "I know, that's how I felt about it. And I had to listen. But at least we found him."

"Virgil put the bed in his own room? So he never believed me when I told him about the curse."

"So *why*—"

"Why did he switch the beds? Because he figured out that you care. He knows you believe what he calls 'the fairy tale,' and he wants a hold over you." Clay hesitated. *Better tell her the truth. She can't kill me while we're in the thick of this. And if I can't talk her out of being mad by the end of it—well, I know I can.* "He thinks you can protect him from prosecution."

"Me? Wait a minute, prosecution for what?"

Clay filled her in on the FBI-in-the-house thing.

"Mellish!" she exclaimed. "That's why he was poking around Virgil's room! Plus, he found something, don't ask me what. But he was in the closet, and he sounded, I dunno, like, 'ah-hah.'"

"That's good," Clay said. "Virgil will love knowing the FBI is saying 'ah-hah' in his closets. There's worse."

Jewel looked happy. "I can't believe what a relief it is, knowing Mellish wasn't a burglar about to kill me. Of course, if I'd known he was FBI then, I could have got out of there before Virgil declared his undying passion and took Griffy to bed."

"He what?" Clay said, distracted from a mission he didn't want. Then he remembered the worst news. "The worst news," he gulped, "is that Virgil had a videotape recorder running in Sovay's bedroom."

Jewel looked puzzled. "To catch Sovay and Randy doing it?"

Clay shook his head. "That's probably why he planted the recorder. But he also caught you and me doing it."

Jewel took it big. Her jaw went slack and her eyes bugged out and her lip curled and her teeth came together with a click that made him wince.

He hurried on, ripping off the Band-Aid. "He thinks the FBI planted a mole. He wants us to identify him and

he wants you to stop their investigation, divert it or whatever. I don't think he's thinking. I've never known Virgil
to resort to blackmail. He's always said that blackmail
means maintaining too long a relationship with the mark.
Sooner or later they get mad enough to fight back, no
matter how dumb or shortsighted that is. And then
you're dead. Because even if they don't succeed in killing
you, they've smeared you enough to attract the law."

He saw the wheels begin to turn. "He seems upset
enough to blackmail you with this tape."

"He's blackmailing you, too," she said. "Or do you
plan to disappear if the shit hits the fan?"

"No, no, I'm in." He put his hand over hers on the
Kauz file. "We're in this together." He looked deep into
her eyes.

Jewel met his eyes and sucked in a long breath. What
was she looking at? Ever since she had a second dose of
the Venus Machine, she'd been looking at him funny.
Like she saw too much.

"So do we toss Mellish to him?"

"No! We do not expose undercover FBI agents to their
suspects. I have a plan," she announced.

"Plan is good." Distraction complete. "Tell me the
plan."

She gave him a long look. "I don't think so. You're
not such a red-hot team player, buddy."

"C'mon, partner. You can't hold out on your partner."

"You did!" she flashed.

He turned up the charm. "So lead by example. Show
me how to do better. Communicate."

"I'll tell you some of it. Some of it isn't gelled yet."

"Okay," he said to keep her talking.

She gnawed her lip, and he reflected that the Venus
Machine hadn't changed one thing. She was as tough as
ever. She seemed to have recovered over the videotape.

She said, "Put these things together and let them rattle

around in your head. One, mayoral race. Two, Kauz believes in his own bullshit, so he can't shut up about it. He's charming, but he's got this blind spot."

"Ah." Clay knew all about blind spots.

"Three, he invites the society press to this block party tomorrow night, knowing also that Virgil's birthday party will draw the cream of the neighborhood to this house, where he has his spectro-psyche-thingy and the Venus Machine handy, and he can show off what a hell of a magician he is."

Clay scratched his head. "The guy is no oil painting."

"He's charming," Jewel countered in a grudging tone. "He talks a good line. And the Venus Machine could—"

"You think it really works." He smiled.

"Well, I do," she said, looking embarrassed. "I haven't had much fun with it so far. Griffy's loving it. Never mind the personal aspect, something *happens* when you throw the switch. Let Kauz crank up his malarky mouth and—and *suggest* things to a party full of movers and shakers—in front of a camera—who knows what their reactions would be?"

She was still skirting the fact that she had bought into the good doctor's scam. Clay played along. "Disaster waiting to happen."

"If we can engineer it. But we can't play too dirty."

"Why? Oh. Because the press will be there and they're unpredictable?"

She rounded on him. "Because it's wrong."

"So?" He shrugged and turned up both palms. "Why mention playing dirty? Just how dirty is too dirty, by the way?"

She sent him a contemptuous glance. "He'll need volunteers to try his stupid machines. But these aren't self-selected fashion victims like the customers at his spa. Hopefully, they're less gullible. They'll decide if they like his goofball ideas and his machines or not."

"So we make sure they hate it."

"No! We do not *make sure* of it. That's playing too dirty."

"You're such a Sunday-school teacher," Clay said, mystified.

She flapped her hands. "I knew you wouldn't get it. There's an opportunity here. I'm not sure what. I'm asking for your help with that, but here's where you need to put a leash on your criminal imagination, okay? Help me think how we can maximize this opportunity *legally and fairly*."

"You want legal and fair, you should get another partner." He wasn't insulted. "Do you hear yourself?" There was no compromise in her razor-blue eyes. He sighed. "Why don't you let me work on it, come up with a few ideas, and I'll run them past you for legal and fair."

"That's what I'm asking. Oh, and find a reason why Virgil will let me into that bedroom so I can get Randy out of bed."

"I have lock picks," he said, pained.

She showed him a palm. "Thank you, I'd rather know I'm not being taped."

"Relax, officer. I'm on it."

She looked a lot calmer, which rewarded him, but he hadn't a clue how he was going to fix this. It would be nice if she would tell him the rest of the plan.

Get her into bed again and quiz her in the afterglow.

"You're looking frazzled. Why don't I stay here tonight?"

She rolled her eyes. "Scram."

That night she dreamed about falling. There was no ground under her, just endless blue-gray clouds that parted, rushed at her, smacked her in the face with cold mist, and parted again, down, down, down. Far below her, Randy fell. She flapped her arms helplessly, trying to fall faster, trying to reach him before he hit something. She came closer, agonizingly slowly.

When she was close enough to see his face, his eyes opened.

Looking into his eyes, she saw the ground at last, rushing up to meet them. As she grasped his hand, they splatted.

Her eyes snapped open. She jerked upright in bed.

Her heart thundered in her ears.

CHAPTER
25

Next morning, Clay overheard Griffy and Virgil talking in the breakfast room. He hid outside, behind the door.

Virgil sounded odd. "You look well rested, my dear." *My dear?* Since when did Virgil bother sweet-talking Griffy?

"I feel fabulous." She yawned like Marilyn Monroe after a few drinks. Clay heard a smooch noise. "I slept soooo well."

"Come back here," Virgil said in a playful voice. "Mmm-mmm-mm." More smooch noises and cooing and murmurs.

Behind the door, Clay gagged. He wondered if he should go away for a few minutes.

Then Virgil said, "My dear, you need to be my sister a little longer. Soon it will be over."

"She must know I'm not your sister," Griffy said.

"Now, Griffy," Virgil said in a more familiar tone. "If you'll just be guided by me—"

"I can take care of myself," she said in a sharp voice that astonished Clay. "I did it for years before you met me."

"Nonsense." Virgil said it too quickly.

"I won't be used like this!"

"Of course not. But a job at this delicate stage—"

She interrupted him. "Last night you said, 'No more

jobs!' You have all the money you need." Power rang in her voice.

What's with Griffy? Clay thought. She wasn't timid or self-deprecating anymore.

"I need money to support you and your habits," Virgil said, losing diplomacy points with every syllable. He sounded upset and out of control. Not like Clay's dear old dad at all.

She said stiffly, "I guess I better get cheaper habits. Or get my own money. Like your new girlfriend has."

Jewel came clattering down the stairs, and the voices in the breakfast room went silent. Clay walked in with Jewel.

Virgil was his imperturbable self over breakfast, but Griffy looked stormy. *Not a good sign.* Clay was glad when Jewel suggested that they go out and pick up some things Griffy had ordered from the party goods store.

"And bring that tracking unit," she whispered.

"Do you think he knows Randy put horns on him?" Jewel said on the way to the car.

Clay smacked his forehead. "That's why!"

"What's *why* what?" Jewel wasn't in the mood to play twenty questions. She'd spent another night alone, listening to the creaking in the air ducts. Though sleep had been welcome, the bed had felt empty. Was it possible that three weeks of Randy and-slash-or Clay had ruined her independence?

He said, "Virgil's anxious and Griffy acts like she's God. That's a turnaround. Randy must really do something for women."

"He does. Did you see her face at breakfast? I see that look in my mirror every morning. I never realized how freakin' X-rated I look."

He sent her a sidelong glance. "Are you missing Randy? Little jealous of Griffy?"

"Of course not." She slammed the Tercel into gear and peeled away from the curb. A Hummer driver goggled at her and stalled, and she pawed in her purse for her sunglasses. "Fucking Venus Machine effect." She turned on the radio so she wouldn't have to listen to more of Clay's remarks.

"*Thank you, caller,*" Ask Your Shrink was saying. "*And this message is for Coral, out there, whose boyfriend won't let her sleep. Check in with Your Shrink and let us know how the sleeping pills worked.*" With a groan, Jewel turned it off.

Poor Randy. *Hang on, buddy, I'm gonna save you.*

"You're looking fresher these days, 'Coral,'" Clay said. "I trust you got your eight hours last night."

She prayed for lightning to strike the car. Then her phone rang. Ed. "What?"

Ed roared, "That friggin' fruitcase has called a press conference tonight!"

"I know." She listened with half an ear to Ed's opinion of the press conference, the fruitcase, and her incompetence. When he paused for breath she said, "It's just society coverage. Kauz is showing off some machines at a block party."

"Hinky machines?"

"You're quick. But they're gonna backfire on him tonight." She motioned to Clay to turn on the tracking unit. "And the press will be waiting to see it all."

"Terrific. Don't fuck up."

"That's our song, isn't it," she said to the dead phone. She glanced at the tracking unit in Clay's hands. "You got him?"

"I got him." He directed her south and east. She took the angle down Michigan and slowed to a crawl.

Jewel had a bad feeling as they got closer and closer to the Hancock Tower. This was getting annoying. She didn't like to crush the spirit of a budding entrepreneur, but if Buzz wouldn't do what he was told, she would have to throw him to the cops.

"There he is," Clay said. Half a bock ahead, Buzz pedaled away from the Hancock, dodging tourists and suits, pointing his bike south along Michigan. Had he noticed them already?

"If he's going where I think he's going—"

"I think he's going."

Jewel blasphemed and looped around a loading taxi. Buzz stopped smack in front of Giorgio lo Gigolo, *goddammit*, and got off the bike. She double-parked half a block behind him, threw on the flashers, and turned over her Official Business card. "Can you carry that thing and grab him at the same time?"

Clay examined the tracking unit. "Not if it means wrestling. I doubt it would survive a fall on concrete."

"Never mind. He's seen you once. He might not recognize you. You walk ahead and take a position south of him, not too far away. If he gets back on the bike, he's gone."

"Gotcha."

Clay moseyed past Buzz as directed and Jewel followed, ducking behind other pedestrians. Buzz kept looking up and down the street and checking his phone. *Appointment.* When his head was turned south, she ran up and grabbed his backpack strap.

He almost knocked over his bike. "Off-officer Jewel!"

"Don't try to run. How do you think we found you?"

His eyes got round. Clay came up and showed him the tracking unit.

"What," Jewel began, "are you doing here? I told you not to come here. What's in the backpack today?

Dammit, do you *want* to go to jail?" she said, her voice rising.

"I got customers. I got commitments."

She laid a hand on his shoulder, and Clay slid the backpack away from him at the same time. "It is against the law, Buzz. You cannot sell drugs."

"It's a potion."

"It's an unlicensed drug with serious effects."

Head down in the backpack, Clay said, "What am I looking for? This thing is the Black Hole of Calcutta."

"Teeny bottles," Jewel said.

"Oh, thank goodness," someone said, and Jewel looked around. Buzz wriggled out of her grasp, but he didn't run.

It was Beulah. "I was afraid I'd missed you." Her well-bred voice was horribly at odds with her appearance, which was more bag-lady-like than ever: hair like a crow's nest, no makeup, schlumpfy sweatsuit, expensive running shoes with no laces, a scuffed-up Coach handbag, and of course her signature brooch, broad as her palm, with her name picked out in diamonds.

Today, Beulah smelled bad. *Guess she hasn't been swimming.*

Not bag-lady-like was the wad of crisp twenties she brandished. "Three more friends want to try the potion."

Buzz looked miserably at the money. "I came to tell you, I can't get any right away."

Jewel's phone rang. She told Buzz, "Do *not* move," and looked at the number. Ed again. "What!"

"For crissake, get over to Giorgio lo Gigolo and bust that kid! He's selling shit to some woman right there, right now!"

"I'm on it. Who told you?"

"Giorgio called," Ed said. "He's foaming."

She put the phone against her chest. "Clay, go inside, will you, and talk Giorgio off his window ledge? Tell him we're handling it." She told the phone, "We're handling it."

"Uh," Clay said, looking past her.

Ed began, "So help me Jesus Mary and Joseph on a flyin' Swiss petunia—"

Jewel hung up on him. "*Clay*. It's kind of important?"

Clay looked past her, his eyes bugging.

Jewel smelled another funny odor.

"Beulah! Darling!"

"Bunny!" Beulah embraced another bag lady and air-kissed her. This one was dressed better, and her fingernails still showed the ruins of a nice manicure, but her hair was the usual Self Love Lady mess, and she seemed to have slept in her silk Chanel suit. Also, the b.o.

Bunny said, "Did you get any? Because I went to Presbyterian Homes to see Mother and it occurred to me, the potion is just what she needs."

Beulah lit up. "Brilliant! Bunny, meet some friends of mine." She gestured graciously to Jewel.

"Clay," Jewel said in a steely voice. "Get *in* there. We don't want Giorgio calling the cops."

Clay handed her Buzz's backpack and went into the salon.

Jewel tried in vain to get the ladies to move down the sidewalk, away from Giorgio's front door. Beulah rolled over her with a flood of courtesies.

"And you know Buzz, of course, our prophet, our font. Buzz, darling, we're a bit pressed for time. I think I'll need five. There's three, and then for my aunt and for her daily helper. Poor child, she puts up with a great deal from my aunt," she said aside to Bunny and Jewel. "Although." She nibbled a dirty fingertip. "If one means to be generous, one should remember everyone at the Homes. Hmm. . . ." She flipped through the thick wad of twenties. "I have enough cash for perhaps thirty doses."

"I don't got any." Buzz looked at the money with anguish. "The doc's out and he ain't made a new batch or left me none or nothin'. Somebody took my supply off me." He sent Jewel a sullen glare.

"The doc's been busy," Jewel said.

"Oh, do you know the good doctor?" Bunny said. "Buzz has been so discreet about his identity. I realize we are engaged in a double-blind experiment, and we wouldn't dream of compromising the data. But of course, sooner or later, the product will be available commercially. Won't it?" She clasped her hands together. "It is needed."

Bunny might smell, but she was appealing. Something about her wistful pleading made Jewel wish she could give her the darned potion.

A woman came out of Giorgio lo Gigolo and started to walk by with her nose in the air.

"Allison?" Bunny said.

The woman did a double take. "Bunny? Beulah! Where have you been? Dr. Korshak says you've been missing sessions. You don't answer his calls. He actually broke confidentiality to ask me to get in touch with you and make sure you're okay." Allison looked Beulah over. "*Are* you okay?" Her nose wrinkled.

Beulah waved a hand. "That man. A vampire. I don't need him anymore."

Giorgio lo Gigolo burst out of his salon, his face red, his gelled-to-death hair bristling. "This is how I tell you!" he snarled at Clay, who was sprinting beside him. "These horrible women! They ruin my business! Ah, here comes it the TV peoples, that is all I am needing yet!" He clutched his hair.

Pedestrians stopped to watch his angst.

Jewel looked over her shoulder. A news van. *Shit.*

"Go," she muttered to Buzz. "Get out of here. You get on the news, you're busted. Go-go-go!"

Buzz grabbed his backpack, slung it around his neck, and took off on his bike.

On Michigan Avenue, cars were slowing to see what the news van was about.

Jewel sidled left, hoping against hope to hide Buzz's exit from the reporters. She grabbed the tracking unit from Clay and shoved her ballpoint pen into Beulah's face. "Would you repeat that, please? The part about love?"

Beulah looked at Jewel's "microphone" and swelled excitedly. "Why, we want to share the love." She radiated glorious peace and delight.

"The *self* love," Bunny added, shoving in next to Beulah and looking around for the camera.

The cameraman was aiming for Giorgio lo Gigolo. Over the heads of the Self Love Ladies, Jewel caught Clay's eye, mimed a throat-cut and waggled her head.

Clay slithered between the camera and the angry salon owner. Jewel heard him say, "Giorgio, you don't want to appear on television in connection with these women, do you?"

Thank God. My partner has a brain.

Giorgio vanished into the salon.

A reporter elbowed Jewel aside. She was carrying her own microphone and she beckoned to her cameraman, who shoved Jewel yet farther away, out of the shot.

"May we have your name for Channel Eight?" she heard the reporter saying to Allison.

"Beulah!" Jewel yelled. "Don't forget tonight!"

Beulah waved. "I won't!"

As Jewel ducked around the growing crowd of spectators, she saw four familiar faces jaywalking across Michigan Avenue toward Giorgio's, their hair like scarecrows', their likeable faces glowing, their eyes gleaming with charisma. Reading from left to right: Diane, Yasmin, Shirley, and Mrs. Noah Butt.

Jewel trotted back to where Clay leaned against the Tercel. "Let's beat it."

Her plan was in motion. Now to get Clay out of her hair for a while, so she could follow up with the bad-hair army by phone.

Clay was disappointed that Jewel didn't mention his slick work with the Gigolo guy. Instead she sent him off to the party-goods store. When he brought back two huge bags, Griffy was in the kitchen, aggravating the caterers.

Griffy crowed with delight over the bags full of a dozen huge feathered masks in brilliant colors, each with a silky hood that covered the wearer's hair and supported the masks. She chose a mask with long lime-and-emerald feathers sticking a foot into the air. The feathers cascaded over the whole front of her body, making her look like a big green bird. A green silk cloak hung from the back of the mask.

"You can't see my dress! Oh, well, Jewel will have more fun if she isn't being pestered by men. And Virgil loves masks."

Clay hoped they had made up. "Where is Virgil?" He didn't want to get caught searching the house for that tape.

Jewel walked into the kitchen. "He's upstairs, bidding against Dr. Kauz for the Venus Machine." She chose a mask striped blue and white, Chicago Police colors.

Clay frowned. "I thought he already bought the Venus Machine." Sovay was playing with fire if she messed Virgil over.

"Guess not." Jewel whispered, "You were great back there."

Clay forgot Virgil's troubles. "What did I do?"

"You got Giorgio off the street when the cameras showed up. Nice work, partner."

It embarrassed Clay, how good he felt. "Yeah, but those wacky ladies. Ed won't be happy to see them on the news."

"He wasn't," Jewel said, making a face. "He called. Hey, would you go put these signs up in the alley for Griffy?"

He leaned over and pecked her on the lips, and she smiled.

"Aren't you going to pick a mask?"

"I don't need no steenking mask," he said, and swaggered out with the signs before she could see how pleased he was.

While Clay put up signs, Jewel kept Griffy out of the way of the caterers and her own staff. She also watched Mellish, who may have been FBI or a burglar, but he buttled well.

The whole time, she itched to sneak into Virgil's room. Randy was still in the bed, alone, worried she wasn't coming.

"Will Lord Darner be back from Skokie in time for the party?" Griffy said.

"I hope so." If she couldn't get to Randy this afternoon, maybe she would find time during the party. Assuming Virgil didn't think of it first and squat. "Where's Virgil?"

Griffy folded paper napkins into birds and piled them in an antique china basin. "In the collection room. They're moving the machines down to the back garden," she said, referring to the postage-stamp yard behind the house.

Jewel peeked out the pantry window. "But you already have a huge bar out there. There's no room."

"They'll end up in the garage." Griffy seemed weird today. The serenity she seemed to gain after her Venus Machine ride had turned steely. "I told and told them, but they didn't listen."

Jewel waylaid Clay in the garden. "Let's get into Virgil's room tonight. Things are coming to a head between those two. I don't want Randy caught in the crossfire."

"As in?" Clay said, looking mystified.

"As in, Virgil sneaking the bed and using Randy the way you did. Or Griffy might get hold of it. I haven't forgotten how Nina once stole the brass bed so she could keep Randy forever."

No woman who'd had Randy on tap would want to let him go. Jewel hoped she would be different, if and when the time came.

"Good point. Let's go," Clay said.

It didn't happen. Virgil's bedroom was locked, and Clay was unable to pick it. It seemed to bother him that he couldn't deliver. He said, "I'll ask Griffy for the key."

But then Kauz summoned Clay and all the male servants to move the Venus Machine into the garage, and Clay had to spend the rest of the afternoon helping the mad scientists "recalibrate."

The block partiers trickled down the alley at six. Griffy's bar was already set up, so they came to Virgil's house first. The late summer sun was still high enough to glitter on the Venus Machine's brass and mother-of-pearl fittings in the open garage. Kauz, resplendent in a tuxedo, offered rides to all comers.

"Vun treatment on zis device vill make you irresistible to the opposite zex!" he ballyhooed, his accent thickening.

The yuppies lined up to get machinkusized. He was doing brisk business when Beulah arrived with her Self Love Ladies.

This fit in with Jewel's plan. They looked bedraggled as wet hens and smelled almost as bad, but every one radiated happiness and charm.

Jewel steered them away from Kauz and hustled them into masks. "I'm guessing the news cameras will arrive after dark. We want to spring you on them at the right moment." Her plan had weak spots, and timing was one of them.

"I used to love masked balls," Bunny said, fingering her fuschia feather mask in puzzlement.

"I wore a mask every day of my life," Beulah said like a queen-turned-nun. "Thank goodness that's over." But she put on a turquoise mask. Her eyes looked out, sweet and calm as a stone goddess's. "Buzz will be here, if he can find another supply."

"What!" *That kid!* "I'm J-Julia, who are you?" Jewel said to a Self Love Lady donning a purple mask.

"Annette Perini," said the Self Love Lady, shaking hands.

"Annette, I think you all should rehearse your message, decide how you want to present your story to the media."

"Excellent point," Beulah said crisply. "But I do apologize. I've been calling you Jule."

"Childhood nickname," Jewel lied. "You might practice your spiel on different people. Not the media, just people at the party." She saw Griffy come out of the house with a bowl of origami paper napkins. "Griffy, come meet someone!" This could handle two problems at once. "You can start by telling Griffy all about yourselves," she suggested to the Self Love Ladies.

And Griffy will stop "helping" the caterers. Jewel

performed introductions and skated away, looking for Clay. It was time to let him in on more of her plan.

"Remember what I've told you," Beulah said to Griffy, winding up a ten-minute speech that went ninety percent over Griffy's head. "Your beauty doesn't belong to anyone but you. No one can sell it to you or take it away from you."

"That makes so much sense," Griffy said. She felt more powerful today than yesterday. Maybe they knew something after all. The Venus Machine effect seemed to be getting stronger.

Beulah gestured superbly. "We who have passed into Self Love no longer need the crutches forced on us. We can fly!"

Griffy thought of parasailing over the lake, and Virgil's face full of love. She swallowed a lump. "Clay, honey, here's Beulah—"

"Good afternoon," Beulah said to Clay. "I believe we met on Michigan Avenue yesterday."

"She says she can see my green tones," Griffy said proudly. "Where have you been? I wanted you to meet my friends." She had a party to run, and, as nice as they were, the Self Love Ladies did talk.

"Looking for something," he said.

"Looking for what?"

"Something I can't find." Clay seemed grumpy to be stuck with the Self Love Ladies, but Griffy figured he was a big boy. The important thing was keeping Virgil from hiding out in his collection room.

Or in his bedroom. With Sovay.

She swallowed another lump.

She also had a humongous ice cream cake coming for his birthday announcement and she didn't want it to melt while she hunted for him.

So she was relieved to see Sovay come out of the house in her gold-and-black-striped feathered mask.

Sovay walked straight up to her. "We should talk," she said eerily through the mask.

Griffy frowned. "I don't think so."

"You'll be sorry if you don't," Sovay said and turned away, hunching over with her hands in front of her face. She scurried toward the English ivy and Griffy saw something plop among the leaves and disappear.

"Sovay? Are you feeling all right?" Griffy wasn't sure she wanted to watch Sovay throw up in her ivy. She laid a hand on her bent back. "Do you want a glass of water?"

"No!" Sovay stayed hunched over, but she grabbed Griffy's wrist. "Listen." Her voice was muffled. "Virgil wants you to visit us once we're living in the south of France. I'll tell him yes, but only if you agree to let him go without a palimony suit." More chunks came spasming out of her as she spoke.

Griffy marveled that anyone could be so nasty even while she was sick. Of course, being sick could make a person nastier. "I don't believe he has agreed to go anywhere with you."

"Believe it." Urp. "He's buying the tickets now." Urp. "I thought I'd tell you, as one friend to another," Sovay said, looking up with a pointy smile. Then she turned away again to hurl another chunk.

"I doubt if you have friends," Griffy said evenly, "but I'll bring you a glass of water if you want one."

Sovay stood up and wiped her lips with one manicured finger. She didn't speak, but her eyes glittered evilly through the mask.

Behind her own mask, Griffy felt her heart clutch up. "Well. May the best woman win."

"I always do," Sovay said.

Griffy lifted her chin. "In that case, I win, too, because he's not worth having if he would take you over me." *I can go to college. I could get a job.* Her heart was hot and sore.

"Keep telling yourself that," Sovay said and laughed, or choked, as she bent over the ivy again.

The birthday-cake caterer arrived. Griffy swallowed once and went to supervise the setup.

CHAPTER 27

"Clay, honey, would you find Virgil and bring him outside?" Griffy said at Clay's elbow, much to his relief. "His birthday cake is here."

"Will do." He escaped from Beulah-and-friends in her wake. "Thanks for getting me out of there. Those women *stink*."

"I know. I think they don't care. They're nice anyway, aren't they?" Griffy waved back to the nutcase ladies. "There's something so likeable about them."

"They've been taking a potion," Clay said grimly. "It works like the Venus Machine. Apparently it also makes them nuts."

"Oh, no." Griffy sounded dismayed.

"Promise me," Clay said, taking her hands, "you won't take that potion."

She hesitated. "Well, if I—but Virgil doesn't like smelly people—anyway, I don't care," she said with resolution. "May the best woman win."

He put his arm around her. "You okay?"

With a sniff, she said, "Clay, Sovay says she's talked Virgil into going to live with her in the south of France!"

"Oh, *shit*," Clay said, and Griffy raised a finger.

"You mustn't swear, Clay," she began. "It—"

"—Puts off the marks. Thank you, Virgil, for complicating my life again."

She clutched his arm. "Do you think it's true?"

"No. She's just being a b-brat." *Criminy, I can't make myself swear!* "This is what Virgil gets for filling the house full of marks. Actually, it's a good sign, because she wouldn't show her claws if she didn't feel desperate."

"Do you think so?"

"I do. Go back to the party." He squeezed her shoulders. "Serve your cake. I'll rout him out of his rathole."

He found Virgil in the collection room, sitting at the computer, and attached himself to his father's arm without ceremony. "Come on. They're cutting your birthday cake in fifteen minutes."

"At least let me close the program," Virgil protested.

Clay hauled the old man to his feet, surprised at how frail and bony he felt. "Hurry up." He stood behind Virgil, watching the screen while the old man tapped keys. "Ripping off someone's credit card account?" The screen showed a fat balance.

"CD account," Virgil said. The screen went black. "There. Now I can go." Clay moved to take his arm again. Virgil drew back. "You forget who's got the whip hand, boy? I still have the video. Find the FBI mole or I'll send it to your *supervisor*. That'll be a green sheet in your file."

Clay counted to ten. Then he said, "Tell me something. Did it occur to you, while you were conning Griffy that you loved her last night, that you had a witness the whole time?"

"That room is secure. I sweep it every day now. With FBI in the house? What do you take me for?"

"A cuckold," Clay pronounced. All the rage he'd hidden while Virgil taunted him these past few days burst out of him. "I take you for a cuckold. That means a guy whose wife is screwing somebody else under his nose. In your case, right there in the bed with you. Did you think she got all pink and happy only for you?"

Virgil looked flushed. "What are you talking about?"

"The fairy tale, Dad. Lord Darner, who disappeared out of a locked second-story room when you and Jewel were about to walk in on him and Sovay. He's in that bed."

"Oh, horse pucky." The old man went pale and then red.

"He's in that bed. I could prove it to you, if you'd let Jewel be alone in that room for twenty minutes."

Virgil looked shaken. "You *puppy*. You *worm*."

"Cuckold," Clay said, projecting truthfulness the way he'd been taught.

"I can have you arrested. I have the contracts from the Torstensen job, four years ago," Virgil said, starting to tremble. White spots appeared in the corners of his mouth.

Clay went hot. He leaned into Virgil's face. *My God, he's so old. I could break him in half.*

"I always knew you would turn on me if you got emotional enough," he said, and saw his father flinch. "I didn't think it'd be Griffy who sent you over the edge. You love her. You always have, you dope. You thought she was a doormat, and now she's got her ego more than two inches above the floor, and you're *so old*, you can't stomp on it like you used to. Maybe it's time to start treating her like a person." He turned the screw. "If it's not too late."

"Get out. Get out of my house."

Clay closed his hand over Virgil's wrist. His heart hammered so loud, he thought it would come out his ears. "You're coming downstairs with me now and eating some birthday cake."

Jewel meanwhile was fending off one of Virgil's neighbors. She couldn't find Griffy, so she surrendered to hunger and followed the smell of grilled bratwurst up the alley.

Once again her fatal spell got her in trouble.

The grillmeister weighed three hundred pounds, including gut, and he was shirtless, and he had a long-tined barbeque fork in his hand. Beer was apparently making him deaf.

"I'm Jack Allen," he kept saying, gripping her wrist with one hand and trying to slip his fork-holding hand around her. "I developed that condo building over there."

"No," she said, keeping an eye on the barbeque fork. "Let go of me." Crap, she hadn't had to use physical force since college. This Venus Machine effect sucked.

"Where have you been all my life? You're so beautiful," he crooned. "So very, very—"

For Pete's sake, she was wearing a feathered mask that covered everything but her eyes and mouth. "Let go of me or I will hurt you."

Let's see, could she reach his nuts without crossing within range of the fork? Maybe she should shove his bare belly against the barbeque grill. A close spin, a kick to the back of the knee, and push. Sooner or later, he would let go of her.

The drunk gasped. "Beautiful!" His grip slackened, his eyes fluttered, and he sank to his knees.

"Hi," Clay said, his face cold, his hand on the drunk's shoulder. "Time for some birthday cake."

"Jack!" a woman shrieked. She rushed down her back steps and threw a tattooed arm around her fallen barbeque master.

"Thank God," Jewel said. "I was thinking I'd have to leave scars. What did you do to him?"

"Vulcan neck pinch."

"You'll have to teach me that one." Something was the matter with her partner. "What up? Buddha not smiling."

"Virgil," Clay said, drawing her away from the Allen

barbeque. "He's losing his rag over the FBI mole thing. Are we positive it's Mellish? It might be smart to toss him a bone."

"I'm surprised you haven't fingered Mellish already," she said, trying for humor. "Why not, if it'll calm Virgil down?"

"We don't mess with federal agents gratuitously," Clay sniffed. "That's how we stay off their radar."

"Well, jeez, sorry for the suggestion." Poor Clay seemed bent. "How about I go find Mellish and give him a cop handshake, see if he responds. If he does, I'll let you know."

A smile cracked Clay's face. "Great. Thanks." He pushed a feather away from her eyes. "You okay in there?"

"Sweaty. What's that old man been doing to you?" Jewel looped her arm through his elbow and led him toward the sound of "Happy Birthday."

"Just a little family blackmail."

"I'll kneecap him for you. Jack Allen got my blood up."

"I'm not helpless," Clay said.

Boy, we are brittle tonight. "I never said you were."

As they walked down the alley toward Virgil's house, Jewel wondered if she shouldn't continue to cut Clay out of the loop for a while.

Time for a talk with our host. At least she didn't have to conceal her identity from Virgil.

No need to tell Clay all that.

The first person she saw when they came up to the crowd outside the Thompson garden gate was Buzz, shoveling birthday cake into his face. "What are you doing here?"

"Eagin birfgay gake. Hi, Officer Jewel. I didn't recognize you in the mask."

"Did you bring any more of that stuff?"

She yanked open his backpack where it dangled from his shoulder and rummaged. There were a lot of things in the backpack, some of them squishier than she wanted to know about, but no little bottles.

"Okay, you're clean. Maybe it's a good thing you're here after all. Come with me."

She led Buzz behind Virgil's garage, which gaped open so passersby could try out the Venus Machine. "In about an hour there's going to be a press conference here. I want you up front and center. If I point to you, you speak up and tell the press where you got those little bottles."

He squinted at her. "But you said I'd get busted."

"Not unless there are any more little bottles in existence. You don't have any, do you?"

"Hey, if I had any, I'd a sold 'em by now."

She crossed her fingers. "If you won't do this, I'll have to bring in the cops, because there's no other way to stop Kauz. If you play ball," she said, regretting what she was about to offer and also realizing how fiendishly addictive blackmail could be, "I'll take off the anklet."

He hesitated.

She said, "C'mon. There will always be other crap to sell. I'll bust you for that, too. But the anklet's on. I don't need to take it off."

He scratched a zit with his plastic spoon. "Well, I dunno. The Doc's been pretty good to me."

I've been good to you, dammit, and what's my reward? "Buzz, think what the cops can do to you." She leaned over him and looked into his eyes. A picture flashed through her mind of Buzz, miserable, sitting at a Thanksgiving dinner table with a couple of very properlooking parent types. *What?* "The batteries are good for five years."

He looked pale. "Dag, Officer Jewel, you're tough."

She slapped him on the shoulder. "Good boy. See you back here in twenty. In the meantime, you can eat until you burst."

His eyes lit up.

Jewel skirted the crowd and went into the Thompson garden in search of Mellish.

The whole house party was in the garden, along with a dozen neighbors, hanging around a bar and a punch bowl and a two-tier ice cream cake the size of a '78 Caddy transmission. Griffy talked and laughed, her green feathers quivering. Sovay stood silent in gold and black. Virgil looked like a devil in a crimson and scarlet mask, pushing tiny spoonsful of ice cream cake past the feathers into his pie-hole. Jewel spotted Mellish hovering in the background. She wagged a finger at him.

He backed toward the kitchen door, away from her. *Why Mellish, I didn't know you were afraid to talk to me.* She smiled and sprinted forward. She got to his side before he had his hand on the doorknob.

"Hello." No point in subtlety, if he was going to duck her. She flashed her badge, quick enough that he could see metal flash but not so slow that he could see what it said. "May we talk?"

He was taller than she was, and bigger, too. She looked straight into his eyes and got a mental image of a closed door. *What the—?* This stupid Venus Machine effect wasn't working for beans tonight.

"Inside or outside?" he said, not sounding butlery.

She was still puzzling over that picture of the closed door. "Outside. But within sight of witnesses."

A caterer tried to open the kitchen door from the inside and bumped her on the shin.

Mellish seemed unflapped. She made him go down the steps ahead of her and, as she glanced down at his big, shiny, thick-soled, federal-looking shoes, she remembered seeing them before. From under a bed. *Closed door. Closet door!*

"Closet door." She tapped him on the shoulder. "What's in Virgil's closet, Mellish?"

"Yes, Mellish, what's in my closet?" Virgil said behind the butler, and she saw Mellish's eyes flare with alarm.

CHAPTER 28

When Mellish turned toward his employer, however, his poise seemed restored. "Your other smoking jacket, sir. There is ice cream on this one," he said with utter detachment, as if his employer could smear himself all over with ice cream if he wanted.

Virgil glanced at his sleeve. "So there is. Why don't you fetch me that other jacket. Ms. Hess and I will be in the card room." He smiled like a snake at Jewel. "If you don't mind."

Jewel raised her eyebrows, a wasted gesture behind the feathers. "I'd like a word with you, too."

They went inside and Jewel took off her mask, which was smothering her where she stood. In the card room, Virgil unmasked and poured himself a glass of brandy. "Drink, officer?"

"No thank you." She knew what she would have to do. For a moment she wished she still had her mask on, so that her red face wouldn't show. But her best weapons here were her honesty and her open emotions. Virgil could beat her at the sneaky stuff.

"I see my son has already told you about the videotape."

She attacked. "Has he told you about the incubus in your bed?"

Virgil went still. Then he flicked a couple of the fingers holding the brandy snifter. "Ah, the fairy tale."

"Have you listened to that tape, Mr. Thompson? Not just watched, but listened?" He didn't speak. "Obviously you haven't, or you would have thought your blackmail through better." To her surprise, he looked embarrassed. "Didn't you wonder why we chose to have sex in that room?"

"My son has a penchant for foolish thrills."

Me, too, she thought. "Your son and I did the only thing I knew that would bring Randy out of hiding. We didn't know you had already switched out the bed."

"I thought you displayed laudable enthusiasm. Very, ah, invigorating to watch."

Here it came, the blush to end all blushes, and humiliation, and then anger, a healing anger that freed her from fear. Jewel let the blush and the humiliation do their worst. She took a deep, freeing breath. Rage cleared her mind.

"This morning, I saw the face of the woman you've been calling your sister." She leaned forward, though she wanted to hide herself from those lizard eyes. She spoke crudely to push past humiliation. "Randy's been fucking me for weeks. I see that face in the mirror every morning. It's the face of a woman who's been sleeping in a bed possessed by Randolph Llew Carstairs Athelbury Darner."

Her voice went hoarse. "That man—that creature, he's more than a man after two hundred years—he is the *best fuck in the universe*. He can read a woman's mind and give her exactly what she wants. He can do her asleep or awake. He can do her—"

"I don't believe in magic," Virgil said sharply. She saw him smooth out his face.

"I didn't believe at first, either. But Randy can do her—"

Virgil interrupted again. "You're deluded. The bed is

mine, and it stays in that room. The tape is mine, too. Maybe your employer would like a copy. Maybe the mayor."

Jewel raised her voice. "You can wriggle all you want, but I know what you don't want to hear. Randy can do a woman *while she's having sex with somebody else*. And, unless that woman is me, the other man *will never even know*."

"I don't think you know who you're dealing with," he said in a silky voice. "I can send that tape to the media."

"I don't think you know my reputation. I'm a *slut*." His head snapped back at the word. "I've screwed every fifth disease-free, single, adult male in the city of Chicago. Two of them have already put me on the Internet. We won't go into what happened to *them*." She'd hated those Internet pictures. It creeped her to the max to mention them to this evil old man.

Virgil sneered.

She showed her teeth. "But that's not my threat. My best threat is to do nothing. Because *I saw Griffy's face this morning*."

Virgil went still. His face was expressionless.

"If you give me that tape, I'll go up to your room, *alone*, and get Randy out of your bed."

"That's it? That's your threat?"

"No, this is the threat. If you keep the tape, I leave Randy in the bed. And Griffy sues your ass for palimony and takes the bed. Or maybe not. Maybe you can make it up to her somehow, despite the way you've treated her, and maybe she'll stay with you. But if I'm telling the truth, *she will never give up that bed*."

He opened his mouth and she raised her voice again, rolling over him.

"And *you will never know* if Randy is in there or not, because Randy doesn't do guys. That's not his curse. He has to satisfy any woman in his bed. It's annoying sometimes, he can't control himself—he's a bigger slut than I am—but I guess if you've practiced two hundred years, it's hard to break the habit.

"You and your videotape," she said with scorn. "Shall I tell you what it feels like to a woman, to think you're alone in bed and then find out, inch by magical inch, what happens when he starts to make his presence known? How it feels to be having sex with a guy and then realize, hey, there's too many hands touching me, there's too many tongues licking me, too many—"

"Stop!" Virgil was panting, his face dark with rage. "I don't believe you."

"So don't." She shrugged. "All you have to do is tell Griffy you're getting rid of that bed. See how she reacts."

Jewel turned on her heel and walked out, swinging her mask at her side.

Holy Jumping Jack Flash in a basket with fries and slaw. That was terrifying. She decided to stop needling Clay for knuckling under to his dad.

Now to warn Griffy to deliver the next part of the threat.

Out in the alley, the party was picking up speed. Home owners had opened their garages and backyards. Smells of grilled steak filled the air. The Self Love Ladies stood out in their huge feathered masks, but other merrymakers made up for it in itty-bitty cocktail dresses, big sparkly rocks, and shoes inappropriate for a cobbled alley. Everyone was drinking.

After the fight with Virgil, Jewel regretted turning down his brandy. *Though he might poison me.*

Jewel threaded her way past the mob by the punch bowl and through the gate to the alley. There was Griffy with a fingertip in her mouth, watching a girl in a beaded dress sit down in the green velvet chair. Jewel would have felt sorry for Beads Girl, but she clearly spent way too much money on her appearance. The Venus Machine would cure that.

Beads Girl spasmed theatrically in the hot seat.

Dr. Kauz unstrapped her and handed her out. The on-looking yuppies applauded. Every one of the men kissed her.

Griffy bit her lip.

Kauz looked up and saw Jewel. He rushed forward to take her hand. "My star patient! My greatest success! Unmask, my goddess, so that all can see your so-glorious green tones!"

Jewel pulled her hand free. *He's almost where I want him.*

The yuppies bayed like hyenas at the smell of fresh meat.

"Uh, I'm thirsty," she said. She backed away. "Think I'll go get some punch."

He held up a palm. "But no, I have a glass of punch here which I did not touch."

He circled around back of the Venus Machine and reappeared with a plastic cup in his hand. Jewel took it. Kauz sent her one of those deep looks that told Jewel he was thinking about her blood again. She backed away, and he turned his attention to the next victim clamoring for treatment.

She was lifting the cup when someone hissed, "Don't!"

Jewel jumped. The punch slopped over her hand. "What?"

The masked woman grabbed her wrist. "Don't drink it! I saw him open a little bottle and put something in that cup!" The voice was Griffy's.

Jewel regarded the cup with interest. "Holy crap. Thanks for spotting that. Listen, I need to talk to you."

She glanced back at Beads Girl, who was dancing wildly to "Foxy Lady" with three men at once.

"Let's go over here." Jewel drew Griffy around the corner by the Dumpster. "I wanted to tell you, you mustn't do that machine again."

"Why not? You did it twice."

Jewel lowered her voice. "There are side effects when you do it twice. More side effects, I mean."

"What kind of side effects?"

"When I got zapped that second time? I started, well, seeing things."

"Things?"

"It's like, whenever I made eye contact, I could picture what guys were thinking about me. You know how guys think?" She put the doped punch cup down, and Griffy promptly kicked it over. *There goes that sample.* "Why do you think I started wearing shades?" She let this sink in. "I don't know if it'll ever wear off. I hope it does, because there are times you don't want to read minds, even the minds of people you love."

Griffy nodded.

Jewel said gently, "You know, don't you, that Lord Darner isn't in Skokie. He's in Virgil's bed. I saw your face this morning and I knew."

Blinking, Griffy said, "In—in Virgil's *bed*? In *Virgil's* bed? Why—" She covered her masked face with her hands. "You knew—oh!" she said, sounding guilty.

Jewel patted her shoulder. "Weird feeling, isn't it? He's been living with me for three weeks. Something . . . happened the other day and he got trapped in Sovay's bed. Then Virgil swapped that bed for the one in the master bedroom. I think Clay told him too much."

"I knew the bed was different!" Griffy sounded thoughtful. "So that's why I had those crazy dreams. But how—?"

"I'll explain the whole thing later. But do you understand now why Virgil switched the beds? Clay says it's to get control of me and make me protect him from the law. But what I wanted to warn you is, now he's talking about getting rid of the bed."

The tall green headdress quivered. "He wouldn't dare!"

"He will. It crushed him when I convinced him that Lord Po—Darner was in there, doing you when he thought you two were alone."

Behind Griffy's mask, her eyes darted. "He was so sweet last night." Tears appeared in her eyes and she blinked them away. "But then this morning he was such a poop. So I thought maybe last night was all an act. He's a good actor," she said unnecessarily.

What if she loses Virgil and decides to keep Randy as consolation? "Lord Darner hates being trapped in beds."

But Griffy was a nicer person than that. "I'll find Virgil and keep him busy. You go get Lord Darner out of there."

Now for the rest of Jewel's plan. "Thank you, but I have a better idea. Tell Virgil that while he was eating his birthday cake, you had locksmiths change the lock on the bedroom door."

"But I didn't."

"Never mind, tell him anyway. I'll fix it so nobody can get in there, not even with a key."

"But—"

"He'll hate it. You want leverage? This is it. I don't like leaving Randy in that bed one minute more than I have to, but, if you want to keep the old buzzard, you'll need some ammo."

"Not ammo," Griffy protested. "I don't want to *shoot* him."

"If you don't defy him, he'll never know he's not the boss." Jewel waited while the deviosity of this percolated into Griffy's melon. "If you still want him."

"Yes," Griffy said slowly. "I do. He can be awful

sometimes—like now—but when he loved me—he used to love me—"

"So this is how you find out," Jewel said bracingly, before she could break down again.

Griffy sniffed and stood straighter. "I see." Her green feathers trembled with determination. "Yes. That's what I need. Leverage."

"Mind, I still want Randy back." Uh, that wasn't the way she'd meant to phrase it.

"Of course," Griffy said nobly.

CHAPTER

29

It was all very well for Julia to say, "defy him," Griffy thought, striding up the alley in agitation, but she had spent a very peaceful eighteen years letting Virgil run things. That had worked fine. Well, they'd moved more than she had liked. And often he wouldn't let her talk to neighbors. And when they'd lived in hotels, she couldn't talk to the maids, either, or to people in elevators, or waiters, or anyone. But he'd never asked her to pretend to be his sister before.

She squeezed past a dance in a neighbor's garage. She hadn't danced in ages. Virgil controlled way too much of her life. They were playing eighties music, and her feet began to shuffle. Her hips moved, and a nice-looking guy with a receding hairline smiled at her, and she thought, *Why not?* She wasn't in that big a hurry to defy Virgil.

Receding-Hairline Guy was a pretty good dancer.

The mask got in the way of some of her best moves, but the moves were rusty anyway. With a pang she thought of her stripping days, when she could dance for six hours straight, given water breaks. *I was alive. I was on my own, which sucked sometimes. But I got to pick my apartment and my day-off clothes and I didn't have to take elocution lessons from Virgil. Or ring a bell to get my sheets changed in my own house.* She looked over her partner's shoulder and saw the tips of Sovay's feathers bobbing nearby. *Or have snakes to visit.*

So when Virgil tapped her partner on the shoulder and pulled her away from the dance, she was in a fighting mood.

"What is your problem?" she demanded. "I get to dance sometimes."

"We have guests," Virgil began.

She cut him off. "So? I had to send Clay to drag you out of your hole to meet them."

She saw him blink, and she realized he was off balance. Boy, you didn't see that very often. *Julia was right. He must be upset.*

"Dance with me," she said softly, and held out her hand.

He took it and looked into her eyes, swinging her into the dance. "Do I know you anymore?"

Oh God, this was the breakup conversation. "You pulled me out of a dance to tell me you're done with me?"

"You don't listen to me anymore."

"I'm listening. I always listen to you. Your voice is—is always with me." Hot sadness welled up in her throat. "But I'm talking back now." Was that all he wanted? Had she lost him by speaking her mind?

His voice went husky. "Haven't I taken care of you?"

The heat in her throat hardened into a lump, silencing her.

He swung her around. "What is it, Griffy? What do you want?"

The mask was too hot. She pulled away from him to take it off and wipe her eyes. "I think I want to find out who I am. Maybe go to college. I don't want to pretend to be anybody else, I'm no good at that, you know that. I'm not smart enough to keep up with your work. But you didn't—you never brought—" *Never brought your work home with you*, she was going to say, but he had, and he'd always scolded her for talking too much, for her clothes, or her walk. "I think I want to be me. I don't want to pretend to be your sister," she said.

He put his palm over her mouth. "Not so loud!" He moved nearer to her again. "It's just for a few—"

She pushed his hand away. "It's always just for a few. A few days, a few weeks." Over his shoulder she saw Sovay's feathers again, not moving. Sovay was listening, but was he?

He thought he could talk and she would be silent, like a girl in a chorus line with a twelve-pound hat on her head, smiling at catcalls. She needed leverage. She needed *ammo*.

She leaned into the shadow of his big red mask. "I've had the locks changed on our—on *my* bedroom door. You can sleep elsewhere from now on."

He stood still. "You couldn't. When?"

"While you were eating birthday cake. I called them this morning," she added, thinking, *Boy, this lying thing is easy*. "After you were mean to me at breakfast. I told them when it would be good to come." He stiffened all over. She told another lie. "If you don't want me, I know where I can get all the comfort I want."

His red feathers trembled. "You devious little *slut*."

Her heart shrank up cold. *Well, that worked*.

"*I'm* not trying to get a twenty-something into bed," she said, feeling her mouth go puckery with nastiness. This was excruciating.

His eyes closed. "You still don't understand."

Behind him, Sovay's feathers were even nearer now.

In quiet despair, she said, "No, Virgil. I do understand."

She ran back to the house, knowing that even if he followed her, Sovay would be too quick. And he would never put Sovay aside for her.

The yuppies crowded even thicker outside her garage door. She couldn't even get to her own garden gate, so she went to watch from behind the Dumpster, feeling like garbage.

Kauz's voice crowed about the marvelous Venus Machine. "Who vill try? Who is villing to change their life? Who vants to be irresistible?"

Sovay pranced forward in her gold-and-black mask and seated herself in the Venus Machine with a flourish.

Virgil stood among the crowd, his red feathers motionless.

Griffy brushed through the garden, past the wreckage of the birthday cake, into the house, past the caterers in the kitchen, sorry she'd taken off her mask because her face was crumpling and she could feel sobs coming up in her chest.

She squeezed them down and hurried through the empty house to the ladies' cloakroom off the foyer. Her shoes clacked in the darkened marble hall. Panting, she hung her mask on a hook in the candlelit cloakroom, then ran into the lavatory and threw herself into a pink brocade chair to cry.

Jewel saw Griffy run past the cake into the house and thought, *Oh, hell.* The woman was too nice to fight with the likes of Virgil.

She gritted her teeth and followed.

When she found her in the cloakroom, Griffy was sobbing exhaustedly.

"Oh, girlfriend." Jewel went back out and hung her mask on a peg beside Griffy's, grabbed up a box of tissues, and went back in. "I take it he acted like a brat."

"He was *horrible*," Griffy sobbed. "He called me a *slut.*"

Jewel dabbed at her chin. "Huh. That must mean he believes that Randy's in the bed." He would have to give her the videotape now. She tried to feel triumph, but Griffy was so clearly suffering a fallout from her brilliant strategy that she felt guilty. "He'll come around." *I hope.* "If he wants you back, he'll let me get Randy out of that bed."

Griffy raised her head at that. "Oh." She sniffled. "I hadn't thought of that."

"And he'll have to ask you for the key, because he thinks you've changed the locks."

Griffy shook her head. "He's too proud. He'll never apologize."

Jewel squinted. "Are you telling me Virgil can't figure out how to ask you for the new key without apologizing?"

"You're right," Griffy said with a laugh. "But what do I do then? I don't have a new key."

"Let me know when he's asked, and I'll deal with it."

High-heeled footsteps strode into the outer cloakroom.

Sovay sailed in without her mask. She cast a pitying glance at Griffy and went into the potty stall. "My God, what stinks?" she said from the stall, and made a horking noise. Lavish spews plopped into the toilet. "I was told this would be a *high* class party." She horked again. More plops.

Jewel raised her voice. "You know, Sovay, if you're gonna hang around with a high-standards guy like Virgil, you have to pretend to have class twenty-four-seven. It looks tacky if you can't speak to your rivals without throwing up."

"Rivals!" Sovay said in a hoarse voice. "You're pathetic." Hork. "You're a cow and Griffy's a hag." Hork hork. The toilet flushed.

"Julia's right," Griffy said. She went to the mirror, winced, and began repairing her makeup. "Virgil's very fussy. He would never put up with anyone low class."

Jewel patted Griffy's shoulder. "Tell it, sister," she whispered. "By the way, Sovay, Lord Darner says your English accent is fake."

"Fake?" Griffy paused with a hairpin in her hand.

"Yeah, Sovay, where is Lord Darner?" Jewel said. "Last I knew, he was with you, banging the headboard against the wall. What did you do, fuck him to death?"

"Ooh, you're mean!" Griffy whispered.

"Maybe I'll tell Virgil I saw him coming out of your room," Jewel added.

"Liar!" Sovay cried from inside the stall. "You never did!"

"No, I didn't," Jewel said. "Maybe screwing a human snake made him disappear in a puff of smoke."

"Bitch!" Hork. Thrashings from the stall. "You're both pathetic bitches!" Hork hork hork. The toilet flushed again. Sovay swept through the lavatory without pausing to primp. They heard the cloakroom door bang.

"What's her problem?" Jewel wondered. "She can't even speak to me without vomiting. I don't think she's faking it."

"I know she's had two goes on that Venus Machine already." Griffy blotted her lipstick.

"Holy crap." Jewel swiped at her hair with a comb. "What does that thing do to people? Power of suggestion, my ass." She checked the stall to see if Sovay had left a mess. On the floor, something weird wiggled. "You should keep your back door shut, Griffy." She picked it up and showed her a tiny baby snake.

"Eeek!" Griffy drew back.

"It's just a baby," Jewel said.

"Talk about your custom-made magic!" Griffy sucked in a horrified breath. "Lord Darner must have done something to her when he told her that story about the three girls at the well."

"Miss? Miss Griffin?" A caterer came to the door of the lavatory. "Miss, there's a food fight in the backyard. I thought I should tell you, they're throwing cake."

Griffy sighed. "What next?" She went out, masking herself again, and leaving Jewel with her prize.

Jewel stared down at the tiny, bright, green, wriggling snakeling. "Power of suggestion, huh." She went out.

It was just like high school. The mean girls went around picking on people, and Jewel, the farm girl, went to parties with a snake in her pocket.

CHAPTER
30

Griffy arrived in the garden to find the food fight was now an orgy. The cake was gone. The combatants wrestled in twos and threes, having a good time—on the patio, up against the wall, under the messed-up cake table. People moaned. Lingerie flew.

While she stood there, feeling left out, Dr. Kauz came up to her. He hugged her tightly, crushing her feathers.

"My fire goddess! Ach, you are more radiant now than before you drank my potion!" he cried.

She drew back. "I think you mistake—" He kissed her hand and the words died on her lips. She remembered the potion he'd poured into Julia's punch cup.

He pulled his face back. "But I must not presume. Soon enough you will embrace me. Now that you have taken the potion," he said, holding her hand and stroking it, "you are addicted to its power. And only I can give you more!"

She blinked. "But I didn't—"

"*Stumm*, hush, hush." He set his finger on her lips.

Griffy was getting annoyed. What did men think? She would always zip it for them?

"You are my crowning achievement. After one taste, you crave my potion. Only my potion can make you feel desirable!"

She drew back, creeped out by the bad Peter Lorre imitation, but he pulled her closer.

He hissed in her ear, "Now you will always be beside me. Now I tell you my great plan, for you have a part in it, oh yes! With your green tones, you can have any man alive, and I, Kauz, will be the greatest politician of the age! We will be Borgias, ruling the city *mit* magic, *mit* zex, *mit* raw power!" He cackled.

Griffy began to piece it together. *He thinks I'm Julia. He did dope her punch! I'm so glad she didn't taste it.*

"Conceive my delight when our hostess invites me here on the eve of this party. So exclusive, such excellent media coverage!"

She gasped. "You *knew* about the block party?"

"I am a guest of the richest man at the party! It was opportunity I could not pass up." He leaned closer. "To-night I will take such a tiny drop of your blood, and I will run it through the psychespectrometer and also a few instruments I have back at my laboratory. If I can isolate the Venus Machine factor and synthesize it! It is my dream!" He clutched her arm.

She pulled. "Let go of me!"

His tone turned sinister. "Perhaps another visit to the Venus Machine will remind my green goddess of how pleasurable you find the admiration of the masses." His grip tightened.

With a squeak of irritation, she brought her heel down on his instep. He yelped and let go of her, and she fled.

At that moment someone turned out the lights in the garden. She couldn't see a thing. She ran straight into a tall person wearing a feathered mask. "Ouch!"

"Oof! Griffy?" Julia said. "Is that you?"

"Julia! I came to warn you. That horrible Dr. Kauz did put some kind of addictive drug in that cup he gave you!"

"Yeah, hey, no big, I didn't drink any, remember?"

"Well, he thinks you're addicted to it now. He wants to take over the city and make you his fire queen sex magic power goddess. He was totally *icky*." Griffy shuddered.

"He told you all this?"

"He thought I was you."

Julia said, "Duh, you're wearing my mask. See the stripes?"

Griffy looked down. "Of course! It's so dark outside that cloakroom." They swapped masks. "They must have got mixed up."

"Look," Julia said, holding her mask in her hand, sounding embarrassed. "I'm sorry Virgil was so mean about the locks. What I wanted to remind you was, if he doesn't want you sleeping on that bed, it's because he's jealous of Randy. So you have a chance. I advised you wrong about how to use it—"

"No, you've been great. If something awful has happened to Sovay, like if that Venus Machine is making her say stupid things and throw up snakes, maybe I do have a chance."

"I totally think you have a chance. I wish I knew how to make it work. I'd better not give you any more advice."

Griffy felt strong again. "Never mind. He's with Sovay now. Here's my key to the bedroom. You can go upstairs and save your friend." She smiled tremulously. "It would never do to have him in that bed if—if I get lucky."

"Is that what you want me to do?" Julia said.

"Yes. It is."

Julia kissed her cheek. "I should have known. You're always straight, Griffy. I think that's why Clay loves you." Griffy sniffled, and Julia gave her a hug around the shoulders. "If you see Virgil aiming for the house, try and head him off."

"I'll try."

Griffy watched Julia march to the back door, ignoring the orgy going on around her. *That's how I should be. I should know what I want and go after it.* She pulled her mask on.

If only she knew what she wanted.

If only there wasn't a mean old buzzard who needed her.

Under cover of darkness, Jewel sneaked into the house and upstairs to Virgil's bedroom. Peering over her shoulder, she took her penknife out of her pocket and eased the penny out of the crack in the door.

It looked a little creased. Huh. Virgil must have tested Griffy's claim to have changed the locks.

She whisked into the bedroom and locked the door. For good measure, she stuck the penny back in the door crack, hoping it would work from the inside.

She left the room lights out. Faint streetlight from Marine Drive and Lake Shore Drive came through the windows over the top of the curtains. She took off her mask, her dress, her shoes, her underwear and bra, and laid them all on a chair. Trying not to squick at the thought that Virgil and Griffy had had sex here, she slid onto the quilt. Somewhere in the bowels of the house, a tinny alarm trilled.

She said aloud, "Randy?" She got a tingle. "Oh, thank God." They didn't have a minute to lose. Virgil could decide to skunk the party at any moment.

Shutting her eyes, she tried to relax, joint by joint, toes, ankles, knees, hips, shoulders, elbows, fingers. She tensed her neck and released it. *I am so not sleepy.* But as she thought this she felt her edges fuzzing out, felt the slide of arms around her bare waist. *There you are, buddy.*

He grabbed her, turning her to face him. He looked

anxious and angry. *I feared that Sovay had poisoned you.*

What? What happened to "Let's fuck and get out of here"? She already felt her kookamunga swelling up and getting slippery.

She marries men and then kills them for their money. She hates you. I discovered this as I seduced her. He scowled, his face scary in demonspace. *You should have come for me sooner.*

Jewel pulled out of his arms. *We have ten minutes before Virgil walks in here. Do you want to spend them pissing me off?*

He assumed what she thought of as his diplomacy face—stiff, bland, and guarded. *An excellent point.*

Doesn't he believe I'll always come back? she thought, and, when the words came out aloud in demonspace, his face relaxed.

She reached for him, and her hand went all the way into his chest, where she felt a hot coal. Heat ran up her arm into her own chest. She smiled.

Fuck now, argue later. C'mon, I have something to show you. The bed fell away beneath them.

They were falling endlessly through a brilliant blue sky.

Are you afraid because you're aroused, or aroused because you're afraid? he murmured in her ear. This time Jewel laughed.

Slipping out of his arms, she fell a hundred feet, then opened her arms like a high-diver, turning over and over, exulting. She swooped around him, wingless, fearless. *Look at me! I'm not scared to fly anymore!*

When did that happen?

She laughed gaily. *I flew on a parasail yesterday. It was fabulous and scary and fun.* She swooped back up to him, then turned around him in a laughing spiral.

Parasail? Show me.

She created a parasail out of thin air and let wind fill the sail. *Plus there was water.* She gestured. Lake Michigan or something like it appeared below them, impossibly blue, cold, bright, powerful. She swooped closer to him, looped her arm through his, and carried him out over the lake, towed behind nothing, swinging wildly, dipping, whirling, swaying left and right under the parasail as the cold lake spray speckled the soles of her feet and made her shriek.

At some point he disappeared. She looked down. He was on the sand below, smiling up at her, watching.

She descended until she could drop on all fours beside him. With a wave of her hand she banished the parasail. *Thanks to you,* she said, standing. She put both hands on his bare chest. *I wouldn't have dared try it, I mean the real thing, if we hadn't been flying every night.*

They lay on the sand, which, being demonspace sand, did not get into her butt crack or carry fleas, and he rolled with her until they lay half-in, half-out of the surf. She burned all over with hunger, hunger for his hard, heavy body, hunger for a quick explosion, and she felt so hot that every wave hissed and sizzled over her skin. He kept them rolling on the fringe of the waves so that the sand and sky and water revolved along with a kaleidoscope of sensation.

Hurry up! We have to get out of here!

You wouldn't hurry with me, would you? he said, and she jerked her head back at the sound of his voice, the wrong voice.

He was Clay. Clay down to the shaggy blond bangs and crinkly blue eyes, his long body slimmer and lighter, Clay's voice, Clay's—*Randy! You don't have to do this.*

The smile was Clay's pouty-lipped smile, but the anxious look came from somewhere else. *I thought you might like it.*

She pulled a hand free and wiped wet hair out of his

eyes. *Randy, you are you, and you are good enough. Be yourself.*

He smiled an un-Clay-like smile and passed his hand over her eyes. *No woman has ever said that to me.*

When she opened her eyes, he was Randy again, Randy with the big, hard body, black-eyed Randy lifting her hips with one hot hand, sliding inside her with that amazing instrument. She squeezed tight around it. A cry broke from his lips.

He rolled her under him one more time.

Quick, now! Make it fast—she began. But he was already driving into her with a thump and a grind that made her judder. *Thump,* the world heated until she thought she would go up in flames, *grind,* and she cried out, and then a wave washed over her, sizzling, turning to steam when it hit her skin. *Just do me, just do me,* she thought, feeling sizzling heat and the splash of cold water and his cock like a freight train running through her body, just *do* it just *do* it just *do* it just *do* it and then the whistle blew in her ear and she came apart with a *boom.*

Twenty seconds later they were spooned together, her belly to his back, sweating on the coverlet.

Jewel listened to her heartbeat slow. "Why'd you take that bitch to bed?" It might ruin the mood, but she had to know.

He sat up, rubbing his face and scalp with his hands as if he was thrilled to have his body back. "Because you annoyed me."

She suppressed a smile. "Hey, I'm sorry about the tracer anklet. Buzz made me understand how humiliating it is. It doesn't work well in a building anyway."

"No," Randy said. "No. I've realized how easily I might be separated from you. It was a good idea." He flashed her a big-black-cow-eyed look. "Also, I thought to search her mind. And I learned that—"

"She's a black widow. That's what we call it. I know. Clay showed me his files. He searched her room, too, but either he found nothing we can use, or he snitched her jewelry."

"The poison is not in her room," Randy said. "She's too wily for that. I read her mind. She searched our room. She found your badge. She knows who you are. She was going to try to force you to leave the house. I thought if I seduced her and took away proof, I could threaten to show it to Mr. Thompson." His tone got an edge. "Had you rescued me sooner, I could have warned you."

It was a harebrained idea, but his heart was in the right place. She put her hand over his.

"I tried to find you. I did. Clay got me into her room, but we didn't even realize Virgil stole the bed and put it up here already." She swallowed. "Stupidhead Clay told him about your curse. I was so afraid Virgil would want to use the bed the way Clay did, to make money," she confessed. "I was scared shitless for you."

Randy started to smile. "I believed you might be glad of an opportunity to be rid of me."

"I kind of was," she admitted. "But I, uh, I kind of missed you."

The smile got bigger. "I shall remind you that you said so." He slid off the bed. "Did you bring me any clothes?"

She hadn't. "I was in a huge hurry to get in here and get out. Which reminds me, we need to get moving! That press conference will start the second the media arrive."

"Fortunately Virgil was once taller than he is now," Randy said from the walk-in closet.

To Jewel's horror, someone opened the door, letting a sliver of bright light into the room. She froze, naked on top of the coverlet. So much for her penny.

"Fuck!" she breathed, and shut her eyes.

Don't panic, Randy. Don't panic don't panic don't panic—

She heard a chunky, thunking noise and a heavy body hit the floor. "Randy?"

chapter 31

The light flashed on. Randy stood by the door, rubbing his fist. On the floor lay Mellish, the eternally intrusive.

"Jeez, what did you hit him with?"

Randy showed her his fist.

"Wow." He was still naked. "Get dressed, okay? Let's boogie before he wakes up."

While Randy dressed himself out of Virgil's closet, Jewel went to the in-wall entertainment center and started pressing buttons. Something clacked and squeaked. A black videotape cassette popped out of a slot.

Was it the right one? She bit her lip.

"Go out in the hall and keep watch, will you? I have to get dressed, and this is not a good moment for Virgil to find us."

For a miracle Randy did as she asked. While she was dressing, she stuck the tape back into its slot and fumbled with the controls. A smeary, grainy picture appeared, and then Clay said, *Why yes, I'm having a ball. I haven't had so much fun since we hid under a thirteen-thousand-dollar sofa at Field's and then burgled the joint.* She slammed the eject button as Randy stuck his head in the door.

"Someone is coming."

"I'm ready," she said, shoving her feet into her shoes

and grabbing up her big feathered mask. "For the love of Mike," she said, goggling at his outfit. "That was in Virgil's closet?"

Randy had chosen a slick, shiny, purple paisley, polyester shirt with a chest ruffle and frilly cuffs, and a pair of powder-blue stretch pants to go with. The stretch pants left nothing to the imagination. He had added a pair of white vinyl boots, and was struggling to cram his shoulders into a burnt orange crushed-velvet frock coat.

"Hey, Willy Wonka. Ix-nay on the oat-cay. It's summer," she said. "Hotter than Dutch love."

He smoothed a hand over the sleeve. "My father would have worn this coat."

Her eyebrows climbed into her hairline.

The maid came up the stairs. "Oh!" She fell back against the banister, clutching her heart, or something near it, with both hands. "Oh, it's you, Lord Darner!" Her eyes bugged out at those stretch pants.

Randy preened.

Jewel poked him in the ribs. "Peacock."

When they got to the kitchen door, she could see over the garden wall into the alley. A cameraman was coming through the alley. A sleek-looking blond woman walked backward facing the camera, talking into a microphone.

Jewel held her breath. If they came into the garden first, they would be distracted by the orgy. If they stopped at the garage first, she'd be screwed.

The cameraman turned in through the garden gate.

She let out air. "Randy, would you mind going outside and talking to that woman with the cameraman? Keep her in the garden until I signal to you from the garden gate. Then bring her out into the alley."

"Talk? What about?"

She frowned. "I don't know, think of something, Put

the moves on her. Give her a guided tour of the Kama
Sutra as re-created in a back yard off Marine Drive.
Dear God, these people have no shame." She looked in
disbelief through the back door at the couples squirming
all over the garden.

Randy studied her. "What?"

"Don't tell anybody who you are." When he scowled
she thought, *Hell, I'm doing to him what Virgil did to
Griffy. Taking away his name. Making him a nonper-
son.* "I mean, you can call yourself Lord Darner. You're
still undercover."

"This I can perform." He lifted his chin, tugged the
lapels of the orange coat, and swaggered out the kitchen
door.

I'm getting better at managing him. "Now where the
heck is Clay?"

"Right behind you," Clay's voice said faintly. She
turned to find him transfixed, watching Randy. "Where
in the world did he get those clothes?"

"Virgil's closet."

"I can't decide if it's Carnaby Street or Mardi Gras."

"Pay attention," Jewel said. She handed Clay the
videotape. "Burn this."

Clay stared. "I've been searching the whole house for
that. Did Virgil let you into his room after all? Because
that door was so locked, even I couldn't pick it."

"I pennied it shut."

"You what?"

Jewel squinted. "Holy magooley, is that Buzz over
there?"

"Hey, was that the mask you were wearing before?"

"Yeah. Blue-and-white stripes," she said, staring.

Leaning his partner against the brick garden wall, a
naked Buzz humped as if his life depended on it. Jewel
made a *euw* face. "Will you look at the tattoos on her."

The tattooed woman seemed enthused. She and Buzz

were having a good time. Jewel shook her head, then shook it harder. Some pictures weren't meant to be given headroom.

"Listen, Clay, we need to orchestrate this press conference. Beulah and the Self Love Ladies are out there somewhere. Randy's got the camera crew nailed down, I hope—" A glance in Randy's direction showed her that his lordly charm was doing its usual good work on the society reporter. "Great. Your job is to get Buzz decent and out in the alley by the time the reporter goes out there to interview Kauz."

Clay scowled. "And how do I do that? Tap him on the shoulder and say 'May I cut in?'"

"Remind him that I promised to take off that tracer anklet if he shows up at the press conference and does his bit."

"That ought to work," Clay said. "Anything else?"

She stood there, blinking. Clay seemed calm. *He's working with me. Like he's my partner.* She smiled. "That's all I can think of."

He glanced at Randy and the reporter. "I'd guess we have about ten minutes."

The cameraman was getting close-ups on the orgy. Bare flesh flashed unattractively under the moving light. But the reporter had her hand on Randy's crushed-velvet orange sleeve.

Jewel gave Clay a thumbs-up.

He pulled her close, kissing her in a clinch that made her head swim. "Little hint," he said, as she punched his arm. "Con artists and undercover cops do not 'thumbs-up' each other in front of the marks." He released her with a pat on the fanny.

Okay, his manner could use work. But, by golly, it was nice to have someone she could rely on.

She sent Randy another glance as she stepped over

naked partyers and passed through the alley gate. *Two someones.*

Thankfully, Beulah had her group organized. They were at the garage door of the house across the alley, sucking down raw oysters and drinking beer. Jewel hissed, "Meet me in ten minutes right over there by Virgil's garage."

Beulah bobbed her turquoise-feathered head.

"Say, I found out where Buzz has been getting that potion. It's that guy over there, with the Venus Machine. Dr. Kauz. He wants to run for mayor because he's such a great magician."

Beulah trilled, "Oh, is *he* the mysterious doctor? How marvelous to meet him at last!"

"He'll need your testimonials," Jewel said, feeling evil. "Wait for my signal."

"We'll be there! Won't we, girls?"

The other masked Self Love Ladies bobbed their feathers.

Jewel saw Virgil's red mask crossing the alley. She came up beside him. He was staring at Randy's peacocky high-disco costume. Below the feathers, his mouth trembled, and the old turtle eyes blinked. Then he turned and blundered past Jewel, almost knocking her down.

This ought to be good. I wonder which one he's running to?

She followed. To her delight, he sought out Griffy where she leaned against the opposite alley wall, watching the back of Kauz's medicine show. Kauz's voice could be heard, ballyhooing the marvelous Venus Machine over the noise of the crowd and music coming from up and down the alley.

The green-feathered figure turned toward the red one, then jerked her shoulder.

Jewel couldn't resist. She worked her way closer.

"Please," she overheard Virgil say. "Give me another chance. You don't often hear me say that."

Griffy's feathers shook, *No.*

"You haven't let me explain," Virgil said, raising his voice, and Griffy put up a palm. "I was never going to marry Sovay. She's a mark. She's got twenty million dollars and she's a crook. If I take her, she can't go to the cops."

Griffy still looked stiff and furious, even under the enveloping mask, and Jewel held her breath.

"I saw you flying in that contraption yesterday and I realized something. It's you," he said, moving closer to her. "It's always been you. Griffy, I don't know how to tell you how I feel—"

She pushed him away with a shriek and stood up, pulling off her mask at the same time. The woman under the mask was Sovay.

"You *scum*!" she shrieked, spitting out something she'd been eating. "How *dare* you abuse my trust! Bastard! Monster! Heartless, heartless bastard!"

At every *bastard* something flew out of her mouth and landed on the alley bricks. The partiers nearby drew back. A woman screamed, and more of them drew back. A clear space widened around Sovay where she half crouched, spitting with rage.

Jewel looked down at the bricks. Half a dozen toads and snakes squirmed there. Then she yanked out one of her own feathers. Gold and black! She had on Sovay's mask.

"You shriveled old monster! Nobody wants you!" A stream of reptiles shot out of Sovay's mouth like sluggish bullets.

Virgil backed away, looking down at the menagerie accumulating at his feet, and bumped into Jewel.

Jewel told him, "I hate to tell you this, but I think you're gonna have to repeat that tender speech." Virgil spun around. She said, "You knew I was listening, and you thought I was Sovay. You wanted Sovay to hear." Virgil was still watching Sovay give a diva-grade performance. "So I guess your plan worked. But will Griffy ever hear that speech for real?"

Virgil looked at her. His turtle eyes were round with some emotion. Then he blundered away through the crowd.

That's weird, I don't see what he's thinking.

Sovay watched with indignation as Virgil fled.

The society reporter and her cameraman came through the Thompson garden gate, followed by Randy.

Kauz, who must have been watching for the camera light, raised his voice. "My name is Gustavus Katterfelto Kauz," he pronounced. "And this is my magnificent Venus Machine!"

The camera moved into the alley in front of the open Thompson garage. Jewel peered over the heads of the crowd.

Kauz spread his arms in a victorious gesture for the camera.

"You!" Sovay shoved forward. "You did this to me!"

The camera swiveled toward her just as a bunch of little snakes and toads flew out of her mouth and plopped on the ground.

Kauz clutched at his chest. "*Mein Gott!*"

Sovay pointed a finger. "You've had me in that machine all evening! And look at me! Look what you've done to me!" *Plop! Plop! Plop! Plop! Plop!*

The crowd gasped.

The cameraman bobbed like a chicken pecking at flying grain, pointing at her face, then at the critters falling to the alley bricks. The reporter, dammit, came

out of the garden gate just then. She'd missed everything!

Jewel took her little friend out of her pocket and
tossed him with the old high-school accuracy.

Just as the reporter turned to Kauz, the tiny green
snake flew between them and landed on the reporter's
sleeve. The reporter looked at it and screamed. The camera swerved to her.

Kauz brushed the snake off her sleeve. "No, no, it is
not true. This unfortunate woman, she is inebriated, un-
hinged."

"Sir?" the reporter said, recovering and thrusting the
microphone at him.

He put his chin up. "I am Dr. Gustavus Katterfelto
Kauz."

"Doctor, do you contend that this woman never received a treatment in the Venus Machine?"

"Of course not!" Kauz stated.

"Yes, she did!" someone yelled.

"She took my turn twice!" yelled someone else.

"You mean you have all been using this machine?" the
reporter said, and the camera swung wildly between the
Venus Machine and the crowd. Hands waved.

"I did."

"Meee!"

"I tried it."

"I did, too!"

"How about those people in there?" She pointed into
Virgil's garden.

"I assure you, they did," Randy said without a blink.

"I assure you." Kauz wrung his hands. "She has
never—she was never my client!"

"Liar!" Sovay spat. "I was at your spa three days ago!
You ignored me for that cow, but I was there, and I got
twelve-hundred-dollars' worth of your so-called treatments!" Snakes and toads showered onto her shoes.

The crowd took one giant step back.

Jewel heard retching all around her.

This is perfect. Kauz will never run for mayor now.

Jewel looked around for Beulah. Beulah waved, and Jewel beckoned her forward.

Beulah stepped into the camera light. "Please," she said, pulling off her mask with a flourish. "Friends!"

The noise level lowered. *Spooky.* In the cameraman's assistant's harsh, wobbly light, Beulah looked magnificent, fascinating, messy as hell, supremely confident, and totally nuts. In a likeable way. "Please, everyone!"

Even the murmurers fell silent.

"Friends, calm yourselves." She signaled and the Self Love Ladies unmasked. "We have benefited from the doctor's genius. He created the Self Love Potion! One dose will silence that poisonous voice that says, 'You are ugly, you are old, you are undesirable.'" Beulah said thrillingly, "You are *not* ugly! You are beautiful!" She opened her arms. "Desire yourself, and everyone will desire you!"

The partyers didn't look happy, but Jewel noticed they didn't run away. Toads hopped between their ankles, and snakes slithered past their shoes, unnoticed. *Must be some potion.*

"Good people," Kauz said. Sweat stood out on his bald forehead. "Let us be reasonable and think like scientists!"

Oh, that's going to get their interest.

Past Kauz, Jewel saw Buzz, now wearing pants, *Thank you, Clay,* sneak behind the Venus Machine. *Stealing something.* That boy was the sharpest opportunist she'd ever met.

The reporter stuck the microphone in Beulah's face. "Ma'am, how long has it been since you visited a beautician?"

"Ten glorious weeks!" Beulah announced. She had tremendous presence. She smiled, and Jewel felt the crowd around her relax.

"Are you sure you can attribute your change of heart to Dr. Kauz's potion?"

"I can. As proof, I offer the testimony of my friends here, all of whom walked in the night of self-loathing before they received a dose. One single dose. The man is a genius!"

One by one, the Self Love Ladies stepped forward. Mrs. Noah Butt from Water Tower Place was there, and Annette Perini, and Bunny from Giorgio lo Gigolo's. The camera light wobbled over them. The gleeful reporter took sound bites from each one.

"Then that's why my customers don't come back," Kauz muttered, his brow furrowing.

Another masked woman stepped into the light. "You told me that that potion was addictive," she accused Kauz in Griffy's voice. The camera swerved toward her. "You said that after one taste I would keep wanting more and more and more. You said I would never be free of you, and you would control me and make me a fire goddess and rule the city with sex and magic and power."

"Julia?" Kauz said, looking baffled.

"But it's not addictive!" Beulah protested. "We have all taken it"—she pointed to her friends—"just once! One dose, and we are free of the tyranny of the beauty industry."

"Then the formula is wrong," Kauz blurted.

The reporter pointed her microphone at him. "Dr. Kauz, have you received permission from the FDA to sell this potion?"

"Yes! I mean, no!" Kauz tried to stand tall, which made him about five foot four. "That is to say, there is no potion. I have never met any of these ladies before—"

"Hey!" Sovay yelled.

"—Except this unfortunate madwoman here, tonight only."

Jewel looked at Buzz, still lurking behind the Venus Machine. She stuck her thumb in the air.

Buzz nodded. He called out, "Not so fast, Doc." As the camera light swung toward him, he put his palm up to hide his zitty young face. "I seen you in your la-bore-atory lotsa times, and you had the potion, and you told me all about it. You said the customers would want a new dose every week. Only nobody ever ast for it again. I guess it worked permanent or somethin'."

You did? Jewel thought. *Buzz, when are you going to quit lying to me?*

Kauz looked hunted. The reporter swung back to him.

"Dr. Kauz, is this potion addictive? What are the withdrawal symptoms? Do you know of any side effects?"

He exploded. "There are no side effects. Besides, potion is sold out, no more available." He made an umpire's "safe" gesture with both arms. "There is no potion! And if there were, I would take it myself with complete confidence! Everything of my making is safe and wholesome!"

"Not sold out yet!" Buzz called. He lobbed something over the Venus Machine. "Here ya go, Doc!"

Beulah leaped into the air like Michael Jordan and caught it. "You found more. How wonderful!"

The reporter swerved to her.

She showed her catch to the camera, then held it aloft. Another teeny little bottle.

She turned her heartwarming smile on the camera. "Dr. Kauz's masterpiece is harmless. It works permanently to bring one to perfect inner harmony and self-love. *We* are not addicted"—she gestured to her scruffy, smelly friends, who waved at the camera—"except to loving ourselves!" She brandished the bottle. "This is the key to true beauty!"

"How about that, Doc?" Buzz yelled.

"Drink it!" someone yelled from the crowd.

"Come, Doctor." Beulah stalked toward Kauz with the bottle raised in both hands, like a high priestess bringing the offering knife. "You have given so much to so many unhappy lives. Will you not partake of your own bounty?"

"Yeah, Doc," Jewel called out, as Kauz edged away from the light. "If it's harmless, you won't mind trying it yourself."

The camera swung toward her, but she had her mask on, and the camera returned to Kauz.

Kauz looked trapped. He blinked at the circle of watching faces. His face smoothed out more with every blink.

"Very well. *Natürlich*, I will try it. You shall see." He took the little bottle from Beulah and showed it to the crowd. "Behold!"

He unscrewed the top. The cameraman swooped closer. Kauz put the bottle to his lips and swallowed dramatically.

"Hey, Doc, you dropped your potion," Jewel called out.

The reporter looked down. The camera moved with her. There in the puddle of light sat the potion bottle, still screwed shut, laying on the driveway.

Everyone looked at Kauz.

"I am scientist," he squeaked. "How can I observe if I am part of der experiment?"

"Dr. Kauz," the reporter began. "Did you give an experimental drug to all these women—"

But Kauz picked up the potion bottle, opened it, and, with a gray face, drank it down.

Jewel took a deep breath. It was now or never for her secret weapon. "Yo, Gussie! Who are you?"

Kauz blinked. His little round face seemed to close. Jewel realized that, behind the round glasses, his eyes were closed, too. *Gosh, I hope he doesn't croak from it.* Then his eyes opened, and he smiled. He threw his arms wide.

"I," he said in a new voice, "am Gussie Kauz. And *youse*"—he pointed with both forefingers at the crowd— "are all beautiful!" His smile was splitting his face.

For once he seemed almost, well, likeable.

Uh-oh. The potion! Jewel glanced wild-eyed from the Self Love Ladies to Kauz. *I bet his green tones are going over the top. I should have thought of that! Now what?*

"That's the man," yelled a voice outside the circle of light. "That's the guy that made a slut out of my wife!"

Jack Allen, the condo developer with the bay-window gut, shoved forward through the crowd, a police officer at his side.

Allen pointed at Kauz. "Arrest him!"

The reporter and the cameraman fell back to let Allen and the cop through.

"Sir, is this your equipment?" the cop said to Kauz.

Kauz lifted his chin. "It soitenly is." *Soitenly?* He sounded like Curly the Stooge. "You wanna make somethin' of it?"

"Dr. Kauz," the reporter said, shoving forward. "You aren't German, are you?"

"On my mudder's side. But!" He stood tall. "I am a soyentist." His finger pointed at the sky. "*And* the woild's greatest magician!"

The cop explained to Kauz that he was under arrest for disturbing the peace and read him his rights. Then he ordered the garage door closed, hiding the Venus

Machine. Kauz nodded and smiled. The cop held him by the elbow, and Kauz marched away with his head high. The cameraman followed them down the alley.

"Never fear, dear Doctor!" Beulah cried. "We will visit you in jail!"

"My husband is an attorney!" called Mrs. Noah Butt.

Jewel walked into the Thompson garage. "Everybody out, please," she told the stragglers and closed the big door after them. That was one mission wrapped, anyway.

Buzz popped up from behind the Venus Machine. "Aren't you forgetting something?" He pointed at his ankle.

Clay came into the garage through the garden door with the key to the tracer anklet. "I thought that went well."

Jewel beckoned to Buzz. Clay unlocked the tracer from Buzz's ankle and the kid rubbed himself, looking blissful.

"You were great, Buzz," she said warmly. "You'll stay out of trouble now, right? Because you know how bad life can be if you don't, right?"

"I'm gonna be fine," Buzz said. "My new girlfriend will take care of me."

"Your new what?"

He puffed out his skinny chest. "I'm gonna be a gigolo!"

"Buzz?" Someone knocked on the garage's garden door. "Oh, there you are!" The woman with the tattoos came in, now wearing clothes, and took Buzz's arm. "Bad boy! You need *such* a bath. Come home with me. We have a Jacuzzi in the master suite."

"Uh," Jewel said. "Buzz?"

"You're not the boss of me," Buzz reminded her.

She put a hand on his shoulder. "Don't get yourself—"

Tattoo-woman shoved between them. "I beg your pardon, I'm Mrs. Jack Allen. Jack Allen, the developer?

He developed that condo building at the end of the block. You'll tell our hostess for me, thank you for a lovely party, won't you, dear?" She ran a scornful glance up and down Jewel. "Come, Buzz." She scooped him up and they left.

Jewel sighed. "If anything else happens tonight—!"

Randy stuck his head in the door. "Jewel? Sovay seems very ill."

"I hope she chokes," she muttered, but she followed Randy out into the alley behind the Dumpster.

A bedraggled Sovay knelt on the bricks, limp and hiccupping, sending baby reptiles out of her mouth with every "hic."

"Oh, hell. Come on inside. I'll get you a drink."

"I am wanted in the collection room," Randy said to Jewel.

She waved him away. "I'll deal with this." He went.

"Four times," Sovay gasped. "I sat in the Venus Machine four times." She seemed to have stopped retching, anyway.

Four! Holy crap. Jewel watched and waited.

No horns sprouted from Sovay's forehead. No steam came out of her ears.

Disappointed, Jewel led her into the house.

CHAPTER 33

The caterers had gone. The servants were in bed. In her deserted kitchen, Griffy sat at the window, too tired to take off her mask, watching lights flash and listening to the crowd roar in the alley. That high-pitched whirring noise still came from the air duct. Virgil would yell at her for not calling for repairs. She wished she had the guts to tell him another thing or two.

Then Mellish came staggering into the kitchen from the back stairs, nursing his jaw. He saw her and stood up tall.

He looked a lot less like a butler and more scary.

"Is your partner around?" He felt his jaw again. "He packs a wallop. Look, I'm sorry I didn't identify myself earlier, but this case has been a long time closing." Then he pulled out his wallet and showed Griffy a shiny badge that said FBI.

Her heart leaped into her throat.

"Years," Mellish said, fishing in the freezer. He pulled out a bag of frozen corn and laid it against his jaw. "Ow. We had our perp ID'ed early, but getting solid evidence has been a bitch and a half. We're not asking you to put your case on hold. I'm almost ready to make my bust. Tomorrow maybe. Tonight if I get lucky. Work with me, okay?"

Griffy swallowed and nodded, her feathers trembling. *Virgil! They've come for you!* Her heart started thumping.

Mellish turned the frozen corn bag over and pressed it against his face again. "Mind if I have a drink?"

"I'll get it," she whispered. "Sit."

He took a stool by the counter and shut his eyes, leaning against the frozen corn.

She walked behind him, silently took a heavy aluminum saucepan off the dish rack and, with all her strength, swung it against the back of his head.

He went down like a rock. Blood ran onto the tile.

"Oh God. Ohmigod, ohmigod," she whispered. Voices sounded near the back door. Terror lent her speed. She wrapped a dish towel around his head, rubberbanded it in place, grabbed his hands, and dragged him around the corner into the pantry.

"Please, please, I hope I haven't killed him," she prayed under her breath. "No! I hope he's dead and he can't get Virgil. But please, I hope I haven't killed him."

His long legs stuck out of the pantry. After a struggle, he folded, and she was able to shut the door.

She went back to the kitchen, cold with panic.

There was blood all over the floor.

She snatched up a roll of paper towels, ran the whole thing under the tap, and knelt, wiping furiously, tearing off three wet towels at a time, trying to keep the blood off her dress and the trailing feathers at the bottom of her mask. When the blood was gone, she stuffed the gory evidence into the kitchen garbage can.

"—Maybe you'll feel better with a glass of milk in you," Julia said, coming in from the garden. She still wore her mask, and she was half carrying Sovay.

"Maybe I'll feel better with a Scotch in me," Sovay mumbled.

"Hey," Julia said, propping Sovay against a tall kitchen

stool. "You're talking. But no snakes or toads. Why is that?"

Sovay sighed. "They come out if I say something bad." Her makeup had run, her hair was in her face, and her slinky white dress had smudges all over it. She still looked lovely.

Griffy threw her mask on the counter. "The Scotch is on that shelf." She fetched a glass and some ice. Sovay might be an awful person, but she looked like she needed a drink. Griffy needed a drink herself. "How do you mean, say something bad?"

Julia found the Scotch.

Sovay watched her pour and sighed. "Don't be stingy. I'm hoping to get really, really, really"—she looked beaten—"really drunk."

Griffy said, "How bad does it have to be?"

Sovay took a long drink and set the glass down. "I don't know. I experimented with that for a day or two. If I kept quiet, it was all right. Then that *bloody* machine did something else to me and I can't seem to shut up."

Julia said, "You used it the first night I did, didn't you?"

Sovay nodded, sucking down another long drink. "It's been hell." She looked at Griffy with dull eyes. "I hope you're happy with him. The old bastard."

She hiccupped and a small toad jumped out of her mouth and landed on the countertop. Griffy stifled a giggle.

Sovay said listlessly, "There you are. Something bad. And I should like to bloody-well know who is the judge of what bad is, and how the hell they can be watching me."

"I expect you're your own judge," Julia said.

"*I'm* the judge?" Sovay said.

"The power of suggestion made you connect the fairy story with—with whatever you've been up to. Nobody else could have done that."

Boy, Julia sounded smart. Griffy wondered if she was right.

"Fuck," Sovay said. "Figures."

"Don't swear," Julia said and, when Sovay gave her a puzzled look, she added, "It puts off the marks."

Something chirped.

They all looked at the toad on the counter. It blinked. Its throat throbbed, and a high, musical trilling came out.

"The fan belt!" Griffy exclaimed. She looked from the toad to Sovay in wonder. Then she remembered Mellish in the pantry. "Um, Julia, can I talk to you for a moment?"

She led Julia around the corner and opened the pantry door a crack. Mellish lay on his face. He hadn't moved. Blood soaked the towel rubber-banded around his head.

Griffy felt terrible. "Ohmigod, he's dead all right."

"What the—" Julia bent over him. "I can't see anything. This mask is driving me crazy."

She reached up to take it off and Griffy stopped her. "Better not," Griffy whispered. "What if he isn't dead?" Then he would arrest Virgil.

"What happened?"

"He's FBI. He's after Virgil. I killed him."

"Not good." Julia stood up and looked down at the remains of Griffy's butler. "Does he know you hit him?"

"I was wearing my mask."

Julia said, "The one on the counter in there? Groovy. Because it's my mask."

Griffy looked at her with horror. "Then whose mask are you wearing?"

"Sovay's. I noticed that outside. So we're okay there."

Mellish groaned. Griffy's insides did a complicated jump between relief and dread. He got up on one elbow, craning his neck to look up at Julia.

Julia took a can of silver polish off the shelf and whacked him on the forehead.

Mellish collapsed.

Calmly, she yanked the cord off the waffle iron and tied his hands together behind his back. Griffy watched, heart in mouth, while she tied his ankles with the rice-cooker cord.

They went out and shut the pantry door.

Julia turned the key in the lock.

"Is he dead now?" Griffy whispered.

"Naw. FBI guys have cast-iron heads."

Back in the kitchen, Sovay was almost comatose over the Scotch bottle. Julia laid her mask on the counter next to the mask Griffy had discarded. She looked at the two masks. "Excellent. Let's go give our news to Virgil."

And with that she picked up the mask Griffy had been wearing and carried it out into the garden.

Griffy hurried after, grateful to have somebody smart in charge. "I wonder who has my mask."

"Green, right?" Julia said. "Sovay left it behind the Dumpster. Do you want it back?

"Thank you, no."

Outside, the party was over. The garden was a disaster area, cake and ice cream everywhere, potted plants overturned, and articles of intimate clothing soggy underfoot. The alley gate hung open. There was no light in the garage.

"What happened with those TV people?" Griffy said.

"You don't want to know. But don't expect Kauz at breakfast. If Lord Darner hasn't got lost again—" She stuck her head out the alley gate and came back, looking displeased. "*Now* where are they?"

Griffy went into the garage and turned on the light. She gasped. "The Venus Machine! It's gone!"

"Halle-fucking-luia. Maybe it got stolen. Or else the cops took it for evidence against Kauz." Julia seemed cheerful, in spite of having bashed an FBI agent in the head with a can of silver polish.

"No," Griffy said. "If I know Virgil, I know where it is."

"I have the tape," Virgil snarled halfheartedly, standing on the second-floor landing.

Clay was thrilled to be able to say, "No, you don't. Jewel found it when she got Randy out of the bed. I took it to the basement and burned it."

The longer he looked at Virgil, the more he realized he had won. Strange feeling. It was amazing how different Clay's perspective was after being in bed with Jewel two nights out of three. He took another step up toward the old man.

"Dad, I never wanted to be in the game." Virgil looked at him warily, and he added, "I know you feel betrayed because I took this job, but I'm not that good a con man." For once, Virgil didn't comment. "I want to do something I'm good at."

"Seducing women," Virgil said with a weak sneer. He looked old and shell-shocked.

"Selectively, yeah."

"She won't have you. She's all wrapped up in the tea bag."

"Lord Pontarsais and I," Clay said, "have an understanding."

"Patsy," Virgil snapped. "She'll dump you."

"Not if she doesn't know she's got me."

Virgil looked pained. "Boy, did I teach you nothing? You don't hand me a weapon like that and expect me not to use it."

Clay smiled warmly at him. "You won't use it."

"And why not?"

"Because you love me. Because you want me to be happy."

His father looked shamefaced. "I suppose I must."

Clay flushed. As displays of affection went, that was strong language for Virgil.

Virgil started up the stairs again, still tottering but with his spine straight.

Clay caught up with him. "She'll come after you."

"She tell you that?" Virgil said, looking at the floor, but Clay saw the skin on his dome go pink.

"No, but I know Griffy. She doesn't give up."

Virgil took the last four stairs two at a time. With his hand on the collection-room door, he met Clay's eyes. "I may be in jail this time tomorrow."

He might have been saying, *Fuck you, son,* or *I wonder if it'll rain.*

Clay blurted, "Anything you want, you got it. I know a good lawyer."

The claw on the collection-room doorknob relaxed. "It isn't that bad yet."

Clay nodded. "Keep me posted."

In the collection room, the Venus Machine was in pieces. Clay and Virgil got to work, reassembling it. Randy stood by, handing them tools and parts.

"I don't see what's so urgent," Virgil grumbled. "I can put this together any time."

"We have to fix, uh, Julia," Clay said and, for a miracle, his father didn't argue.

Then Jewel and Griffy marched out of the service elevator.

Clay flinched at the sight of all that determined womanhood.

"Virgil, we have a problem," Griffy said crisply.

His father looked taken aback. "Griffy, this may not be a good time—" Clay savored the moment.

"The butler is with the FBI," she stated. "I hit him over the head and so did Julia and then Julia tied him up. He's in the pantry."

Virgil seemed to be struggling to change gears.

Clay said, "Did he see you?"

"I was wearing a mask," Griffy said, "but I think he thought I was Julia."

"We could try to pin it on Sovay," Clay suggested.

"Already done," Jewel said, and exchanged a look with Clay that warmed him down to his toes.

Virgil's head was shaking but he didn't seem to realize it. "This is it, then," he muttered. "They must have something, or they wouldn't be here."

The old man took a deep breath. Then he approached Griffy and took both her hands. "Sweetheart, give us a chance. Please. I've been—I've made mistakes, but I can—"

"I've decided that I want you, Virgil, but I don't need you. I have to tell you that."

He turned her so that his back was to everyone else. Clay heard him say in a low voice, "I'm saying that I love you. I want you to stay with me."

Her voice wobbled. "I always wanted that. But I want to be me, too."

"Who else would you be?" Virgil said, sounding puzzled.

She lifted her chin. "You get to be whoever you want to be with everyone else. But you're always you to me. I can only be me. I'm not your sister. I'm me. If that's not enough—"

Clay's father's face cracked. "Griffy—oh Griffy, you are enough. I'm a bad hand at showing my feelings. I'm sorry. I love you."

The glorious hesitations and apologies and begging tumbled out of him, and Clay grinned with silent glee.

At this moment, Randy took Jewel by the arm, led her outside, and shut the door. Clay hid behind the Venus Machine and held his breath.

Virgil didn't seem to notice. "My love?" His voice trembled.

She squared up to him, her forty-two-year-old lip quivering. "What about Sovay? Why did you bring her here? Why did you make me pretend to be your sister? I know I'm not smart like her—"

"It was just money. I wanted it." Virgil waved that aside. "Sovay is nothing."

"Nobody is nothing," Griffy said in a firm voice. "I love it when you talk nice to me. But you need to learn to listen to me. And I'm not talking about Sovay." She took a deep breath.

"Would you still love me if I did go to college?" Griffy's chin was wiggling, but she smiled with chorus-girl tenderness.

Virgil exchanged glances with Clay. His look said, *See what happens when you fall in love with a dumbbell?* Clay's look said, *You conned her. Now you have to fix it.*

"Go to college if you want to," Virgil said helplessly. *No, not the truth!* Clay rolled his eyes.

"When Julia got her second time on the machine?" Griffy swallowed. "All I could think was, I want my Virgil back. I want him to love me. And then I did it, and then you loved me. But it was all the Venus Machine! Maybe I'll get you away from Sovay, but what if that's j-just the m-machine, not m-m-m-meee?"

Her face crumpled, and Virgil wrapped himself around her.

"It's not real, honey, it's not real. It's just a con," he kept saying.

"Poor Virgil. Stuck in a world with no magic." She touched his face. "I don't think it's a beauty machine at all. I think it's a wishing machine."

"There's no such—" Virgil started to say, and stopped.

Clay frowned at him. *You have to fix a con with another con. The mark will never believe that you fooled him. Lied to him, yes, as long as you say, "But this is the truth, this time." His pride won't accept that. So you fix a con with another con.*

A look of despair crossed his father's face, as if he'd read Clay's thought. He took her by the shoulders. His hands trembled. "Honey, it's a fake."

Clay could have strangled him.

She seemed to pull herself together. "No, really. Should I get the reverse treatment on the Venus Machine?" She looked at him with big, dumb, serious, blue eyes.

I could have told you she wouldn't accept that answer!

Virgil looked hunted. "What can I say?" His hands rubbed together as if he couldn't stop them. "If I tell you the machine's a fake, how can I explain how beautiful you look to me? If I say, go ahead, reverse it, would that be fair to you, when you seem to get so much confidence from it? You need the truth from me, don't you?"

She sniffed, nodding.

He pulled her hand to his chest and his mouth twisted. "You're better at honesty than I am. What do *you* want?"

He held her hand, looking scared. *Virgil, scared!* Griffy was entranced.

"You first," she said. "Tell me what you want."

"I want to set things right with you. With us. It's been a lot of years." He touched her hair so sweetly she had to bite her tongue to keep *I love you* in. "The other night, when you stepped out of that contraption, you looked like the girl I brought home eighteen years ago, and I realized you were in there all the time." He smiled. "My big-hearted stripper girl, inside the clothes I chose and the jewelry I bought and the elocution lessons I forced you through. I didn't know how much I took away from you. The you I want is the you I couldn't change."

She sniffled and tossed her head. "Does that mean I can say *dese*, *dem*, and *dose* now?"

He looked horribly uncertain, and she smiled. She decided to put him out of his misery.

"I'll tell you what I think. That machine didn't do anything. It was you. I saw what you did for Julia. She used to be like I used to be. Young and beautiful and wild. Giving it away wherever she wanted. Somehow she lost all that—that free glory—but you gave it back to her, Virgil. I saw that and I wanted you to give that to me, too."

He swallowed. "Honey, if you need to be free—"

"I need *you* to be free." She put out both her palms. "You have so much power and wisdom. You could use them for good, if you wanted. You made a stripper into somebody worthy of you."

"Oh, Christ!" He covered his face. "I'm not worthy of you, and you know it."

She touched his hand until he looked at her. "I fell in love with a good guy. Being good to people is harder than taking them." She smiled through tears. "That should interest a workaholic like you. A new challenge."

He drew a deep breath. "What should I do? I can do about anything, but I don't know if I can be a do-gooder."

"Sure you can. You can help Clay convince Sovay and Julia that the Venus Machine is fixed so it will cure them."

Virgil sent Clay a sideways glance. "He might not thank me for that."

Clay stuck his head out of the Venus Machine. "I could use your help. Julia is the toughest mark I've ever met, and the most honest, so it's hard to fake her out. It'll take both of us." He told Griffy, "It's not real, you know. It was never real. I'm sorry if—if that ruins something for you."

"My boys. Always doing things the hard way." She kissed Virgil's cheek. "There's always one person who can make the magic happen for you."

"Now, that I can do," Virgil said gallantly, putting his arms around her.

CHAPTER 34

Out in the stairwell, Jewel faced her sex demon.

"Virgil sets an improving example," Randy said. "Let us make peace. I want to live on good terms with you."

She blinked. "Well, I want that, too. This situation drives us both crazy. I think we can make it more bearable." He nodded. She said, "I guess I should be more patient. I know you used to have, like, this big estate, and all these servants my-lording at you, like Mellish does. It's gotta kill you to be so dependent on me. I—I guess I can try to be less bossy. I mean, who am I, I'm not a lord." She gave a lame laugh.

"Well," he said, raising his eyebrows ruefully, "you are no person I would have met in the ordinary course of life."

"I'm no what?" Her apologetic mood skidded.

He pursed his lips. The orange crushed-velvet coat and ruffles looked right on him. "We are of different degrees."

"We are what?" Jewel was getting the impression he was insulting her. "Do you mean you're a lord and I'm—"

"Common. Well, solid yeoman stock," he amended. In his eyes, she saw a picture of herself in a peasant blouse with a yoke over her shoulders and two pails hanging from it. She was curtseying to Randy-in-lord-costume.

A milkmaid! I'm a milkmaid next to His High Lordyness!

"Perhaps the lesser landed gentry. I understand your family were farmers who worked their stock."

She gasped. "And this is *how much* lower than a lord?"

He lifted a hand, as if to smooth over the insult. "This is scarcely the moment for a lecture on the order of precedence. You would never have been a servant. But we could not have met, let us say, at a ball, as equals in polite society."

"I suppose I would be too low for you to fuck!" she exploded. "I would hope I'm higher than those *whores* you skanked around with, or, wait, was that *after* your mistress shitcanned you for being lousy in bed?"

"Whatever a gentleman chooses to do, if he does it with good *ton*, cannot but be acceptable," he said stiffly.

"Say that in American. You're in America now. Without a green card, may I add."

He looked tight and snooty and lordy and offended. *I have to start treating him like an adult. He's a hundred and ninety-eight years older than I am.* He didn't have the tools to be her roommate in her poky little apartment. It was up to her to set rules, make it work. If she could just keep him from getting emotional! *I suck at emotional.*

She relaxed. "Let's make peace. I want to live on good terms with you."

"I said that first," he huffed.

"That's how peace negotiations start. We pick a goal together. Is it a good goal?"

After a moment, he nodded. He started to speak, but the door to the collection room opened and Clay called them back in.

Virgil stood holding a voltmeter in his hand, touching the probe to the Venus Machine and grunting.

Griffy was opening a beer bottle. Jewel took it and sucked down half in one ice-cold swallow.

Clay led her to the Venus Machine. "Voilà!"

Jewel scowled. "Voilà what?"

He beamed. "It's fixed. Took some doing, but once I worked out what the ratios should have been on the lateral receptors, everything snapped into place."

She drank more beer. "Hm. No, alcohol doesn't help. What are you talking about?"

"We set it up wrong. God knows what Kauz did to those poor people at the party. If you still have discomfort from your last go on this machine, I think we can normalize that."

She looked in his eyes and saw herself, smiling. "This won't electrocute my heinie like it did last time, will it?"

"Checking that now," Virgil said, looking very technical with his voltmeter and his frown.

"If you don't mind, I'd like Clay to check it, too," Jewel said. Virgil looked at her. "Since you messed up last time."

Virgil snorted, but he handed over the voltmeter.

"They're going to cure Sovay, too," Griffy offered. "As soon as we know this works on you."

Jewel sent her a *You're too nice to live* look. "Sovay's in the kitchen, getting snockered."

Griffy raised her voice. "You hear, Virgil? You're to cure Sovay. She doesn't deserve what happened to her."

"What does this do again?" Jewel said.

"Well," Clay said, "the symptoms of arousal resemble the symptoms of a heightened sympathetic nervous system."

"So it's kind of based on real medical principles," she said, blinking.

"Oh, Katterfelto didn't know squat about real medicine, but he knew plenty about the medieval invisible body, and he applied the work of Renaissance thinkers toward a unified field theory."

Griffy cleared her throat. "I think she just wants to know how it works."

"Quite so, quite so," Clay said quickly. "Anyway, making it simple and leaving out all the theory"—he made a face at Griffy—"a woman is more attractive when she's aroused. Her senses are heightened, her circulation system runs at a higher level—that means pink cheeks, bright eyes, a little heaving-bosom action. She's excited by what she sees and hears, and that makes her interesting, mating-wise. She's prepared for mounting, if you want to be biological about it."

Griffy frowned. "I think that's too biological."

Jewel rolled her eyes. "I am a farm girl." She remembered Randy's crack about solid yeoman stock and scowled at his lordship. "But this is all newage."

"I think it's a wishing machine," Griffy said.

Clay shrugged. "I only know the three-hundred-year-old theories. If it screws up, who you gonna blame, the theory or your body? If I were you, I wouldn't blame my body." He put down the gadgetry, held out his arms, and twiddled. "C'mere."

Cautiously Jewel walked forward.

He took her face in his hands and kissed her, a long, deep, firm kiss that left her cross-eyed.

"What was that about?" she said groggily.

"I wanted to do that one more time, before I turn you back into chopped liver."

She slapped him, loud but not hard.

He kissed her again, even longer.

Griffy started laughing. Virgil whistled. Randy sniffed.

Clay stepped back and flourished a hand toward the green velvet chair. "Will you take a seat?"

They didn't strap her in this time.

Just as Clay was about to throw the switch, Virgil stopped him and they debated for what seemed like eternity. Clay argued that they had to keep the voltage low and not stimulate any secondary chakras, whatever the fuck that meant.

A wishing machine.

Jewel wondered if she could get what she wished for if she imagined it. And that was? *God, who ever knows what they want?*

She knew she was was sick of seeing men's thoughts. Sick of guys trying to hump her leg.

Before she could think further, Clay said, "Ready?" and the big lever went clunk.

She didn't feel a thing.

Clay said, "How was that?"

"Allow me." Randy stalked up to Jewel in his orange crushed-velvet and ruffles. "Stand up."

She stood.

"Look into my eyes."

She looked.

No weird pictures. Definitely no picture of herself curtseying to him in milkmaid costume.

"I value you," he said in a low voice.

"I know you do. I almost wish you didn't," she blurted.

A funny look crossed his face. He backed away and put his hands in his coat pockets. "She's cured," he announced to Clay.

She wondered what he had been thinking about her just then because, obviously, if she had been able to see it, she would have killed him. So it was a good thing she couldn't.

"My brain hurts."

Clay patted her. "Never mind. The important thing is, you're cured."

Griffy said, "But what do we do with the Venus Machine? Sovay sold it to Dr. Kauz, but—"

"He's in jail," Clay said. "The cops may want it—"

"I'm keeping it," Virgil said flatly. "And the psyche-spectrometer. I thought we had a deal, but she got annoyed with me after last night and sold it to the fruitcake."

"Hey!" Jewel said feebly, thinking she ought to be acting more like law enforcement in this situation.

"What will you tell Sovay?" Clay said.

"It all got stolen out of the garage," Virgil said.

"That's true," Clay said.

For once Jewel didn't feel like arguing. She felt cold and limp, like leftover noodles. "Can I go to bed now?"

"Not yet," Griffy said. "The pantry is full of FBI."

"Oh, *shit*, right," Jewel said, and everyone else groaned.

Virgil felt behind himself for the workbench stool and sat down with a bump, looking gray.

At that moment the service elevator opened. The cook came in in her bathrobe. "Sorry to intrude, Mr. Thompson, but I thought you should know. It's about Mellish."

Everyone froze.

"Well?" Virgil said harshly.

"He's gone, sir. And he took Miss Sacheverell away with him." The cook frowned. "He said to tell you he works for the FBI, and he charged her with murdering her last five husbands. He said he found the poison she used on them in your closet."

Closet! Jewel made a noise. *That's what Mellish found!*

"I guess I can't cure her after all," Virgil said, not sounding sorry.

"Don't be mean," Griffy said.

Virgil said evilly, "Don't waste your pity on her. If she's killed five husbands, she deserves a few toads. If she uses her looks, she could get off scot-free. Provided she can keep her mouth shut."

"Toads?" Clay said.

The cook said to Virgil, "Sir, I hope you won't be angry with me, but I didn't think it my place to interfere—"

"No, no." Virgil waved that away. "It's fine."

"Tell me," Jewel said to the cook. "Did Miss Sacheverell, well, use any bad language to Mellish as she left?"

"Oh my, yes, how she cursed. Toads *and* snakes. Snakes is new," the cook said, sounding impressed.

"Toads and snakes?" Clay said to Jewel. "*What* toads and snakes?"

"Weren't you a little surprised by the toads?" Jewel asked the cook.

"Well," the cook said, "I've been cooking them all week, but I didn't know where they came from, if that's what you mean."

Jewel smiled. *I love Chicago. Nothing fazes us.*

Randy made a face.

Clay raised his hands heavenward. "*What toads and snakes?*"

Virgil said, "Tastes like chicken."

CHAPTER

35

Next day, Jewel sat at her workstation, trying to write a report without saying, *They're all criminals, but we got the ones who counted.* Ed called her into his office.

"I'm not done yet." She closed his door behind her.

"Screw the written report. I wanna know what happened."

She drew a deep breath. "Well, you were right about Kauz's spa. He was beta testing a potion through a retailer. He hoped to get people addicted to it so he could control them."

"And you know this how?"

"I didn't hear him say this myself, but he told a witness."

"Will the witness testify?"

"If we can get him for making the potion."

"So? Subpoena her ass."

"Well, turns out the potion wasn't addictive. Nobody ever wanted more than one dose. It made them, uh, eccentric."

Ed's forehead wrinkled. "What the fuck? You got a sample?"

"Well, no. I took the last supply off his retailer—"

Ed nodded. "Buzz."

"—But it, uh, got destroyed."

"Shit." Ed brightened. "But you put an anklet on him."

"Had to take it off. It was illegal. But Kauz got busted."

"So he's put away."

"Overnight, for disturbing the peace. But his spa is closed, and his reputation is in shreds since the news footage."

"*Footage?*" Ed said dangerously. "Anything hinky?"

Jewel swallowed. "A little. The perp—our other perp—started spitting live toads and snakes on camera. Mostly it was just, like, socialites getting naked in a Marine Drive garden."

"Holy Jesus. The Fifth Floor must be shitting bricks."

"The snake-spitter lady blamed Kauz."

Ed looked relieved. "That's good."

"And the eccentrics told the press how wonderful he is."

"Lemme get this straight. I send you after a magician—"

"More of a mad scientist."

"—Mad scientist and his pusher, and he gets a slap on the wrist, and you lose your samples of the drug, and you had the pusher on a tracer and then you let him go. Don't tell me the pusher ain't that homeless kid because fuck that." Jewel opened her mouth and shut it. "Plus we got a broad who spits toads on TV, and the mad scientist gets a testimonial."

"From crackpots, Ed. The whole block party was vomiting."

"Block party? A whole *block*? How many people saw this?"

"Probably the toads and snakes made them sick," she added conscientiously. "But the people in the orgy missed everything."

Ed looked like his head hurt. "What about your other perp? This is the gold digger with the hinky machine?"

"Turns out she's a serial black widow. The FBI got her."

Ed seemed to weigh this. Then something outside his office caught his eye. "What's that guy doing here?"

Jewel looked through the venetian blinds. Randy and Clay sat at a workstation. "Basic computer training. He worked well with us on this—"

"He *what*?"

"And Clay felt he could be more helpful with some skills—"

"He's not a city employee!"

"It was a three-investigator job."

Ed turned color and jabbed a finger at her. "Look, missy." He stuck his head out his door. "Get in here, you two."

The boys trooped in, looking innocent.

Ed announced, "I got youse all here at once so's there can't be no misunderstandings. You"—he pointed at Jewel—"are the senior partner on this team. You"—he pointed at Clay—"are the junior partner. You"—he pointed at Randy—"do not belong in this office at any time. *Capisce?*"

"He's my stealth teammate," Jewel said quickly. "We work well together."

"Fuck that. Tell me you work well with golden boy here."

"Clay was great. Full of initiative and ideas." She didn't look at Clay. "And Randy was a huge help. He wrestled Buzz to the floor at Water Tower Place." Ed looked pained. "He also sweet-talked this socialite until she quit threatening to sue—"

"I don't wanna hear this."

"And then he was, uh, in the suspect's bedroom and—"

Both Ed's hands were in the air. "I *don't* wanna *hear* this."

"And he protected our cover by clobbering the butler for me—well, he turned out to be FBI—"

Ed clapped his hands over his ears. "La la la la la, I ain't listenin' to you!"

"I mean it, Ed!" she protested. "He has skills we need."

Randy raised his eyebrows to Clay.

"Oh, say, can you see!" Ed bawled.

Clay put a hand on her arm. "Not so much detail, partner. Stick to the big picture."

Ed stopped singing and took his hands off his ears.

Clay said, "Sir, we did the job. We shut down Kauz's spa and ruined his mayoral campaign before it could start. We got rid of the hinky machine complaint. Buzz is out of the picture."

Ed glowered. "For the next ten minutes."

Clay put one hand on Jewel's shoulder and one on Randy's. "As for Randy, we need him. He's good. You're not paying him. You don't know who he is. You'll never know what he does. The existence and activities of this division are classified anyway. To use your own phrase, sir, don't fix it if it ain't broke."

For a long minute Ed breathed tensely through his nose. Then he turned his back. He told the ceiling, "I don't know nothin'. I don't see nothin'."

Clay gestured. Randy opened the door, and Clay hustled the three of them out of Ed's office.

Packing her briefcase, Jewel said bitterly, "Thanks a lot. How come he listens to you and he sings 'The Star Spangled Banner' at me?"

"Because I'm a better liar," Clay said. "A skill you need to hone."

"I do not lie to my boss!"

Clay looked at her pityingly. "No wonder you're stuck in the Hinky Division."

"So explain this, smarty-pants," she said, nettled. "Was that thing magic or wasn't it? I mean, it did all kinds of things. And," she warned Clay, "skip the chakras and potentiometers and shit, because I don't believe a word of it."

Clay raised his eyebrows to Randy. "Over to you, Lord Credibility."

"It used the power of suggestion," Randy said.

"Griffy called it a wishing machine," Jewel said. "But then you told that fairy tale, and Sovay started spitting toads and snakes."

Out of the corner of her eye she saw Clay turn to Randy and mouth, *What toads and snakes?* She ignored them.

"What I can't figure is, did you suggest that and it went into her, like, subconscious mind, and she did the magic to herself? Did she punish *herself* for talking mean? That doesn't make sense. She killed all those husbands. Why should she care about talking mean?"

Randy looked at Clay. "Everybody's got a sticking point," Clay said. "Look at Virgil. Sucks at blackmail, won't do it."

"He didn't suck that bad," she said darkly. "But Sovay?"

"The power of suggestion?" Randy said again. "Griffy's primary weapon of defense was her sweetness—"

"I'm glad you admit it!" Jewel put in.

"—So when I criticized Sovay for shrewishness, she may have acknowledged the fault, if only in her heart. The Venus Machine did the rest. Or she did."

Jewel considered this. "I don't know what's scarier, the idea that the machine did it to her, or that she could do it to herself just because you suggested it. I mean, *you* don't have magic powers—outside of bed—right?"

He said, "That we cannot know, unless you care to conduct further experiments."

She put her foot down. "No!"

"You'd need a control group, too," Clay said.

"Absolutely not! Brrr! No fucking way."

"Although Virgil may charge rent on the machine," Clay said.

"Fuggeddaboddit. Oh, that reminds me. Did you know all along that was the wrong bed, that day in Sovay's room?"

Clay widened his eyes. "Absolutely not."

"You've always said we should experiment," Randy said.

She whipped her head around. Was it possible they were double-teaming her? "No experiments. Anyway, I think Ed's getting used to having you around."

Her partner turned to her incubus. "Say, 'Thank you, Clay.'"

Randy totally shocked her. "Thank you, Clay."

Boy, if these two get comfortable, I'm screwed. Thank God they're jealous. "C'mon, let's pick up some Thai food."

Later that evening, after carryout Thai in her apartment, Jewel let Clay resume the computer lesson with Randy in her living room while she phoned Nina for some overdue girl talk in the still-sooty bedroom.

"So you hate undercover, after you've bitched for it for years?" Nina said, cutting to the emotional jugular as usual.

"I don't know." Jewel lowered her voice. "I know I'm not in Clay's league. *He's* perfect for it."

"I'll bet."

"I couldn't have done it without him. Though I may smack him if he keeps hogging my thunder."

"Go ahead. He won't mind, and it'll relieve your feelings."

"I know what'll relieve my feelings," Jewel said, lowering her voice still further. "Thank God I have a sex demon on tap."

"Girlfriend." Nina gave a raunchy laugh. "You ever think you need therapy?"

"All the time. But if I talk about my job, Ed will have to have my shrink killed."

Nina's laugh quacked so loud that Jewel held the phone away from her ear. In that moment, she heard Randy say from the living room, "We can transfer moneys from her bank into ours?"

Uh-oh. Jewel walked into the living room.

Clay was explaining, "But if we use our regular mail account, the e-mail trail leads straight to our door. Well, Jewel's door. Which would be bad. So what do we do?"

"What's going on here?" she demanded.

"Create a false Internet identity and backloop it to the mark's e-mail account?" Randy said in the voice of a star pupil.

"Talk to you later," she told Nina, and hung up.

"Very good," Clay said. "Same with the cash transfer. This is where a PayPal account works for you. Oh, hi, Jewel. We're bringing Randy up to date on Internet fraud."

She narrowed her eyes. "Sounds to me like you're stealing."

"Just from Sovay. Did you know that woman has twenty million dollars?" At Jewel's expression he said, "Don't worry, we'll leave her enough for a good defense lawyer."

Jewel ground her teeth. "Clay. No."

"You didn't object when Virgil cleaned out Sovay's CD account."

"What? He *what*? Don't tell me this! Argh!"

"Besides, Randy needs some money of his own. C'mon, partner," Clay wheedled. "The man's got his pride."

She was still thinking about Sovay's CD account. "Virgil *what*? Never mind." She did a mental headslap.

Randy turned from the computer with such puppy-dog

eyes that she felt guilty. "Now I can pay to have your bedroom cleaned and repainted."

She swallowed. "Randy could have had a *job*, if you hadn't sold him downriver with Ed."

Clay waved a hand. "Ed would never have hired him. No paper trail."

"I thought you were getting him an identity!"

"I'm getting it, I'm getting it. Faking a solid ID takes time. Not like you'd use on a weekend scam, I mean, but something that'll last him years."

Jewel couldn't take any more. She clapped her hands over her ears. "Oh, say, can you see!"

CHAPTER 36

"Star Spangled Banner?" Randy said after Clay left. They'd laid newspaper over the sooty bedroom carpet. Now Jewel tossed him an end of a sheet. He caught it and snapped it open. His naked muscles came and went behind the sheet like a peep show.

She felt a little light-headed. "National anthem. You know. I think it dates back to the War of 1812."

He tucked in the sheet. "Ah. I became an incubus in 1811."

"You've heard it watching football games on TV."

He caught her looking at him and his magic schlong swelled up and rose in a slow, stiff salute. His dark eyes seemed to grow bigger. "Jewel. If I may speak of serious things."

The Relationship Conversation. Red alert! She touched her dry lips with the tip of her tongue.

He smiled. "Did I thank you for rescuing me once again?"

"I think so."

"The forced solitude gave me time to ponder. I begin to understand what causes me to—what's your term?— 'zap' into bed."

"No kidding?" She tossed the sooty coverlet into a corner.

"It is the difference between myself perpendicular and myself prone. I am two men."

This she knew already. "The sensitive new-age guy who tries to please women." *Do we have to talk about this?*

He bowed. "And the buff bastard who always wins. You have a gift," he said ruefully, "for bringing these two halves of myself together and, er—"

"Rubbing them the wrong way?"

He shook his head. "I don't know that there is a correct way for my two selves to confront each other. I've realized there is no escaping the confrontation, if I'm to be free."

It always came back to that. He wanted to be free.

"I don't blame you for wanting it." Her heart pinched.

"So it is high time I begged your forgiveness for—for not knowing whether I am an earl or an incubus."

Those big dark eyes made her nervous. "Apology accepted. Now say you don't think I'm too skanky for a lord to know."

He smiled. "That rankles, does it?"

"Someday I'll make you eat those words." She shrugged. "Let's go to bed." She climbed between the sheets.

But he wasn't done.

"Miss Griffy, in the spa, spoke to you of women's needs."

She groaned. "I won't go there if you don't."

He went there. "She said, men who want a relationship think that if they know about sex, that should be enough."

Ugh, ugh, relationship talk! Whatever happened to the guy who wanted to fuck all night?

He touched her cheek. "She said, too, that sex is easier

than love. She said, men don't understand themselves. They want sex to be enough, but it never is. What do you think?"

I want sex to be enough. "I think that's a sexist generalization." *Does that make me a guy?*

"What do you want, Jewel?"

She felt claustrophobic. She wanted to get dressed and run home. But this was home, and he lived here. "Um, a good bra without an underwire?"

Smiling, he shook his head. "Ask me for something only I can give you."

He stood there, naked, as if unaware his Washington Monument was aimed at her and bobbing as he talked, talked, talked. Her brain shut down. *Oh say, can you see, by the dawn's early light.*

"Randy, I have what I want. I have a great job, wonderful friends, a nice apartment"—she looked around at the sooty walls and ceiling—"a new partner."

His face darkened.

She added hastily, "And I'm getting used to you. Both the hard parts and the fabulous parts."

He began to smile.

"I—I don't know how to make this work," she pleaded. "I mean, what's the goal here?" *That* was too close to the bone, and she backpedaled. "The first priority is getting your life back, for real, once and for all."

"I complain too much of my losses, don't I? Yet your losses are no less profound. Your privacy. Your liberty."

She couldn't bear to think about her losses—especially the loss that would come when he was free at last. When he left. *What's the matter with me? I'm not the clingy one—what so proudly we hailed at the twilight's last gleaming.*

"Bright Jewel. I may know your heart, but not touch it."

"Shh." She rose up on her knees and stopped his mouth with hers. Her throat was packed full of hot words she could never say, painful thoughts she didn't dare think.

They kissed. Pleasure flooded her, easing her tight throat.

She lifted her mouth. "Are you done talking yet?"

Smiling, he kissed her and pushed her on her back, carrying her down slowly, never letting their bodies part.

She sank into demonspace.

He wafted her to a flowery meadow lit by a moon.

He looked different. *You have a ponytail! With daisies?*

I learned about the Haight making one's hair grow. "Make love, not war." He smiled at her surprise. *I shall take that for my new family motto.*

She laughed. *Okay, you look hot in the ponytail. How did you find out about the Haight?*

I read Griffy's mind last night.

Euw! She so hadn't wanted to know that.

You know what I am. His eyes were full of light. *Jewel, let us make love, not war. What is my lady's pleasure tonight?*

She felt dizzy. *No sex in the air.*

I will not frighten you tonight, bright Jewel. I must try to imagine new pleasures for you. I have never known a woman like you, he said in a deep voice that sent shivers down her back. *Together we will discover fresh delights.*

He stroked her with feather-light fingertips, strumming her back, her buns, her knees, up the insides of her thighs, skimming her sex, up her belly, up the undersides of her breasts, flicking her nipples, brushing her throat.

Her skin flamed all over as if his fingers were hot coals, making her wriggle and moan. *A light touch,* he said deep in her ear, wrapping her in his velvet voice.

He ran a hand over her from throat to knee, and all his fingers turned into licking tongues. *Ohmigod*. He stroked her face with his other hand, and those fingers became tongues, too. She moaned. Lick, lick, lick, he licked her everywhere rhythmically, a little faster than her heart could pound.

Another handful of tongues sneaked down her leg toward her ankle, and another, oh, she couldn't keep track, she writhed under dozens of tongues, licking every inch of her body at once.

For God's sake, Randy, fuck me! She twisted, striking out, but even though her hands met his and his fingers laced through hers to hold her, it seemed he had still more hands, more tongues-fingers-tongues to lick her with.

He hoisted her up until she straddled him and sank slickly, gratefully down onto his cock, feeling anchored while his hundred tongues licked, licked, licked. Now she could thrash in his arms, but she was pinned to him at that one spot, Randy big and hard inside her, something to struggle against, while pleasure and confusion made her lose herself.

His tongues began licking in unison, one for every few inches of her body, as if she were an ice cream cone, and he bent her backward until her head fell back and she arched against him and her hot button met the root of his amazing thing.

And then he bit her gently, once. All over. *All* over.

Pleasure shocked through her.

Time stood still.

Her bedroom came back around them, still and quiet and dim and safe. They lay face-to-face on the tangled sheets.

"That was interesting," she said when she could speak.

"Not vastly original, but a popular selection," he said with a smirk in his voice.

"God. I think I came out the soles of my feet that time."

"Was that fast enough for you?"

"God yes." She pressed her face to his neck, her heart thumping.

He brushed her hair away and kissed her ear. "I promise I will neither scare you nor rob you of sleep."

She drew in a shaky sigh. "Big talk. Now if you can keep surprising me in bed."

"I can promise you—hm—" He shifted and she dared to look at him, admiring the planes of his angular face and his shock of midnight-black hair. "I can promise at least three hundred and eight new experiences."

She laughed. "That's next month taken care of, then."

ACKNOWLEDGMENTS

I owe thanks to many people for their help with this book. In almost chronological order: Rich Bynum, a writer's dream husband; Nalo Hopkinson, for The Connection; Pam & Bar Man Mordecai, Larissa Lai, and Hiromi Goto, for being there from the start; Beata Hayton, for The Other Connection; "Mr. Balantine" for invaluable insider info; MJ Carlson for straight dope; Don Maass, smarter than I as always; Betsy Mitchell, editor and major saint; Ysabeau Wilce, for brainstorming and lifesaving; Simone Elkeles and Amey Larmore, for synopsis genius; Officer Sue Heneghan, Chief Greg Shields, and Ed Myer, for advice on tracer anklets; Arrit McPherson, for advice on parasailing; Cat Eldridge, for encouragement and support above and beyond all my desserts; the fabulous team at Ballantine Books for taking such good care of my books and making them look so great; and my wonderful readers, Jackie Wallis, John and Pam Nikitow, Theodore and Sylvia Halkin, Pam Telfer, Marianne Frye, Mindy "She's So" Fine, Yvonn Yirka, Kate Early, Nnedi Okorafor-Mbachu, Kari Hayes, Bev Long, Martha Whitehead, Marilyn Weigel, and the ladies of Chicago-North RWA.

SPECIAL THANKS

To the heroes of the Chicago Department of Consumer Services, who make the city a better place to live, in so many ways.

Read on for an excerpt from
Jewel's next adventure!

The Bearskin Rug

Coming from Ballantine Books

"Might I indeed be arrested for driving with too much spirit?" Randy said to Clay as they waited in Jewel's Tercel for Jewel to get off work.

Clay shrugged. "I guess."

"But on television only criminals and comely women are detained for driving."

"Sadly, life is not enough like TV. I wish she wasn't doing this stupid job." In Clay's view, undercover should take place only in the haunts of the rich and famous.

It was four-thirty. Men in fancy suits came out of the office tower, looking at their fancy watches, talking on their phones. They jumped into cabs or private cars or marched briskly into the bar on the street level of the tower.

Clay drummed on the steering wheel. "Where's all the women?"

"Is that why I am not permitted to drive this evening?" Randy said with an edge in his voice. Good, it was about time he started acting needled. Clay had been needling him for nearly three weeks, since the end of the last job. He'd begun to think the haughty Englishman had no nerves at all.

When Clay didn't answer, Randy said drily, "Perhaps I drive not too badly but too well."

Bingo. *The mark takes the fly*. "It's rush hour, dude," Clay said in a kinder tone. "You'd hash it, and she would hate that. Didn't they have traffic cops where you came from?"

"We had no traffic control of any kind. Bow Street Runners had more important things to do than to harass gentlemen for the speed of their horses." Randy was silent a moment. "I once drove from London to Brighton in four and a half hours. Not at 'rush hour,' as you call it. By moonlight, before dawn. Match bays, two teams, one stabled in town, one on the Brighton road." He sounded wistful and off guard.

"Fast, huh. How fast was considered fast?"

"Sixteen miles an hour at a canter. Faster if you put 'em along, but one could not, of course, spring 'em in town."

"And you never hit anything?"

"I was no whipster," Randy said with amusement. "Any man may own blood cattle if he can afford them, but he won't drive them hard more than twice. Horses are tricksier than cars."

"Cars are hard," Clay said indignantly. "Try handling a clunker like this on the expressway in the rain at rush hour."

"It's not raining now."

Clay let that remark lie between them a couple of beats. "Don't think I don't know what you're up to."

"I want to drive. There is no subterfuge."

Clay huffed. "Criminy! All right, all right." He switched seats with Randy.

Randy settled behind the wheel with a satisfied little wiggle.

"Seat belt," Clay said.

"We are stationary."

"Seat belt."

"Such petty tyranny," Randy said.

"It's the law."

"Which you honor so much."

Clay said with as much annoying patience as possible, "A con artist has the sense not to get busted for a lousy seat-belt charge."

At that moment the office building started tossing out dozens and dozens of women. Out they poured, fat ones, skinny ones, tall ones, short ones, every single one dressed like a real female, high heels flashing, all legs and hair and flirty clothes, chattering and giggling and shouldering against each other through the door of the bar on the street level.

Clay sighed. "Ed should have sent me in there."

Randy looked at his watch. "She's late."

"She's the boss. And she won't let you drive."

"She wants me to acquire independence."

"The least you could do is stay home once in a while and, like, do the laundry or something. Run the vac. Cook dinner."

"If you have tired of teaching me," Randy said pointedly, "I will ask her."

"All right, all right. Let's work on your identity. What's your social security number?"

"Two zero four, nine one, nine eight five three."

"Born?"

"Guam, 1980."

"Employment?"

Randy paused. "Companion," he grated.

"I'm thinking we change that to houseboy," Clay said thoughtfully. "A companion doesn't skank off and bone the suspect in the middle of an undercover operation and then disappear for days when the person he's companioning needs backup," he said, referring to how Randy had messed up on their last undercover case.

"*You* found my absence convenient," Randy said, now sounding pissed off.

"I certainly did. Jewel knows who she can count on. Plus, she's good company," Clay said, alluding delicately to the fact that he'd got Jewel into bed twice while Randy was waiting for Jewel to rescue him from being magically trapped in the suspect's bed. "I was surprised you gave us a chance for quality time—surprised and grateful."

Randy grunted.

Clay pushed. "I've been meaning to ask you, how many times did you do my stepmother while you were haunting that bed?"

"I never kiss and tell," Randy said drily, and Clay felt himself go hot. "She's a very sweet woman."

Sheesh! So Clay had a little Oedipal something for his stepmother. Randy sure knew where to stick the knife in. Clay said with less than his usual finesse, "One thing Jewel told me. She can't wait to get you shut of this curse thingy. She's sick of having you underfoot."

"I'm sick of the curse myself. Perhaps when I am shut of it, and can support myself, I'll be able to woo her in form."

"*Woo* her!" Clay blurted. "Is that what you call it? Sending her to work bowlegged every morning?"

The one area where he felt definitely outclassed was this sex demon thing. If Jewel had been one of these giggly virgins clattering out of this office tower on high heels, she'd have tried Randy for one night and never slept on that brass bed again.

On the other hand, if Jewel was one of those virgins, Clay wouldn't be the least bit interested.

"Do you call what you do wooing?" Randy sounded genuinely curious.

Clay didn't have an answer to that one. He'd put off closing the deal with Jewel a hundred times this summer, blaming Randy's eternal underfootedness. He couldn't pursue his interest in her until Randy was out of the way. Could he?

While he pondered this question, Jewel opened the driver's door of the Tercel. "Out."

"Clay said I might drive," Randy said, sounding like a four-year-old.

"Not after yesterday's performance. Out." She seemed to be in a temper.

They played musical car seats. Clay got out and got into the back seat. Randy took the front passenger seat, looking smug.

Clay felt pretty smug, too. *Let him think he has an advantage, sharing the front seat with her when she's like this.*

Randy could take the edge off her.

And then Clay could soothe her.

Jewel got in, handed her purse to Clay in the back seat, and banged the door. "Morons."

Nobody said anything while she turned on the traffic report, then switched to "Ask Your Shrink."

Ask Your Shrink was taking call-ins. "—*Wife is never interested! Is that fair?*"

"No, it isn't," said the soothing voice of Your Shrink. "*You could take her to dinner or a spa. Offer her chocolate. Get her drunk.*"

"*It's ruining my marriage!*"

"*Or, if the marriage is more important than the sex, you can try taking saltpeter to match your libido levels to hers—*"

Jewel slapped the radio button to off.

"How was your first day at work?" Clay said.

"Sucked. My boss is hot and knows it, the girls screw their bosses, and the office manager is a wimp. My best informant so far is taking child support, and pipe, from a man forty years too old for her."

"It must have been bad."

"Why do you say that?" she said dangerously, changing lanes and cutting off a taxi.

"You're driving crazy."

"Fucking moron!" she yelled at the taxi.

"And swearing."

"Forced abstinence. Those girls—" She snorted. "I'd call them women, but they're so desperately afraid to seem adult. They get sexually harassed, they dress up like ice cream frappés to fucking type and answer the phone, they sneak and they backbite and they get chewed up in politics between the white guys in suits, and then they lose their rag because I cuss a little."

"Sexually harassed?" Randy said.

"So is that where the orgy came from?" Clay said.

"I have no friggin' idea. The slick willy I work for is part of it. What do these motherfuckers *think*? This is their own personal private stag movie? Sunday driver!" She slapped the horn and leaned on it. "Jesus Christ on a bicycle!"

Clay leaned forward from the back seat and slid his hand over her mouth.

She shut up.

"It must be bad," he said. "You're channeling Ed." He pulled his hand back, peeked—her lips worked—then he slid his hand back over her mouth.

Randy said critically, "Ed's diction during a seizure is more elaborate."

"Funkier," Clay agreed. "More creative."

"Sometimes he fails to blaspheme," Randy said.

"And when he's really upset Ed doesn't use the F-word. I think he actually forgets it," Clay said.

"Difficult to believe," Randy said.

Behind Clay's hand, he felt Jewel smile. He took his hand away and relaxed into the back seat. "So, the orgy. What do you know?"

She drove silently for a minute. "I don't know. There's a woman I can talk to at lunch Wednesday. Maybe more, once I've been around the place. I made a lot of friends by telling Steven to call his own cab today. Of course that's why I may not be working there by Wednesday." She looked at her watch. "Plus I'm meeting the complainant at six at the Billy Goat."

"What is sexual harassment?" Randy said.

This should be good, Clay thought.

"It's something you could use to learn more about, roomie," she said to Randy. "When someone puts unwanted moves on a coworker or subordinate." She stopped the Tercel at the light. "Any kind of unwanted advances, a look, a verbal approach. Touching, exhibitionism, showing her feelthy pictures."

"You see me as one who tampers with chambermaids?" Randy said, going lord on her.

Jewel said calmly, "I think that a guy who has been a stealth fuck to more than a hundred women over the past two centuries might not realize how important consent is to a woman."

In the back seat, Clay's ears flapped.

"I always obtain consent," Randy grated.

"Oh, bull. You can't take 'no' for an answer. Prying into her dreams—and disguising yourself as whatever she wants—is not the same thing as asking, in English, under circumstances that allow her to refuse freely—"

"I take 'no' from you!"

"—Allow her to refuse *without consequences*," Jewel said, raising her voice. "I'm not going to argue this with you."

Randy shut up.

Darn. Just when Clay was getting a nice clear view into something he'd been dying to know about for months.

Clay glanced at her in the rearview mirror. In her navy polyester, with her chin sticking out and her eyes ablaze, she looked all cop. Very hot.